ON THE WAY TO
THE MELTING POT

ON THE WAY TO THE MELTING POT

A novel by Waldemar Ager

Paa veien til smeltepotten

Translated by Harry T. Cleven

Prairie Classics No. 4

PRAIRIE OAK PRESS
Madison, Wisconsin

First edition, first printing
Copyright ©1995 by Harry T. Cleven

Prairie Oak Press
821 Prospect Place
Madison, Wisconsin 53705

Text and cover design by Prairie Oak Press

Printed in the United States of America

Library of Congress Cataloging-in-Publication Data

Ager, Waldemar, 1869-1941.
    [Paa veien til smeltepotten. English]
    On the way to the melting pot: a novel / by Waldemar Ager; translated by Harry T. Cleven.
        p.   cm. -- (Prairie classics; no. 4.)
    ISBN 1-879483-23-8
    I. Cleven, Harry T.   II. Title.   III. Series.
PT9150.A4P213   1995
839.8'2372--dc20   94-33998
                                               CIP

The publication of this book has been assisted by a translation grant from Norwegian Literature Abroad (NORLA), The Norseman's Federation (Nordmanns-Forbundet), Oslo, Norway.

PREFACE

WALDEMAR AGER (1869-1941), author of the satirical novel *Paa veien til smeltepotten* (On the Way to the Melting Pot), was one of the most important Norwegian-American writers, yet few readers today, even those of Norwegian extraction, are familiar with him or his books. This is perhaps not surprising, since of all the persons who have ever produced works of literature down through the ages only relatively few are long read and remembered. Those who have attained "immortality" are those whose themes are universal and timeless. Shakespeare, Dostoevsky, Ibsen, and Tolstoy fall into this category. The great majority do not. They may have been good writers, but their message and their characters may appear so limited to a specific time or cause that they are neither universal nor timeless. This is especially true of ethnic writers in America who published during the latter half of the nineteenth century and the first decades of the twentieth. They depicted the struggles and issues facing their own people in their newly adopted land. Many of the ethnic writers had a particular axe to grind. What is more, they wrote novels, short stories, poetry, and essays in their native languages, limiting their public still further. Subsequent generations are no longer conversant with the language of their forebears or the issues that were of concern to them. Relatively little of what they wrote has been translated into English. Consequently, most of these authors, and what they wrote, are largely forgotten.

Waldemar Ager came to Chicago as a boy of sixteen, but later moved to Eau Claire, Wisconsin, where he lived until his death. He worked primarily as an editor, but left behind him several novels and short story collections. He was very active in the temperance movement and was in great demand as a public speaker.

Ager was much opposed to the common conception of America as a melting pot. Ager knew that his immigrant countrymen had to live, work, and raise their children in America. But he felt it was essential that they hold on to their identity as Norwegians. He was a firm advocate of the Norwegian language among Norwegian Americans. "If the language died out," writes Øyvind T. Gulliksen, Ager "feared that it would not be possible to keep up a vital Norwegian-American Culture."[1]

Ager wrote his satirical novel *On the Way to the Melting Pot* in 1917 as a protest against cultural assimilation. It was a time when there was a growing antagonism toward the use of foreign languages in America, in large part as a by-product of anti-German sentiment. Einar Haugen points out that the title of Ager's book was obviously borrowed from *The Melting Pot*, the much-discussed 1908 play by the English-Jewish playwright and Zionist leader Israel Zangwill (1864-1926). Zangwill described America as the place where "individuals of all nations are melted into a new race of men, whose labors and posterity will one day cause great changes in the world." "Ager," writes Haugen, "showed his distaste for this image by twisting the Norwegian term for 'melting pot,' *smeltedigel,* into the Norwegian-American and mildly derisive *smeltepotte.*"[2] Haugen devotes an entire chapter to the plot and characters of *On the Way to the Melting Pot* in his Ager biography. One of the best books for understanding Ager's thought in general is *Cultural Pluralism versus Assimilation: The Views of Waldemar Ager.*[3] Another helpful source for understanding Ager is Odd

1 Øyvind T. Gulliksen, "In Defense of a Norwegian-American Culture: Waldemar Ager's *Sons of the Old Country,*" in *American Studies in Scandinavia,* 19 (1987), 39-52.

2 Einar Haugen, *Immigrant Idealist: A Literary Biography of Waldemar Ager. Norwegian American* (Northfield, Minnesota, 1989), 88-90.

3 Odd S. Lovoll, ed., *Cultural Pluralism versus Assimilation: The Views of Waldemar Ager* (Northfield, Minnesota, 1977). The book contains an essay by Ager, "The Melting Pot," translated by Lovoll, which is a direct reaction to Zangwill's drama.

S. Lovoll's foreword to another of his novels in English translation, *Sons of the Old Country* (Lincoln, Nebraska, 1983). This novel, which deals with immigrant loggers in Wisconsin, was translated by Ager's son, Trygve, and is still in print. Though the foreword deals specifically with this novel, Lovoll also provides much additional background about Ager and his views.

Ager, like so many other ethnic writers, had his axe to grind, too. He fought a losing battle for the preservation of the Norwegian language in America, and he may have realized this himself even as he wrote *On the Way to the Melting Pot*. One senses the pain he feels for his people in America who are neither wholly American nor wholly Norwegian. Some of the characters in his book are pathetic and comical without realizing it and Ager was certainly drawing from individuals he knew in real life, however exaggerated for purposes of satirical emphasis. What would become of the Norwegians in America? And what would become of their children and grandchildren? What about their rich cultural heritage? We sympathize with Ager and his concerns. Not only that, but he is in line with other American authors who wrote about their ethnic groups and with whom he shared similar themes, such as Abraham Cahan (Jewish), author of *The Rise of David Levinsky* (1917), Pietro De Donato (Italian American), author of *Christ in Concrete* (1939), and Maxine Hong Kingston (Chinese American), author of *The Woman Warrior* (1976).

"Ager's novels," writes Gulliksen, "are not much read today."[4] This is understatement. Ager was well known during his lifetime and much has been written about him, yet he is not even listed in popular surveys of Wisconsin writers. His house in Eau Claire has no plaque on the wall to indicate that he or his large family ever lived there. He wrote what might be termed "time-piece literature." But he was a great storyteller, and he gives us helpful insight into the immigrant experience, although not all Norwegian immigrants would have agreed with his views. Ager deserves to be read, in fact should be read, because he helps us understand our past and, perhaps, what we have become. In spite of his narrow audience and

---

4 Gulliksen. "In Defense of a Norwegian-American Culture," 39.

theme he tells us something about the pain and struggle that went into the making of America. I hope this English edition of *On the Way to the Melting Pot* will bring him an expanded readership.

I am deeply grateful to Mary R. Hove and Odd S. Lovoll, who have carefully reviewed and edited my translation.

Harry T. Cleven
May 1993, Oslo

I.

MRS. LEWIS OMLEY was very busy in the kitchen. There was a pile of empty tin cans just outside the door. Wherever she turned there were empty cups, dishes, and paper bags which gaped expectantly at her. Several things were cooking on the new *range*.* It was no easy task keeping an eye on it all. She had to get finished. She could expect the people home from church any moment now. Her face was red from the terrible heat, beads of sweat collected on her eyelashes, and she kept using her apron to wipe her eyes.

Slumped over the table with one knee resting on a chair was Sophy, with the cookbook in front of her. Whatever her mother needed to know Sophy had to look up for her.

Mrs. Omley was both nervous and worried. The dinner steamed and bubbled on the stove. There was a hissing sound now and then as something boiled over. Hidden forces were at work, and Mrs. Omley was feeling far from secure. She paced about with as much tension as a general during a battle. It was her good name and reputation, and that of her family, that bubbled away on the stove.

She was preparing an American-style dinner, and that was no simple task. She had to serve something extra-special today because her fourth child was being baptized and he was a beautiful boy. It was really only

———

*Italicized words appear in English in the Norwegian original.

the children one had to live for, and one couldn't do too much for them. And besides, she wanted to show off for the other women.

Mrs. Skare had served *flødegrød* and *bakkelse* and the like when one of her children was confirmed, and everyone had said that such just wasn't done in this country and that one had to conform to the customs of the land where one happened to be. For that matter an American woman who was married to a Norwegian was among Mrs. Omley's invited guests, so she had set out to make a "boiled dinner." The ladies in the Presbyterian church had served a dinner like that last winter and it had been written up in the newspapers. Lewis had read about it in the *Daily Chronicle*. But she had later regretted her decision and she regretted it now because the dinner had to cook such a terribly long time. The day was burning hot and the smell of cooked cabbage permeated the whole house.

"Are you sure now that it's proper to put out *cranberry sauce* with salted meat and cabbage like this, Sophy?"

Sophy, who had stayed home from church in order to help her mother, rolled over a little on her side and thrust her clenched little hand against her temple as she rested her elbow on the table. "I d'know; it says *meat* which has got to be *kjød* because *meat* is *kjød* in English, so then it must be *kjød*."

"Ja, well, we have it ready now so we might just as well use it, but had I only known—Ja, it can't be changed now. Take a look to see if they're coming."

Sophy rose up slowly and stretched. She was thin, but just as tall as her mother. She pulled herself over to the window and looked out.

"They're coming!" she exclaimed gleefully and was about to run out but her mother restrained her.

"Now you've got to be a *nice girl* and help me set the table."

A look of annoyance appeared in the girl's pretty, blue-violet eyes. *"Well*—what are *you* going to do then? *Am I supposed*—?*"

"I don't want any *monkeybisnis* from you, Sophy. Hurry up, quick now, right away—is it maybe asking too much that a big, tall girl like you help her mother a little? Now be a good girl and help your mamma, Sophy—you see how much I have to do."

Mrs. Omley could never remain angry long enough to complete a lengthy sentence. And whenever Sophy got angry and spoke English, it was as though something so fine and *ladylike* came over her that her mother often felt ashamed at the thought of her own plainness. She couldn't understand everything Sophy said at such moments, but she felt a mother's pride when she saw Sophy straighten up and answer like a fine lady.

Sophy puckered her otherwise pretty mouth so that her upper lip rested on the bottom of her nose. This also made Mrs. Omley's heart beat faster because it made her think of the children in the wholesaler's family in Norway where she had worked as a maid and Lewis as a servant. There was something fine about Sophy because she wrinkled her upper lip just the way the upper-class people did—the wholesaler and his family were that kind of people—may our Lord hold his hand over her. Sophy could be clever, too, when she wanted to be, but it was not so often she wanted to be. The clatter of the dishes proclaimed that she was being clever now and that the table was being set quickly—just so she didn't break any of the things which had been borrowed. Mrs. Omley now remembered that the plates should be heated when the serving was to be fine and the food was fat. But she decided it would not be a good idea to have Sophy remove them from the table. She cried so easily and Mrs. Omley didn't want her sniffling when people arrived.

"And then you can collect those little dishes, both ours and those with the blue rings we borrowed from Mrs. Overhus. We'll use them for the dessert. And you may just as well start to dish up the green peas on the saucers with the blue rings and put tomatoes on the others."

"Then what are we going to use for the coffee cups—and for the ice cream and that pudding and the pie and all that?"

Mrs. Omley wiped the sweat away from her eyes and looked perplexed. "We'll have to use the saucers, and of course the coffee and pie and ice cream follow all the rest, so we should be able to get them washed. And Mrs. Overhus has promised to help," she continued as she removed a steaming kettle from the fire.

She lifted the lids, investigated and sampled. Her sweat nearly blinded her. It was piping hot. There were beads of moisture on the enamel-painted ceiling, the windows were veiled with dampness, and the smell of boiled cabbage extended all the way out to the front gate.

It had been a difficult task for Sophy to find room for all the dishes on the dining table. But now they were set out as in the finest restaurant. The carriage with the women and the pastor had already arrived, and Mrs. Overhus, who had held the baby during the christening, was changing the child as she eagerly reported how good the boy had been in church. It was apparent from the way she said this that the baby's behavior had depended a great deal on the one who held the child. Little ones like that surely had their thoughts, too, even if they didn't know it themselves, and they had to be taken care of. She also had to tell about the remarkable dexterity of the new pastor. She had always had her own solemn intuition whenever she held such a poor, innocent little thing at the font. If the child started screaming when the minister made the sign of the cross, then she drew her own conclusions. In that case, either there was something the matter with the child or there was something wrong with the minister. She would never feel comfortable with regard to such a minister. There were many things in nature which were not as they ought to be and were hidden from human eyes. Fortunately, however, it was perfectly obvious that all was in order with regard to herself and also with the child and the minister and everything else.

Mrs. Overhus wiped away a well-intentioned tear when she placed little Melvin Clarence in the baby carriage which also served as a cradle. Then she put on the apron she had brought with her and went out to the kitchen to help. Mrs. Omley was one of the younger women she liked most. She was such a pleasant and straightforward woman and they had shared both gladness and sorrow. She could mix her tears more easily with Mrs. Omley than with many who had been in the country much longer. She had also been with her when she was ill. A person would have to search a long time to find the likes of her, even though she had been in the country only ten years.

The dinner was a great success. Sophy and her best friend Mabel Overhus did the serving. The young newcomer Lars Olson didn't know quite how to tackle the food, but Omley explained the procedure to him, and others, equally inexperienced, seized on this means of rescue and, watching Lars, attacked the steaming cabbage and the piping hot meat according to the same instructions. The minister sat at one end of the table and, after saying the prayer, confined himself to the green peas, which he speared onto his fork and ate individually and thoughtfully as he conversed with the American woman married to a Norwegian, who was unmistakably the most distinguished person in the gathering. This American woman's Norwegian husband, whose very humble position in this world was that of a plumber, sat quietly and timorously like a person who has done something wrong, and held his big hands with their dirty-looking, battered fingers as much out of sight as the eating allowed and seldom used more than one hand at a time. Mabel and Sophy scurried busily around the table and repeated incessantly, *"Won't you please have some more?"* They spoke only English and therefore the guests responded, *"Yes, all right,"* and *"Thank you ma' am."* Nels Hill, who had been out among people before and liked to show it, said eagerly, *"I don't care if I do,"* stroked his mustache, and coughed dryly with dignity. The contrast between him and those who were at a real party for perhaps the first time was readily apparent. When the newcomer was asked whether he would prefer coffee or tea and responded to the question with, *"Helst kaffe, takk,"* Mabel turned to Sophy and asked, *"What does he say?"* Sophy blushed bright red and answered, *"Coffee, I guess."* But she was angry with Mabel because she had asked her what it was he had said—right here at the table where everyone could hear it. Tears welled up in her pretty eyes.

It was Sophy's cross here in this world that she had been born in Norway and had even gone to school a little there, so it was practically taken for granted that she ought to be able to speak Norwegian. This expectation always stuck to her. It happened that older women spoke Norwegian to her even when others were present. And that seemed so unjust to her, because she couldn't help the fact that she had been born in Norway and not here. It was a humiliation inflicted on her by her parents. That Mabel should take advantage of her unfortunate lot in such a way was despicable.

The meal was eaten for the most part in silence. The minister tried to get a little merriment going by making some joking comments to the two girls doing the serving. They all laughed then, partly out of respect for the minister and partly to show that they had understood what had been said. But they didn't like to say anything themselves although they thought of several things in Norwegian which they would have said in English if they had been certain they could say them right. The person who talked the most was Mrs. Stenson, who had worked for an American family of quality before her marriage. She said again and again, *"Isn't that lovely?"* and then the others chimed in enthusiastically and in unison, *"Yes, isn't it lovely?"* She was even about to say this to the minister when he told her that he had a toothache, but *lovely* got changed to *awful* just in the nick of time.

When the adults had finished at the table, the children took their places. The serving was done efficiently because each mother stood by and assisted her own offspring.

When the meal was finished, the women sat in the parlor and the men sat out on the veranda in order to smoke and talk.

There was soon a lively discussion going in the parlor and the conversation centered mostly around the children, who ran in and out making noise and wanting to grab everything that wasn't fastened down.

Mrs. Stenson knew how to put herself forward here, too. The woman in the American family where she had been a nursemaid was very fine but sickly and high-strung. Mrs. Stenson was an exceptionally fit woman, the true picture of health, but her sickly mistress had made a very strong impression on her. Mrs. Stenson had often, since little Mehala had come into the world, impressed the other wives with words and expressions which were far above the ordinary when she described her fine mistress, Mrs. Rutherford Vincent, to them.

When the other women were scolding their children in bad English saying *"shut up"* and *"I'll knock the stuffing out of you if you don't behave yourself,"* they became silent and showed almost religious reverence when Mrs. Stenson started in. Her round, ruddy face took on an expression of suffering, her eyelids lowered wearily, her nose turned up sharply when she let loose a voice that was unfamiliar and somewhat strained: *"Be a little lady now—Mehala, dear—don't do that darling! You make me, oh—*

*so nervous. Your poor mama is all in. Puds Næsa di, Darling! Mama's angel child mustn't plokka Næsa. Saa ja! Now run and play nice and don't disturb your poor mama anymore—I am ALL IN." ***

The angel child Mehala groped obediently for her little Norwegian snub nose. Mama breathed a triumphant sigh and leaned back and didn't even see the little red tongue the child stuck out at her, which also was Norwegian. But the women were impressed. Just imagine being able to remember all those words at once! How they wished to be able to direct something like that to their own children on special occasions, but there is so much here in this world that the children of simple folk must do without. And they were so certain this would have done them good. It certainly appeared to do Mrs. Stenson good.

Lars was having the time of his life in the dining room, which now had been cleared. He was the only bachelor in the gathering and here he was keeping Mabel and Sophy company. The minister had also sat there for a while, but he had a bad tooth and wasn't getting much sympathy from these young persons. He therefore removed himself to the parlor where there was no lack of sympathy and Lars was left alone with the two girls. They had made the discovery that he had pretty curly hair, and that he was handsome when he laughed. They competed in telling him the names of things in English and every time he said something wrong all three of them laughed. Here, where they didn't have to worry about feeling embarrassed, both girls spoke Norwegian quite well, and when they used words which Lars didn't understand he would ask what they meant and there were explanations and more fun. It irritated Sophy that Mabel was able to speak Norwegian so well now.

When Mrs. Omley came in from the kitchen, Lars felt obligated to say something to her and then said that apparently the minister had gone off somewhere. "Oh, he probably had a *tutik*, the poor fellow," Mrs. Omley said with compassion. *"Tutik?"* Lars repeated questioningly. Sophy tried

---

*Ager uses this speech to illustrate the confusing, often comical mixed language used by the immigrants.

in vain to remember what *toothache* was in Norwegian, but Mabel beat her to the draw and said glowingly, "It hurts in his *tut*." "*I tanna si*," Sophy quickly corrected her. Lars couldn't keep from laughing and Mabel was sorely offended. Lars then made his exit, joining the men for a smoke as the girls put their heads together to write a notice for the society section of the *Daily Chronicle*. They had saved a couple of samples that others who had had dinner parties had put in, but they didn't have the best one they had seen, in which the word *sumptuous* had been used. They couldn't find that clipping, but they reworded another for the paper in which the guests' names were preceded with *Messieurs* for the men and *Mesdames* for the women. Lars they changed to Louis and that looked nice—but not Olson.

Lars had found himself a spot on the steps and here he sat as he listened to the men's conversation. They were sitting in their shirtsleeves in the heat, eagerly engaged in discussion. There was a pail of beer in the shadiest corner. They spoke only Norwegian, so Lars was able to follow their conversation. It struck him quite forcefully how much finer the women were than their men.

They discussed politics. The subject came up peacefully with the newly baptized infant Melvin Clarence, whom the minister had referred to as a possible future president. This led to the question whether the Norwegians would support one of their own people or if the Americans would allow the son of Norwegian parents to become president. Some said yes and others no. Thore Overhus, who was the proprietor of a sizeable furniture store and was without doubt one of the most successful men at the gathering, believed that all Norwegians who had attained to high offices had been elected to them by their countrymen. No one had got ahead without the support of his own people. When a candidate for office had a volunteer campaign committee of hundreds of his countrymen working gratis for him in the city on the basis of common origin, all went well. These office-holders rode into their positions on broad Norwegian shoulders and that is what sustained them.

But Nels Hill would not listen to this. According to him, Norwegians cut each other down. They couldn't stand to see anyone else get ahead, not even the least little bit. That had been his firsthand experience when he had run for alderman. It was his own people who were the worst. And it was the same thing in business too. For his part, he wouldn't vote for a Norwegian running for any office.

The mention of business brought the plumber into the arena. He was surprised that the Norwegian businessmen got as much patronage from their countrymen as they did. Weren't they the ones who bowed and scraped and acted pleasant whenever an Irishman or a fairly well-dressed woman walked in who had the advantage of being fluent in English? Then they stood and rubbed their hands together in obligingness and politely asked, *"What can I do for you?"* But if a Norwegian woman came in they shrieked, *"Aa ska di ha for no' ida, di da Mor?"** And how willing they were to give the *engelske* everything possible on credit. It was almost something of an honor to be cheated by one of the English.

The plumber had a sharp tongue when he was at a safe distance from his wife. He was much more silent when he was in her presence because then she was the one who had a sharp tongue.

There were many objections to what the plumber had said, but all agreed that such Norwegian merchants did actually exist.

"You've really been lucky to get yourself such a fine American wife," Nels Hill said with sarcasm.

"Ja—I got myself an American one right away so I wouldn't have to try and make one out of unfit material like it says in the catechism. Only our Lord could do that. I wanted to have a fine wife and that's the same for all of you, too. And when we get it the way we want it we have no reason for complaints. The wife is good enough," he continued. "She can make music and paint a little—and declaim and—"

"But, can she darn socks?" interrupted Nels.

"No, but I can," the plumber answered him dryly. They all laughed.

"But how did it happen that you got yourself such a fine wife?" Stenson inquired.

The plumber flicked the ash from his cigar with a reflective look.

---

*"So what do you want today, then, Mother?"

"It went a lot easier than I thought it would," he said. "She told me I have the ugliest hands she ever saw."

"Yes, and then what?"

"Then I put one of them around her waist so she couldn't see it anymore and I told her she had the prettiest hands I had ever seen and that I intended having her hand in marriage."

"And she took you up on it?"

"Yes, right on the spot."

They laughed again. If they were to have any fun, they had to have the plumber along.

He smiled cunningly. "With God's help—and millinery stores—you can all have fine wives too, but it will take time and money—I just looked ahead a little more than the rest of you."

No one thought this was funny any longer and the conversation took another direction.

"It's a bit awkward as far as language is concerned when the husband and wife aren't from the same country," Thore Overhus said rather cautiously. "The two of them can communicate better when they speak the same language."

"Certainly!" said the plumber. "But my wife speaks Norwegian quite well, and she reads it too. She learned it after we got married. We speak Norwegian a lot. She has reached the point now where she speaks English only when she gets angry or when she's with your wives who consider Norwegian too ordinary. When we speak English at least she's fluent in the language, and when we speak Norwegian then I'm fluent in the language. But when you speak English with your wives, neither of you knows the language very well. My wife is proud of what Norwegian she has learned, but your wives are proud of the Norwegian they have forgotten. They don't even speak it to their children. If my wife and I had had children, they would have learned both languages. At least, that's what my wife says now," he added.

Nels Hill became sarcastic as he said, "What use would that be to the children, anyway? This is America, an English-speaking country. Isn't it bad enough that we older ones are looked down on without our children being looked down on, too?"

"Surely no one is looked down on here because he knows languages," the plumber said abruptly. "But here parents have their children learn Latin or German in high school and don't even teach them the only language the parents know—and know well. They go to school and learn about the Greeks and Egyptians and Romans and all that, but they don't know anything about their own ancestors. They know more about Julius Caesar and Jesse James than they do about their own fathers."

"No," objected Stenson. "Now I want to say that as far as my children are concerned, I wouldn't wish on them the pain of being plagued with two languages. It's enough that we older ones have that torment. English is good enough for me."

"Yes, it's enough," said the plumber. "And there are people who get by with just one shirt, too—then they have an easier wash."

The minister, who had meanwhile come in, thought he ought to say something here. He was still new in this call and had replaced an older minister because the congregation wanted to have English services in addition to Norwegian. In his heart, he hoped and wished that the total transition to English would be made because it would be much easier for him. His childhood had been darkened by the Norwegian religion school. Only English had been spoken in his home, but his father, who was a strict Lutheran of the old persuasion, had required that he should go to Norwegian religion school and learn the catechism and its explanation in Norwegian.* And he had attempted to memorize it in the shadow of the rod. First, it was the Ten Commandments and the rod. Then it was the Articles or the rod, and the Lord's Prayer and the rod or the threat of the rod. He had sat and chewed on long words like *nidkjærhed, miskundelse, vederkvægelse, retfærdiggjørelse*, and *vederstyggelighed* and the like that nearly suffocated him and made him feel sick.** No sooner had he learned them than they shifted position and danced around in all the questions and

---

*Congregational school, meeting mostly in summer when public schools were not in session.

**Zeal, mercy, comfort, justification, and abomination.

answers as though they were living creatures who put themselves in his path with nothing but malicious intent so that he should get either a scolding or a whipping. When he got older and entered college he quickly learned how to manipulate them and learned to speak Norwegian fluently. But he never managed to get rid of a feeling of terror from his childhood instruction although he also had great respect for it. He became a pastor according to his father's wishes, and then he had to take his Norwegian along as baggage, and he did too, but only as a necessary evil.

Norwegian, for him, was a foreign language. He could, however, understand those ministers who vehemently held on to Norwegian. They were fine, well-educated men, and as far as their knowledge was concerned—yes, he had the inbred reverence and unquestioning respect for the knowledge which had come directly across the sea. But there was another kind of clergy who always made him smile. They were some of the Norwegian-born immigrants who had started at the seminary rather than at the sawmill. They went about speaking their poor, affected English on all occasions, and no one was as English as some of them were. They had to baptize in English and confirm in English—and such English!

Yes—and such Norwegian! They were fellows who could *mixe*.* He had to laugh every time he thought about one of the neighboring pastors who had been the speaker at the Reformation festival. He said that Luther had *"katta te Piser alt som Pavemagta vart founda paa—og at Luther-anerne i de Dagene ikke havde manglet Bagben som nu i vore Dage."* It was *"backbone"* this pastor who had been in this country only six years had meant to say and not hind legs.**

When he thought about his own Norwegian it was as though a private chamber took shape within him where his own "I" fell down on its knees and thanked God that he could speak decent English and was not like this sinner.

---

*mixe—to mix Norwegian and English.
**"He said that Luther had 'cut to pieces everything on which papal power was grounded—and that the Lutherans in those days had not lacked *hind legs* as now in our day.' "

When the minister expressed his opinion to the group he said it must be obvious that the time was close at hand when everything would be in English. It was best, of course, if the children could speak both languages, though not essential now that what they were taught about Lutheranism and the hymns and confessions were all translated into English. The future of the church depended on the younger generation, and for them Norwegian would be a foreign language which they could barely speak or understand with great difficulty, while the English language was much easier both to speak and to understand.

Nels Hill could attest to the fact that English was so much easier than Norwegian. Lars involuntarily sent him a look of admiration which Nels received almost shyly. Nels was from the same area in Norway as Lars and had been in the country only seven years, but he was nonetheless already much more proficient in English than in Norwegian. Lars felt proud of the region which had fostered them both. He was struck by their self-sacrifice since they were all speaking Norwegian even though English was so much easier!

"I suppose the day will come when only English will be used in church," one of the men threw out as a feeler.

Yes, the minister thought the trend would have to be in that direction. But the time for that was not yet ripe because there remained much to be done. There was, for example, the matter of raising funds for the community's schools because new buildings were needed. And locally, there was the matter of a new church which would be more suited to the young and more in keeping with the needs of the times. He believed the older people could understand that the younger ones made other demands on the church with respect to God's house than they had, of course, because they had required less. A modern church could not be financed and built without the older members, so there could be no talk for some time to come about dropping Norwegian services. The older people were essential when a new church was to be built for the young and for the Yankees whom they also had to attempt to reach and bring under the influence of Lutheranism. If they were to attract these people, then they had to build a structure which was both fine and modern.

All this was taken for granted. The only person to raise any objections was the plumber, who did so in an ironic manner. "So you're saying," he said, "that we should use Norwegian to collect funds for the schools and to build a big, fine church, and when that's been accomplished we dump the Norwegian because we no longer have any use for it. Then we can get the Yankees with us in the same way we Norwegians build fine houses for the Americans—the day we're finished then it's *goodbye*. They pay us off—the carpenters, the painters, the bricklayers—everyone gets his due and the American moves in. But now you're saying that we should build it and pay for it both, and when we're all through we say, '*Værsgo** go in,' and it's to be understood that as soon as they come in through the front door then we are to be kicked out through the sacristy—because then the building has been built and paid for and we're no longer needed—and besides, we're so unrefined that our presence could frighten our children and the Yankees away from hearing God's Word.

"Isn't that what they do in the community, too? Some of what comes in through Norwegian work contributes to eliminating Norwegian work, indirectly anyhow. If the intention is to hang *Norskdom*, then those who are going to do the hanging ought to be obliged to pay for the rope with which the hanging is to be accomplished. As it now stands, we have to pay both for the rope and for our own funeral. 'Go now forth and dig your grave,' they say, and we are never more diligent than when we are permitted to do that. And in the funeral oration they declare how we have provided for ourselves and for them. They were really some splendid fellows. May they rest in peace and blessed be their memory."

There was a pause. Then he continued as though he were just talking to himself. "When our church was built, the building was done by poor newcomers who missed Norwegian services. They lacked higher education and fine clothes, but they worked hard to erect the church. They went off to work on the church when they were finished at the sawmills, without any supper. They carried boards and planks on their backs a distance of a half a mile to save on transportation. If now there's such a great need

---

*Shortened form of "*vær så god*" (be so kind, go ahead).

for a church for the young people, then they ought to be permitted to build it themselves. There are not many of them who are broken down by hard work. It is easier for them than for those of us who arrived here thirty-five years ago."

The minister gently reminded them that it wasn't so easy for the young nowadays since such great demands were being made upon them in every respect. Many of them did not earn much more than what they needed for food and clothing and education together with suitable amusements, and many still hadn't chosen a life's occupation.

All this was just as true as could be and no objections were made. It was quite unthinkable that present-day youth could be expected to do what young newcomers had done twenty-five or thirty-five years earlier. It was not possible to draw parallels, because those earlier ones were simple folk who were accustomed to obtaining for themselves what they wanted, and who had no one else to depend on. Besides, they were able to deny themselves a great many things in the way of both food and clothing which our young people neither would nor could do without.

The conversation touched upon other themes as well. It was especially the difference between Norway and America which was discussed. In Norway, a person just had to accept things the way they were. A simple man was looked down upon. A simple man's son or daughter must never think of dressing or acting or becoming educated like upper-class people. Here all were of the cultivated or educated class and did not have to remove their hats or be obliged to greet anyone. The poorest man could become president, and there were excellent schools where one could learn everything.

But America was also a country in which the immigrants themselves could get ahead. Nels Hill, who now was foreman of a railroad section gang, told how, as a nine-year-old boy in Norway, he was sent out to herd sheep. He had worked and toiled on a farm in Norway for miserable pay. He attributed his present position not only to his own ability, which he demonstrated from time to time and to which he briefly alluded, but also, and much more, to the conditions here in this country which were such that a simple man could work to advance himself.

William Stenson, who was county clerk and therefore held public office, could tell how, back home in Norway, he had sought employment in vain as clerk in the sheriff's office, and now he was about the equivalent of a *sorenskriver** according to Norwegian terminology. His lifestyle also testified to what opportunities there were here for people who sought to get ahead. For his part (and considering that the minister was present) he could not explain his advancement as being due to his competence alone; God had also stood behind and guided events to his advantage— and to the shame of those back home in Norway who had not deemed him fit to assume even a subordinate position in a sheriff's office.

Lars became wide-eyed. This was truly a remarkable country. Here he was, sitting together with a railroad foreman and a *sorenskriver*, and the *sorenskriver* had asked him two times for a match and once to move over a little so that he too might have a place on the steps. As to Overhus, Lars knew that he owned and operated a large furniture store and was supposed to be very wealthy.

He was reminded of incidents from his childhood and from his period of training at the paint store, where he had been bullied. He had had to carry heavy crates of paint on his head while the apprentices strutted alongside him, gesticulating with cigar butt in one hand and ruler in the other. They should just see him now in such fine company.

He listened with wonder to the great opportunities which were open here to the young. One had a son who was going to become a doctor, another a son who was going to become an engineer, and the son of a third was going to become a lawyer. None of them were going to learn a common trade as they would have in Norway. They were all going to become important men.

But it was also said that the experiences of these men had not been any dance on a bed of roses. Thore Overhus told how he and his wife their first winter in Chicago had often sat and turned a dime back and forth not knowing if they should decide to buy bread or coal with it. Stenson could tell about winters when he worked as a lumberjack in the forest while his

---

* Judge of a rural district.

wife went hungry doing laundry—about sickness and death, and how they
had worried about getting the bodies buried of their two oldest children
who perished in a diphtheria epidemic. It had been a tough struggle, but
with God's help they had made it through.

Lewis Omley had not entered much into the conversation. He had been
thinking with contentment about the little one in the cradle, his first child
to be baptized in English. There was something special about that. The
boy would certainly become somebody. Yes, and the other boys too. His
eye caught sight of his two little boys, who just then were out playing in
the street. There was just a little over a year between them and they played
so well together. They were playing catch. They stood a considerable distance from one another as they threw the ball back and forth. The small-
est boy stood on one leg and swung out with his arm like a pro, and turned
and crouched until with deliberation and forethought he tossed the ball to
his brother, who in deep earnestness went through the same motions when
he returned the ball. They had kept on with this since right after dinner
and showed no signs of fatigue. The thudding sound of the ball hitting the
mitt as it was being caught resounded regularly like a gunshot and Omley's
heart beat hard with a feeling of joy that welled up inside him. This was
the way boys played in the finest American sections of the town. No one
could tell by looking at these small boys that their parents were only ordinary uneducated Norwegian folk.

II.

THE CHILDREN, the children! That was the all-encom-
passing theme in the living room—the children and
their abilities or lack of them. What they ate and what
they didn't eat. What they took "lessons" in and what these lessons cost.
How much it cost to keep them properly clothed when they were small
and how much worse it was when they got big. To this were added reports

as to how busy the parents themselves were. The grown-up daughter of one had to have a newly ironed blouse at least every other day, so there was a good deal of washing and ironing to be done. The daughter of another woman had so much "*company*," so many who came to visit. A third had a daughter who went to parties among Americans, even the finest ones, almost every single day. All of them had "lessons" and all of them seemed to be unskilled when it came to all types of housework— the mothers outbid each other in presenting evidence of this lack of skill because it was the most unmistakable sign of refinement and high aspirations.

With respect to some of the individual children, they were quite different from ordinary Norwegian children right from the time of their birth, so to speak. Mrs. Nelson was not at all among those who put herself forward, because she was a widow, and she was poor, and everyone knew it. She had nothing fine except a son who went to high school. But she had to tell how intelligent the boy had been when he was little. She gave him two bottles. The one was just a cheap one that had cost five cents, but the other one was a gift to her from some Yankee woman she had worked for, and sure as shooting, that was the one he had to have.

There were two or three who tried at the same time to have the floor in order to brag about their own children. Mrs. Overhus was the winner and told that Mabel, when she was learning to walk, had not crawled on her tummy like other children but that she had pulled herself forward with one hand and one side of her b— she was going to say "behind" and not at all what the women perhaps thought she was going to say and she changed it to hip. She nonetheless understood by their expressions that she had put her foot in her mouth and became quite flustered while she scraped across the sofa with the sweaty palm of her hand to demonstrate for them how Mabel had got along in this world when she was a little baby.

This attempt had been so unsuccessful that a pause ensued during which no one said anything, but it appeared as though they were thinking all the more: "Was that anything to tell?"

Besides, it was better to show what the children were now. Mrs. Omley called on Sophy, who took music lessons for thirty-five cents an hour:

"Sophy, Sophy! You must come and play *'Old Oaken Maiden's Prayer'* for us, Sophy!" Sophy was not at all unwilling to do this, but she did have to correct her mother a little. There were two different pieces to which she was referring. The one was *"Old Oaken Bucket"* and the other, *"Maiden's Prayer."* However, she obediently played them both while the wives sat very meditatively and thought how much more difficult pieces like *"Silvery Wifes"* and *"Blue Danubb"* were, which their daughters could play almost without looking at the music or having to bother about keeping time.

Now came the coffee and with it the cake platters. With the cake platters came the children. Mrs. Hill had a fat little boy with her who watched with greedy eyes as the cakes were being sliced. Mabel gave him a *smultring.** A storm started brewing in the little face—his eyes sought his mother and he fought bravely to hold back the tears. His mother quickly drew him over to her and exchanged the doughnut for a piece of banana cake which quickly disappeared inside the child's spacious mouth. "He doesn't eat doughnuts," she whispered with a mother's pride to the one sitting closest to her, and she was glad that she had been able to make the switch before the boy had a chance to howl because he didn't get what he liked best right away.

But the little incident had not passed unnoticed. There were women whose children were not accustomed to having doughnuts available to them, and they thought to themselves that the Lord could always fix it so that the Hills would just be grateful that they had doughnuts to give to their children. They were not that well-off, and God did not let himself be mocked by people who did not have any more than they did.

The telephone rang and Sophy went to take it: "It's Mrs. Stenson they want."

"Is it Helen?"

"Yes."

Helen was Mrs. Stenson's ten-year-old daughter, who was at home with two smaller children.

"What does she want?"

---

* Deep-fried Norwegian doughnut.

"She says she wants to know how long you're going to stay here, and that it's about time you come home because you've been here plenty long enough."

Mrs. Stenson got up in a hurry and called out to Stenson on the veranda that they would have to go because Helen had phoned. Helen was obviously not to be fooled with.

This gave Mrs. Hill an excuse to say that she too had better be going, and this also gave her another opportunity to put on her large new hat with two long ostrich feathers which flapped against her back when she tossed her head, which she did when she wore her hat because it was a hat that had cost eight dollars and fifty cents. This was a direct challenge to the others and Mrs. Overhus kept fingering the lace on her elegant ten-dollar blouse, and Mrs. Stenson threw her eleven-dollar white silk shawl around her shoulders, while Mrs. Benson took up her eighteen-dollar gold watch and compared the time with the living-room clock.

There was at least one dissatisfied woman, and that was Mrs. Newhouse. She had neither new hat, new shawl, nor gold watch, but she had had an expensive operation. Here these chatterboxes had spent the whole time talking about their kids and she had let them go on because she had carefully figured that she would have a good opportunity to talk about the operation following coffee. She was the only one here who had been through a real operation. When she stopped to think about it there weren't many among the Norwegians who had ever been through anything like that, though there were more among the Yankees. When it came right down to it her operation had cost as much as six hats and five gold watches, if not more.

She consoled herself and gathered her things and prepared to leave with the others. But she would have departed in a lighter frame of mind if she had had her chance like the others.

After a while the house was emptied of guests. The party was over, the people went their ways, and everything became deserted and silent.

But out on the street could still be heard the regular sound of the ball that the boys threw back and forth with those professional motions of arms and legs.

Thore Overhus and Lars stayed and sat for a while after the others had gone. Overhus had to wait while his wife put together the things she had lent to Mrs. Omley for the occasion. Lars had slid over to the spot which had been occupied by the county clerk and felt it was a good place to be sitting.

"It's strange that more Norwegians don't make the journey to America," Lars finally said only to have something to say. He couldn't just sit there like an oaf and not say anything.

Overhus took his time and cleaned his pipe and cleared his throat before he responded. "It's just as strange that more Norwegians don't make the journey back to Norway," he said. "You have to pay for what you get here too, and some things get plenty expensive, and what you pay with you don't get back again."

Yes, Lars understood well enough that many things were expensive over here. But a person earned more so he could better afford to pay.

But now Mrs. Overhus was ready and Lars unwillingly raised himself up from the spot where the county clerk had been sitting.

III.

L ARS WROTE a long letter to his sister in Norway the next evening after he returned home from work. He found it easier to write to her than to his parents, and they would read it anyway. He wrote that he had got work for two dollars a day, which was more than seven crowns in Norwegian money, and that he lived at widow Nelson's, and that her son, who was a student, and he, that is Lars himself, were the best of friends. He also said that he had been to a fine dinner party at which almost everyone spoke English and that the dinner itself had all been "in English." Among the guests there was a *sorenskriver*, a rich merchant, and one who held an important position with the railroad, in addition to a fine American woman and the minister, who had to be included as one of the Yankees since English was the language he used for the most part. Mr. Omley, his host, was also his employer, and it was not uncommon in America that the masters invited some of their most trusted apprentices when there was something special taking place at their homes. In that respect there was a great difference between America and Norway, where a worker was often looked down on. He also enclosed a clipping from one of the big English-language newspapers, which was called the *Daily Chronicle*. The article reported that Mr. and Mrs. Lewis Omley had given a splendid dinner, etc., and he had underlined the name *Louis Olson, a late arrival from Europe*—that last part, he explained in Norwegian, meant that he was a European who had just come to America from Europe. He also told about two young ladies, one of whom was a pianist or was being trained to be one. She took lessons and had already made considerable progress. The other was a student and was the daughter of a rich merchant.

The work was quite hard because here one really had to make an effort; that was what counted. His working companion was an American named O'Roorke, so he had to talk English all day long and had already learned so much that he could carry on a simple conversation even though there were still many words which he couldn't understand.

When he had finished the letter he went out to sit on the steps to enjoy the coolness of the evening. He sat there a long time resting his aching limbs because he had been working hard. The memories from the previous day were vividly before him.

He was thinking about Sophy. He couldn't help comparing her with Karoline Huseby back home in Norway, the girl he had been so taken with. One of his dreams—one which had accompanied him on the journey over—was that one day he would return to his little home place a rich, fine man and show both his and Karoline's people what someone like him could accomplish. But it was as though Karoline's face faded out of the picture for him now that he had seen Sophy, because Sophy was a *lady*. There was something so maidenly pure and fine about her—something so tranquilly, dreamingly fine, he thought. He had read the expression "dreamingly fine" in a book, and it came to mind when he saw her the evening before. Sophy didn't even laugh—she only smiled. He thought of Karoline's noisy laughter as something wholly unsuited to a lady. And now the dream took another twist: he would return home with a wife like Sophy. They would disembark from the steamship and he would lend her elegant assistance down the gangplank and address her in English and she would answer him in that language, and they would converse in English together while Father and Mother and sister Anna would wonder what it was they were saying to each other. And they would go home with them and sit down to the table to eat and he would offer Sophy this and that and politely say, *"Won't you please have some more?"* And she would answer with her fine smile, *"Thank you ma'am."*

Lars worked for Lewis Omley. Omley had decided to become a house painter after coming to America and had learned the trade pretty well. The Norwegians were good at building and it was not long before he was taking on small jobs on his own. He had only one boy who worked with him in the beginning, but the work increased and now during the summer he regularly employed three or four men. He had set up a paint workshop in an outbuilding and here he was at five o'clock every morning to mix the colors to be used during the day. His best worker was the Irishman Jim O'Roorke, who drank a lot. That was to Omley's advantage because he worked for less pay. Whenever he shirked a day, then he made up for it by working that much harder the other days. Omley kept track of the hours but the Irishman did not take into account how hard he worked. He was a hardworking fellow and Omley set Lars to work with him. The newcomers were almost always slow and particular. Jim would no doubt get him up to speed. Omley never miscalculated. He worked with the others himself and no one—not even the Irishman after a spree—worked as hard as he did. He had much work to do and few helpers. He also had a unique ability to drive others. When Lars was about to start working for him, Omley told the Irishman, "Now, Jim, you're going to have a work companion who is going to be difficult to keep up with. If you can manage to outdo him, then you're a better man than I thought." The Irishman just laughed, lit his pipe, and casually blew the smoke in Omley's face. "I may be dumb," he said, "and the wife says it's because I eat too many potatoes, although I seldom eat more than a peck at a time, but the lad must be even dumber if he thinks he can beat me."

Omley said to Lars, on the other hand, that there wasn't much work to be had during the winter and that most of the painters were unemployed, but he usually kept one man on and, of course, he kept the best one. The Irishman had had steady work for three years.

Lars was accustomed to doing good work. It took some time before he learned to be less particular, but he worked hard to keep up with the Irishman, who labored like a machine. When they whitewashed a ceiling together he could just keep up with him and that was all. It was a silent but strenuous contest between young, unpracticed muscles and old, well-trained ones. The Irishman may also have had winter in mind, and that was of great importance, since he had a family and a constant thirst to take into consideration. After working under such pressure Lars was clearly able to understand why the Irishman was stiff and sore the next day. That gave him hope for the winter, because he felt stiff only during the evening.

Omley walked about like an oracle who would not reveal to either of them which one he considered best, but he got a great deal of work out of them and he was glad for that. None profited him more than newcomers and those who drank a bit, but the big painters didn't want to have them. He worked more than anyone, and when he went to bed dead tired he set the alarm clock for four-thirty. What kept him going was his bankbook in which his regular deposits were recorded. Whenever he took a rest his thoughts were occupied with the children. He was willing to spend money so that Sophy could study more music and get more education. When he saw the boys play catch he couldn't help thinking of high school and the university, and the education they would have. His boys would not have to cart around ladders and paint cans. He had seen fine folk in Norway and he had seen them here. It was quite apparent to him that his own dream of becoming a really cultivated man could not be realized. It was not just a matter of having money—or clothes either. There were a number of Norwegians who had a lot of money and were well dressed, but "fine" they were not—not really cultivated people. All of them had done common labor like himself. But with the children it was different. When he heard the sound of the ball and saw those professional motions with arms and legs, how the boys threw it and seized it, that to him was a portent that their interests were already identical with the interests of a world that he felt was barred to him but into which the boys would be lifted. He would guarantee that. Following such thoughts he stretched his weary limbs, set the alarm clock, and went to bed.

The ringing of this clock would also awaken his wife, who was to have breakfast ready at six o'clock.

IV.

LARS DISCOVERED that he had much to learn in the first couple of months. He worked for several days with the redecorating of Willum's large clothing store and had an opportunity to see what an outstanding businessman Willum was. Willum could side with anyone who had a little buying to do. He didn't belong to a congregation because there were two of them in town and he didn't want to offend anyone. He contributed to them both and led the most prominent members of both congregations and their ministers to understand that he liked theirs best if he were to join either. Since both were eager to have this splendid man, that gave him their patronage. He was neutral in politics, though he was actually a Republican, but could state good reasons why he believed the Democrats could and should win when he had customers of that persuasion. He was quite a clever man with some knowledge of just about everything. But in his store he was only knowledgeable about clothing and people and never had any opinions about anything at all and was heartily in agreement with everyone who could afford to buy anything. He knew almost everyone by name and when someone came in who was not one of his regular customers he would whisper something to one of the clerks who in turn would in all confidentiality whisper to the customer the joyous news that Willum had given orders that he should receive a ten-percent discount just like one of the regular customers, but that this must not be repeated to anyone. Almost all the trading was done in whispers and behind secretive facial expressions, and customer after customer sneaked out with their dirt-cheap, well-wrapped bargains under their arms. The more skeptical customers were even initiated into the code symbols with which the items were marked instead of numbers. The other Norwegian clothiers used numbers and that made it easier to prove that they were more expensive. Willum always went around with a smile on his face. His smile didn't even leave him when he went after a clerk who had told the truth about some underwear that could have passed for wool. He could tell some coarse stories that he had heard from some of the traveling salesmen, and he could hum as nice a tune as "Jesus Loves Me" when the smooth-shaven evangelists who held tent meetings in the town came in to look for a good buy in black trousers from the long-bearded clothier.

Lars had long since been finished with the work in the store when he walked down Murdock Avenue one Sunday afternoon dressed in a brand new pair of trousers which he had bought, when he suddenly had a vague feeling of having done something wrong—or that something had caught on his new trousers. Almost frightened, he looked around and discovered the merchant Willum waiting, for a streetcar. He greeted him and went ahead but felt the merchant's eyes looking at him like two wiggly mice in his trouser legs. Nor had many days gone by before Omley asked him if he had shopped for clothes. Lars explained about the trousers and where he had bought them. "Well," said Omley, "it's just that Willum expects us to buy from him since he gives us work to do. That's the way we do things here—and you know I would like to keep you on this winter."

After that, Lars obediently always bought his clothes at Willum's and got a ten-percent discount.

He learned other things, too, because already that summer there was a movement afoot to vote the saloons out of town the coming spring. Lars, who had been a Good Templar in Norway, felt entitled to his own opinion in this matter and had discussed it with Stenson once when he had been sent up to the courthouse to varnish some doors. A few days later he had been given a friendly hint from Omley not to discuss politics. He could, of course, have his opinions if he would just keep them to himself. If, for instance, the saloonkeepers should find out he had a man in his business who was against them, that would soon put an end to the work at the courthouse, yes, and other places as well. And he added that he of course intended to keep him on through the winter since it was difficult for a newcomer to find anything to do.

Mrs. Berntine Nelson, at whose place Lars had his lodging, was a very hardworking woman who did washing and ironing for better folk. She was a widow. As a young newcomer she had married a man from Tistedalen who was killed the first winter, when a tree fell on him while he was working as a lumberman. All she had from their short life together was the memory of their engagement, the wedding in the minister's study, and the tragic funeral. She knew that her husband had come from the area of Fredrikshald, that his first name was Hans, and that he was usually called "Hank." But she did have her son, who took up all the available space in her little brain and big heart.

To begin with, she had taken domestic jobs at places where the boy could come along. When he got old enough to go to school she grew weary of moving from place to place and rented a house and took in washing. She was capable, strong, and willing, and accepted all she could manage. The boy grew up and became strong, big, and handsome, and got all the schooling required by law.

Mrs. Nelson had been able to chat a little in English when she worked out among people, but during the many years she had stood at the washboard it was as though she had rubbed and scrubbed off again the little she had learned. The boy played outdoors with other children and soon spoke only English. All the while he went to elementary school they managed to communicate reasonably well, he speaking English and she, Norwegian. They understood or thought they understood one another. Of Norwegian she had taught him the Lord's Prayer and "Gud boie," the latter as a table grace. But as the years passed it became more and more difficult for them to understand each other. However, they didn't have much to talk about, either. He was a handsome boy and an exemplary boy, who never did anything bad. He was strong too, and as broad as a door across his shoulders. He liked to be well dressed. He didn't earn anything, to be sure, but then he was very careful with his clothes and his mother pressed his trousers for him and used some tailor tricks like steaming and such, so they always looked like new. Henry, as he was called, was likewise always very considerate toward her and patted her stooped back and said kind words to her, which she couldn't always understand but which were touching to her because of the affectionate tone in which they were spoken. He now went to high school and had been there for several years without managing to graduate. He was at present nineteen years old and even had whiskers, so every Saturday his mother had to give him ten cents for the barber so he could be fine and smooth for Sunday.

He was far from proud. In spite of the fact that he was captain of the high school football team and its best player, he did not consider himself too good to help his mother. When the clothes basket stood ready with freshly washed and freshly ironed laundry, then he picked it up and carried it on his broad shoulders to deliver it and collect payment, which he then brought back to his mother.

She obtained the most reliable information about her son from Mrs. Skare, who also had a son in high school. He told his father who then told her how everyone talked about Henry as an exemplary boy, and she often repeated from memory accounts from the *Daily Chronicle* which her husband had read and retold when the high school football team had won a brilliant victory.

Henry was a football player without equal. When he headed the battle line on the field and felt thousands of stares directed at him, then all light-heartedness and goodwill vanished. He was a wall and an avalanche. Where he stood, the attack was broken against his strong limbs, and where he went ahead he opened a way for others. With his thick, light hair bristling, his teeth clenched together, and his eyes halfway closed, he saw everything. Like a streak of lightning he knew what had to be done and saw a way out when no one else could see it. No wonder the high school celebrated victories about which stories were told years afterward. The teachers forgot that the boy's mind was little suited to studies and let him go on since they were reluctant to lose him on the football team. His mother also took calmly the fact that he never finished school, so long as she could keep him at home with her.

Henry was no dreamer. When he was awake he did not ponder anything on earth, and his sleep was dreamless. His most characteristic trait was his smile—meaningless but still genuine, as when a healthy child smiles in his sleep.

Lars liked the young man very much. He could not remember among all his acquaintances in Norway ever meeting a more exemplary or kind boy. He neither smoke, drank, swore, danced, nor spoke indecently. He blushed and became as shy as a young girl when Lars asked him about what he had thought of doing for a living, and his kind eyes shifted helplessly and beseechingly from Lars to his mother at the ironing board.

Henry understood a great deal of Norwegian and Lars talked to him a lot and showed him photographs from Norway and an ornamental sketch from drawing school; Henry smiled and said *"fine"* and showed Lars some of his schoolwork while his mother stood by and tried to be an interpreter. She didn't manage this very well, but enough was understood so that the two young men could compliment each other.

Mrs. Nelson then straightened up and continued with her ironing. It seemed to go better, and her back didn't seem to ache so much when her nice big boy sat with his legs crossed, resting his chin against his arm, and watched her.

She was only a simple woman and there was something grand about the thought that she who was so simple could have such a fine son. It was almost as though she felt embarrassed in front of him.

V.

L ARS DID NOT often have occasion to see Sophy. It happened now and then that she came into the workshop when Lars was there. The Irishman just called her "*the kid*," and Omley he simply called Lewis. Lars could not bring himself to do anything like that. Omley was Mr. Omley and Sophy was Miss Omley. He was not so formal with respect to the two boys, however. When the Irishman chased them out of the workshop, Lars thought he could do the same, and he did, too—although he didn't swear at them the way the Irishman always did.

When Sophy came she usually stood watching him silently as he worked with the colors. There was something so fine about her that it was nearly impossible to believe she had been born in the Old Country, and Lars hardly dared speak to her. Once he did muster up enough courage to ask if she had been to the park. She answered by asking him if he had ever been there and he responded that he wasn't very familiar with things, but that he would like to go with someone who was. Then Sophy asked if he couldn't go along with her and Mabel because they were going there to see the animals the following Sunday. The beginnings of a zoo had been established in the same park, with monkeys and bears.

He looked forward to this the whole week, and Sunday afternoon he met them in his Sunday best and for safety's sake had the entire week's wages in his pocket. Both Sophy and Mabel had long white gloves and white shoes. Lars couldn't help swelling with pride: the folks at home in the Old Country should just see him now! He tingled with a feeling of dignity and they didn't pass a lemonade stand or ice cream parlor without his extending a gallant invitation or indicating something in that direction. The two girls had an amazing capacity, and he paid with joy and gladness. There was only one thing he regretted and that was that the girls spoke only English together, and when one of them asked Lars about something, then the other answered for him, and besides, it appeared as though the one didn't want the other to see that she was the least bit interested in a person by the name of Lars. And they certainly didn't wish to speak Norwegian here where there were so many people around.

Lars rented a rowboat and took them for a little trip out on the lake. They sat the whole while and said amusing things to each other which Lars could not understand. But he dutifully laughed along with them, and for those who rowed near them it must have appeared as though all three of them were upper-class Americans. One thing that bothered him was that he would have liked to smoke, but he had forgotten to get cigars and it was just not acceptable to smoke a pipe in the presence of fine ladies. In his thoughts he sat and wrote letters home telling about this wonderful outing. He was good at rowing, and it was wonderful to have oars in the water again.

One thing was obvious, and that was that Sophy was much prettier than Mabel. Lars realized full well that he couldn't sit and stare at a woman, and that to do so was impolite, so for the most part he looked to the side as he rowed but stole a look at her every once in a while. He was certainly entitled to do that since he was the one who had paid for the rental of the boat. He surprised her because every time she looked at him his eyes met hers, but then there was a simultaneous change of expression as their glances went their separate ways.

Here in the boat it was all right to speak Norwegian and Lars explained the various techniques of rowing and demonstrated how one should row and how one should not row. Everyone knew how to row where he had grown up, and ships came there from all corners of the world. He had thought of becoming a seaman but his parents wanted him to learn something instead. He also had a chance to tell about his home and in such a way that they could be made to understand that it had not been poverty which was the reason for his being in this country.

And the girls were communicative now and kept questioning him about one thing and another. Sophy could just barely remember Norway and the trip across. She had been so terribly small at the time. She remembered, though, that she had been awfully sick and had been throwing up almost the whole way.

At this point—and in English too—she was reproved by Mabel who asked if she didn't know better than to talk about such things. It suddenly occurred to both Lars and Sophy that such conversation was not proper in good company. Lars then came to her rescue with facts about seasickness, which no one who was not accustomed to the sea could be safe from, and about the many he had seen throw up on the way over who surely belonged to the upper class. He had even been seasick himself and thrown up.

Sophy gave him a warm look for this help, and this little episode became one of Lars's most precious memories for a long time to come. It was as though a bond had been sealed between them—they had in a way found mutual understanding at a place where Mabel was not present.

This also became a precious memory for Sophy, because after she and Lars had accompanied Mabel home and were alone, she carefully brought the subject of seasickness up again. They both agreed that under such circumstances it could not be considered the least bit improper to throw up.

Both Lars and Sophy lived on this for a considerable time; it was just as though there was something they shared which knit them together—apart from and in spite of Mabel.

Months later, when there was snow on the ground and they had seen each other numerous times without being able to find anything to talk about, then this subject was brought up again. This was the bond that held them together and from time to time they had to assure themselves that it was still there and that it had not been torn or got caught elsewhere.

Sophy understood that he had come to her defense and Lars understood that she liked it.

VI.

LARS WORKED for Omley the entire winter and the Irishman passed the time with the promise of work later. Omley liked to keep him in reserve. He had discovered that Lars could draw and put him to work painting signs, something he had not been able to offer his customers earlier. He made good money off Lars, whom he kept on pins and needles with talk about hard times and the difficulties for a painter during the winter season. He took on little jobs here and there for himself and permitted himself no rest. Now and then he also got a bigger job and then he would send for the Irishman.

Both Sophy and Mabel had been sent to college that winter. When Thore sent his daughter, then Omley also had to send his. That belonged to the order of things, and Mrs. Omley and Mrs. Overhus each kept a precious little clipping from the *Daily Chronicle* that mentioned their daughters together with others from the town's best families who had been sent to college.

That first winter was a dismal one for Lars. He thought about the Good Templar lodge and the youth organizations back home, and all the bazaars and get-togethers. Here there was almost nothing to do. Everything in the church youth group was done in English, of which he still understood little. And the young people here were so different. They sat stiff and straight in their chairs and neither laughed nor applauded. They always seemed to have secrets which they told each other while the program was going on. Sometimes they had celebrations and surprise parties and then they could have a litle fun among themselves in small groups. But for the most part, they were very dull and awfully *swell*, he thought. There were individuals who spoke good Norwegian. Lars stayed close to them and asked them if they ever played any games. Their eyes opened wide with amazement when he talked about games for grown-up people like themselves. It was obvious they couldn't play games. What did they do for fun?

Fun? Again their eyes opened wide. What did he mean by fun?

Lars made the observation that the young girls never laughed. They only smiled. And they almost always smiled when they talked to someone. It didn't make any difference what they said, they still smiled. The same was true of the salesladies in the stores, no matter what it was they were selling.

The church programs always consisted of songs, music, and declamations. And sometimes the minister would give a talk on church history. Lars didn't get much out of the declamations because he couldn't understand them. Consequently, he didn't attend many of the meetings. Omley had let him know that he would like to see him go to church—yes, he had even let it be understood that it wouldn't hurt business at all if Lars went up to take Communion when he went himself. But Lars still didn't go very often. He was never more a stranger in America than when he set foot inside the church.

There were evenings when homesickness and the thought of Father and Mother and all the others back home gnawed at his insides so that it felt to him like physical pain, a kind of aching within his breast. At such moments he felt unutterably lonesome—a little boy, Lars, on a plank out in the ocean. Who would take care of him if he should get sick? Who cared anything about him? No one! Sometimes he could hear his mother's voice so clearly: Lars! it called. Then he gave a start. Maybe she was dead.

There was so much he should have done for her. And Father, who still went out to sea, as old as he was. He thought he could see him entering the kitchen, pulling the icicles out of his beard while Mother was busy setting the plates on the table. Would he ever see them again? They surely talked about him every evening.

The longing for Mother ate at his heart and made him recall one painful incident after another. Hadn't he complained about the food because it wasn't good enough? Hadn't he made his mother cry the time she had patched his jacket and he had asked if she really intended him to go around with a patch like that? Hadn't there been time after time when he could have walked his mother to the meeting house to spare her having to walk alone in the dark? She went by herself, poor thing, because his father had no desire to attend. Wouldn't it have made her happy if Lars had gone with her?

At times like this, Lars was on the verge of tears. Everything around him seemed foreign and hostile. There were only two people who cared about him, and they were very far away. The inner pain he experienced made him feel as if his insides had been ripped apart and the pieces were trying to put themselves together again.

When he felt this way he would go into town. It helped to get some fresh air.

It was on such an evening that an acquaintance persuaded him to join him in the saloon to play billiards. Lars had heard that this was a game enjoyed by fine folk, but he didn't know that ordinary folk could learn to play. He learned quickly, though, and it wasn't long before he chalked the cue and aimed and supported himself like the others, all the while feeling that he now was to be regarded as one of the upper class since he did something intended for them. There was no better remedy for homesickness. They should see him now! The next day he anxiously waited for evening to come so he could go there again.

There was the added inducement that very little but Norwegian was spoken in the saloon. There was no one there who was ashamed of being Norwegian. Many men frequented the place, and there was much to hear. People said what they thought, and said it in a language he could understand. He stayed away from spirits in the beginning and ordered cigars or effervescing lemonade, but when it was his turn to treat he never held back.

Here there was someone who wanted to listen to him. Here he could talk about his home and his future prospects. There was always someone who understood him and could sympathize with him or praise him. It didn't cost much either. It was worth a couple of glasses of beer to have a sympathetic listener to whom he could open his heart.

On the other hand, he had been putting a certain amount of his pay aside each week and did not at all like the increase in his expenses. It happened that he could squander a couple of dollars in a single evening, and when he converted this to crowns he was alarmed at his extravagance;

and the many bad cigars which found their way into his pocket were of little comfort to him. And yet, there was a kind of secret pride behind all this. He could—if he wanted to—squander a Norwegian apprentice's entire week's wages in an evening without being the least little bit in need. He did not drink often, however. His aversion to drink had not left him and he saw that the saloonkeeper was polite to the customers as long as they had money and impolite when they got drunk and had no money left. There were almost always a few of his countrymen who had no money and wanted to borrow.

It was really remarkable how many people he met here whom he had not expected to meet. There was a young fellow his own age whom he had met on the ship crossing the Atlantic. Then he had done stunts and walked on his hands and astonished everyone with his strength and training. He could bend himself over backwards so his body formed an arch. He had been a member of a gymnastic society and had several medals. Lars became aware of the boy one cold evening when he went around to those playing billiards and offered to sell a silver medal for a dollar so he could find food and lodging for the night. Lars gave him a dollar and no sooner had the boy got it than he went over to the bar and demanded whiskey. Lars thought it disgusting that the others crowded around the boy at the bar so he had to treat the whole gang. Lars followed him out when he left because he felt sorry for him. They went into the waiting room at the station, where they sat and talked for a long time. Lars had hardly been able to recognize the boy. He had grown so pale, hollow-cheeked, and weak, and his courage was gone. He coughed and complained of a sharp pain in his chest. Lars could hardly believe it was the same boy who now spoke complainingly about his stern fate. "It would appear as though everyone here in town has conspired to destroy me," he said. He had been so miserable and then took lodging at a boardinghouse where there was a saloon, and soon there was nothing but cardplaying and drinking, he explained. He knew of course that there were good Norwegian people in town and that there were churches and societies and such—he had also gone to church, but everything was in English and he didn't hear a Norwegian word from anyone and there wasn't a person who had talked to him. He had also attended something which was supposed to be an evening of Norwegian entertainment, but he didn't understand anything of that either except for a talk by the minister in which he said the young had so much to thank God for because they had such an abundance of everything here in this country. "And they all looked as if they had an abundance of everything, too," he added bitterly. The only ones who had treated him with any kindness were the saloonkeepers. But because he had not had any work since last fall and had no money to equip himself for work as a lumberjack, things had gone steadily downhill for him. They had confiscated his suitcase at the boardinghouse, and he had had to sell the coat he had brought with him from the Old Country.

Lars walked back to the boardinghouse with him and paid for a week's rent. When he returned a couple of days later to see how the boy was, he was told that he had been taken to the hospital and that he had pneumonia.

This incident contributed to Lars's staying away from the bar in the saloon as much as possible, a resolve which was to be reinforced later by what he saw and heard. Here in the saloon he met so many drifting wrecks from Norway—men with a good education, skilled craftsmen, men who spoke several languages and knew all manner of things except that they ought to stay away from the saloon bar rail. Many had held good positions in Norway and had belonged to the upper class. Now they moved from place to place and begged for food at kitchen doors and slept under the boardwalks or in the waiting rooms of railroad stations. During the day they went around telling all kinds of lies in order to get money for liquor. When they were in the mood, they could tell humorous stories and talk so well about books and politics and conditions in Norway that it was difficult to pull oneself away. When they got more intoxicated and closing time approached they sat there and wept salty tears from their blood-shot drunkards' eyes, and then it was their own story they wanted to tell. It was the same old tale about how they had come to this country and had no one to turn to—about the language that had put obstacles in their way, about people who had deceived them—and how no one had extended them a helping hand and everyone had conspired to destroy them and their own countrymen were the worst to shove them with both hands. They wanted to talk about good days in Norway, about parents and brothers and sisters from whom they had not heard for a long time.

Then with a firm hand the saloonkeeper wanted to help them to the door and send them out into the cold night with a heartfelt wish that God would damn them and that they would go to hell and away from the saloon. They too spoke English when it came to closing up for the night.

Lars, who always stayed sober, was unpleasantly affected by this. He had heard mostly about people who had done well in America, succeeded in accumulating wealth, and held good positions. He knew, of course, that drunks existed in Norway and had even known a few, but this type was unknown to him. In Norway they apparently sunk faster to the bottom or floated more quickly to the surface. Here such wrecks could drift for years without either sinking or getting back on an even keel. They were like ships adrift; they bumped into kitchen doors and now and then ran into a police officer who also invoked God to damn them as he towed them off to the police station where they were again directed to hottest hell. They washed in and out of the saloon doors to be swept off to another skerry full of breakers, only later to turn up again in the same waters as before. They were neither living nor dead, they neither wholly floated nor wholly sank. They were typically Norwegian wrecks.

When the minister spoke about the consequences of sin and mentioned these wrecks as an example, then he expressed the same opinion as to their course and moorings as the saloonkeeper and the police officer; but the minister spoke condescendingly, which these others did not do.

These wrecks, however, provided good entertainment, and that was what a lot of people missed. They could keep the laughter going for hours among the more proper saloon patrons, who left reluctantly for their homes, laughing, as closing time approached. After a hard day a bit of good laughter was refreshing.

But the wrecks passed from the lit-up saloon out into the darkness and disappeared, with the bartender directing them to hell as a goodbye. They almost never completely froze to death and almost never completely starved to death. Seldom were they completely permitted to drink themselves to death. They could fall and injure themselves and become bloody, but seldom so seriously that they died.

They tenaciously reappeared when presumed dead, and, remarkably tough, they presented themselves again and again to their countrymen, from whom they expected a helping hand that never came.

But what had an even more negative effect on Lars was the hale and hearty newcomer-boys who were always leaning over the bar rail while their dreaming eyes stared ahead as through a fog. They had only two topics to discuss—the day's work and the Old Country. When anyone would listen to them, they could speak incessantly about their family relationships, about their parents, about brothers and sisters and memories from home. They were also happy to treat if they just found someone who would lend them an ear.

It didn't take long before Lars found himself standing among them. When they didn't have anything to laugh about, then they showed their bleeding sores to each other.

He also noticed how these boys little by little graduated into the groups that told lewd stories or spread town gossip. Some of them were more advanced and could manage to swear and strike the bar like old veterans in just a few weeks.

Lars often wished there had been a Norwegian youth organization or a Good Templar lodge in town, and he talked to Omley about it. But Omley didn't like it that a man who worked for him should be at the head of anything which might cause opposition. He warned him, though, against both the saloon and drink. As for a youth organization, they had one within the congregation that was harmless and uncontroversial.

Lars did not like this. He thought of the many young Norwegians he had come to know at the saloon. They always talked about having no place to go and he understood their fleeing from the cold and inhospitable rooms of the boardinghouses because it was unbearable to sit there and wait for nightfall.

He stayed home more now. There were several factors which held him back: the thought of his home, a steadily growing bank account, his aversion to drink and the stench of beer in the saloon, and—more than anything—Sophy.

He often sat evenings and attempted to draw her likeness, but it was simply impossible to come up with anything that resembled her. He could only sit and dream for long periods of time.

The thought of home and the feeling that he was utterly alone sometimes seized him with absolute fear. He was reminded of his first impression of Omley: a pair of cold eyes which seemed to be sizing up everything. Face after face appeared before him—the eyes were always the same. Even Mrs. Nelson, for example, looked at him differently than she looked at Henry. Everyone seemed to be calculating what a fellow like Lars Olson could be worth to them—just what advantages he could bring them.

It had not been like that at home.

All his loved ones back home were before him in his imagination. They had never looked at him in that way. He felt so endlessly far away from his home that he could almost weep.

A strange thing happened toward Christmas: Henry received his diploma and was finished with high school. He had become an adult and could not play on the high school football team the following season. He was mentioned as an example of how too much interest in sports destroyed the desire to study. Lars helped Mrs. Nelson get a glass and frame around Henry's diploma. After his graduation Henry idled away the time because he had nothing to do. He couldn't take any old kind of work, and he had not learned how to support himself in high school.

There were evenings when Lars couldn't stand the boredom and therefore invited Henry to go to one of the Norwegian saloons with him where they could play billiards. In the beginning it was Lars, who had had some practice, who won. But it amazed him to see how quickly Henry—for whom it was so difficult to learn about other things—learned to play. As with the game of football—where it was a question of winning or losing—where it became a contest—then the boy was all enthusiastic and went at it with such zeal that he soon mastered even the most difficult plays. Lars always paid for the game, but these saloon visits took an unexpected turn in that Henry became a real master and the best players wanted to play with him and Lars became superfluous. So he quit inviting Henry, who then stopped going on his own. Lars was afraid it had become a habit for Henry, but it didn't appear to cost Henry the least little bit to give up this amusement.

The rest of the winter Lars stayed at home evenings and wrote letters, drew, or attempted to learn English. He made very slow progress, but the thought of Nels Hill, who in five years had done so well that he spoke English more easily than Norwegian, kept him going. When others could come so far in a short time then he ought to be able to do it too.

Whenever things got too bad he would join the youth of the congregation at their meetings. He got to know several of the young ladies there and was invited to their homes. Almost all of them came from fine families and he would write in his letters that he had been invited out by some of the best people in town. Almost everywhere they had pianos and *parlors*, where there was not to be found a single ordinary chair but only rocking chairs. There he could sit and rock back and forth or look at photographs which they showed him. They also had a card game which they called "Flinch" and which better people used instead of regular playing cards. He seldom saw anything of the parents, since in this country they usually kept to themselves in the kitchen or in a little room behind the kitchen where they wouldn't disturb the young people when they played Flinch. Sometimes the young ladies played the piano, but, for the most part, they played Flinch. If there was nothing else then they had expensive *stereoscopes*, with which a person looked at pictures through a magnifying glass so they appeared more realistic.*

But that was about all the fun there was. The most pleasant thing of all was the upper-class feeling he had from being together with people who didn't have to work and who went to schools of higher learning or took lessons. The rocking chairs with their thick plush cushions were also good to sit in and Lars assumed several elegant positions befitting an

---

* Stereoscopes do not use a magnifying glass but rather two lenses to give a three-dimensional effect.

expensive chair. Now they should just see him at home. He was beginning to become a somebody here in this country now, and it seemed to him he actually grew in the rocking chairs—when they had seats of fine plush.

VII.

MRS. NELSON was very religious and always went to church when there was a Norwegian service. If the service was in English, she sat at home and enjoyed herself alone with her Bible and her hymnbook. She first tidied up in the kitchen and put a tablecloth on the kitchen table. The washtubs were put away in the cellar and she dressed up and sat there by herself. Henry knew a lot of people and on Sunday mornings preferred going to one of the American churches and was often gone the whole day.

Lars could hear that Mrs. Nelson sat there reading, and that the reading often went rather badly. Her glasses weren't very good and she also had the habit of crying a little when she read God's Word and then she couldn't see well. She was apparently also afraid of disturbing Lars because when she should have sung there was a slow hum instead, and he could hear how she finished with a deep sigh as she got up to put on the coffeepot.

When the coffee was ready she would also bring Lars a cup. He often thought how good she was in this respect.

When Lars had been back in Norway and completely surrounded by familiar people he had never bothered much about church or sermons. The worst thing he experienced as a child was to have to be indoors on a Sunday afternoon and sit still on a chair while Mother read from a book of sermons and sang. This was always the case when his father, who was a seaman, was out on long voyages. How difficult it had been to sit still on a beautiful summer day when he could hear other boys playing out on the hill or down by the pier—or if it was a winter day good for sledding. But now he was far away from Mother and would gladly give anything to be able to hear her read and sing and to walk with her to the meeting house again—which he had so disliked doing when he was little. It gave him a feeling of security when he was with his mother. When she had prayed the evening prayer and asked God's protection from fire, theft, and a quick and hasty death, then he could securely lay himself to rest. He had of course been away from home during his apprenticeship, but that was not being away in the same manner as he was now. He was endlessly far away and there was no one to be alarmed should he become ill—no one who would devise various remedies for him and no one to check if his scarf was wrapped snugly and warmly around his neck. No one used a scarf here and no one asked him if he had got his feet wet or bothered in the least if he had a cough—and—one thought conjured up another—here there was no one who cared if he perished or not—no one who said, "Aren't you going to church today either, Lars?" No one was angry because he didn't go—unless it might be Omley who was afraid of the bad effect it could have on "*bisnissen.*" He even missed the scoldings.

The woman out in the kitchen reminded him of his mother, and one Sunday afternoon when he sat down to write a letter but couldn't think of anything to write about, he heard her sing one of his mother's hymns. Then he made a trip out to the kitchen. The song died out and Mrs. Nelson asked if she had disturbed him. To this he answered no. He waited for her to ask him to sit down but she didn't. He said to her that she must have had a good singing voice and that he was fond of singing and that his mother was also accustomed to sing. Mrs. Nelson looked searchingly at him over her glasses and he understood at once that he was just a boarder by the name of Lars Olson who lived there for four dollars a week.

He drank a glass of water, which was the purpose of his errand, and returned to his room poorer than ever. But when evening came he went into town and found the back door of a saloon open. That evening, for the first time since he had come to America, he drank so much that he felt it in his head.

He was very displeased with himself the following day. Was he to have the same kind of fate as his friend with whom he had made the journey over?

No—he was going to put a stop to this. Lars had to take care of him-self here. No one else was going to do it for him.

He was going to save money, a lot of money—all the money he could. They could just go to hell, the whole lot of them, and Lars could go where he wanted, because it was money that counted.

One of his most enjoyable pastimes when he sat alone was to figure out how much money he would have in the bank in a year, in two years, and in five years. It would be more than a little, and converted to crowns the sums were large.

Once in a while Mrs. Nelson would have a visitor. One afternoon when Lars was at home, a Mrs. Dale came darting in, all aglow and in high spirits. She had come from Norway just a little over two years earlier with a whole flock of children. Her husband was a day laborer and they were quite poor, so one of the daughters, Gjertrud, or Gertie as she was called now, had had to go to work for a family in a neighboring town, since she didn't like to work as a servant girl where there were people who knew her. She had gone three terms to an English school and had done very well. Now she had written a letter to her mother in English. This was the reason Mrs. Dale was so radiantly happy. Every afternoon she had been going around to the neighbor women and friends and drinking coffee as the result of this remarkable letter. One could clearly see that the letter bore traces of wear, but there was no indication of any such thing to be seen on Mrs. Dale. With unwavering enthusiasm she delivered the story of Gertie, who was now so clever that she could hardly speak a Norwegian word any-more and wrote in the English language and they would have to be so kind as to translate it for her, because Ole, her husband, couldn't manage to do that, and now she didn't know what to do because she couldn't under-stand a single word of it.

She was not terribly disappointed to discover that Mrs. Nelson couldn't manage to read it either. It was, on the other hand, something of a disappointment that Mrs. Nelson could outdo her with a son who was so smart that he had almost never been able to say a word in Norwegian. To Gertie clung the indisputable fact that she once had been able to speak only Norwegian. Mrs. Nelson liked to drive this point home. It was good for these newcomer women to be humbled a little when they attempted to make themselves look big after being in the country only a couple of years.

When Mrs. Nelson—on account of her poor glasses—couldn't manage the letter, Lars had to step in. First, naturally, he had to hear the story of the remarkable, advanced daughter. Lars went at it with a profound expression that he felt was suitable for such an important occasion and began to interpret the letter while Mrs. Nelson got the coffeepot ready. This was of greater interest to Mrs. Dale than the contents of the letter. For three or four afternoons she had already enjoyed coffee because of this letter, and with care she could make it last through the remainder of the week. Lars couldn't make out everything in the letter, either, but he did get something out of it and the first words were relatively easy. *"Deer Mama."* That was easy enough: *"Dyre Mama." "I have allready mekt 8 dollars and vil make some moor before I kvit."* Lars explained in Norwegian that she had earned eight dollars and that she would make much more before she was finished. At this point he was interrupted by Mrs. Dale, who asked if she hadn't written thus and so, and quoted from the contents of the letter. Lars admitted that it was something like that which she had written and carefully folded the letter together feeling his honor had been saved. Mrs. Dale wanted to know if he would also help her if she received another letter in English, and Lars promised her he would. If she got more letters like this one, she should just come to him.

Otherwise this was the most dismal winter Lars had ever experienced. The days crept by at a terrible snail's pace and turned into weeks, and the weeks into months. What helped his spirits the most was picturing his homecoming: fine clothing, a thick sketch book, and refined manners. He was going to be industrious and save his money. When he had become a well-to-do man, he would return home in grand style with a gold watch and a fur-lined overcoat. Sophy also entered into these thoughts. It was clear that she should be with him. When something was going on at the meeting house or the Good Templar lodge, then she would play a piano solo and he would speak to her in English and she would respond in the same language and then she would go up to the piano and play "Silvery

Waves" or "Maiden's Prayer" from sheet music and then they would all applaud. It was as though he could see all the astonished looks on their faces and hear the chords from the piano. During the summer he would take her out sailing because that was something he knew how to do, and he would replace the little sailboat with one that was much bigger, and he would have her name forward on the bow as a surprise for her.

There was no better medicine for the unpleasant hollow feeling in his chest than thoughts like these.

Henry was without work the whole winter. As a young man with a high school diploma he couldn't very well do simple manual labor. Like so many other young men with a good education he had made an attempt at being a salesman who went from door to door taking orders for soap, perfume, toilet tissue, and the like, which was much more suited to a young man with an education than physical labor, but he soon grew weary of it. Widows and other trash had squeezed themselves into this kind of thing and made it almost impossible for a young man to get a job. He had also been promised a position as a store clerk, but nothing came of that either. Willum had promised to send for him when he needed a clerk, but no one ever came to Henry with an offer of any kind of position whatsoever.

So it was that he just hung around at home. He was an exemplary young man who had no bad habits. His only fault was that he could not support himself. He helped his mother with the washtubs when they needed to be brought up from the cellar or with the clothesline when it needed to be strung, and he kept a sharp lookout to see that she had all the wood she needed brought into the kitchen. Mrs. Nelson could not help comparing her boy with other boys in the same circumstances, who never thought about carrying in wood for their mothers. She often had to tell him to be careful not to overexert himself when he took, to her mind, too big a load of wood. He also helped her in other ways and sometimes came home with the good news that now there was another family that wanted her to do their washing.

Lars was very puzzled that Henry couldn't find anything to do, but as he became more familiar with things he discovered that there were many young people in houses round about who went unemployed because of learning. In every third or fourth house there was a grown daughter or son who had graduated from business school only to wait for employment that never came.

He discussed this with the plumber one day when they were working together at the same place. Lars thought the plumber was a very sensible man. It was because of the laws, he said—they were so crazy. They forbade the parents to put the children to work before they were sixteen years old. They were through at the public school when they were fourteen and for the next two years they were ruined by idleness and got lazy. Often they were sent to high school just to keep them from hanging around the house. When they had gone there for two full years the parents of course wanted them to finish, but by the time they did finish they were almost too old to learn a useful trade. In high school they learned algebra, physiology, and physiognomy,* and whatever else it might be, but they didn't learn how to earn a living. On the other hand, they sometimes learned to look down on their parents with scorn if they were poor, and the parents learned to look up at their kids with reverence, which was even worse. In high school the children of rich people were mixed together with the children of poor people, and it was the children of the rich who set the rules with regard to clothing and the tone of conversation. The children of the rich had some benefit from their instruction because they could continue at the universities, but the children of the poor came halfway and were at a standstill. The boys were too good for a trade and the girls for housework. The girls learned to figure out how long it would take a man to ride a bicycle to the moon, but they didn't know how long the potatoes ought to cook. They could figure out how many times 28¾ can go into 101½, but they couldn't figure out how much work they could save their mothers by learning to mend their own stockings.

And none were in a worse position than the children of Norwegians: they had learned language and manners and their way of thinking on the street because their parents thought their language and their manners and

---

* A technique of determining character by means of physical features, here used by Ager for comic/satiric effect.

way of thinking were much too simple for their fine children. They thought it was so wonderful that their children learned about Columbus and Patrick Henry and Alfred the Great, but they took it as totally natural that the children didn't know a thing about their own parents or their own family background. They could recite Moses and all the prophets, both major and minor, but they sometimes didn't know their father's full name or the name of the place he came from.

"There are beasts," the plumber said, "who have so little understanding that they eat their own offspring; but the Norwegians in America are even more ignorant, because they let themselves be devoured by their kids."

Lars could not agree with him on this. Here in this country all children had the same opportunity for a higher education, and here no one was looked down on because he was poor. But he had noticed that here also there were people who believed that poor people could manage without an education. They must never look up and ahead but just remain on a lower level. The plumber was one of them.

The plumber didn't get at all angry. He just laughed and reached out his massive hands and seized Lars's hands, which were well smeared with paint and not at all to be despised as regarded their size. "These are paws, Lars," he said. "You won't find the likes of them anywhere in this town. There isn't a day when these claws of mine don't solve difficult problems. They've been down in the dirt and mud and inside walls and dark corners and worked miracles, my friend. They have fixed leaks, damages, and difficulties, and made repairs and made new things, and when I have cut them then I have seen such red blood as can be found in any body of quality. It wouldn't be easy for me to take over bank manager Vincent's place at a meeting of the board of directors, but I would do better at that than he would be able to do what I am going to do now when I go down in the cellar and lie on my stomach and squeeze in to solder a pipe together inside a hole which a cat would think twice about before trying to creep into it."

Lars couldn't hold back from laughing with him. The plumber was one of those people who didn't hanker after anything greater or better than to dig in dirt and filth. But maybe it was for the best that when a person was like that he didn't think ahead to something bigger and better.

A real friendship developed between Lars and Henry. Henry's helplessness and clumsiness impressed Lars. There was something so fine and gentlemanlike about him when he couldn't even manage to light a fire in the stove. Henry, for his part, admired Lars's adroitness and dexterity in all things. Lars was so willing to help, and Henry so willing to be helped. He liked to watch Lars work, and Lars liked to be watched. Once when the lock on the front door refused to budge, Lars removed the whole lock and made a new spring for it out of a thin sawblade, and he also made an extra key for the lock with a file. Henry was struck with amazement to think someone could do something like that without being taught how to do it or without taking "lessons" in it.

When Lars saw how helpless Henry was, he was reminded of the plumber's sarcastic remarks. There was a difference between people. Henry reminded him so much of Sophy. He couldn't imagine her doing simple work either, and he had an inborn notion that it was fine to be helpless in such everyday things.

One did not use pleasure yachts to freight empty barrels to Drøbak.*

VIII.

S PRING CAME, and it came in great glory. The lilacs were full of blossoms, and the apple and plum trees were as white as though they were covered with snow. Lars worked hard during the day, but when evening came it was much too beautiful for him to be able to sit indoors. As weary as he often was, he would go for long walks. He involuntarily made comparisons with the previous spring when he had been at home in Norway. The blossoms didn't have

---

* A city in Akershus county south of Oslo on the eastern shore of the Oslofjord.

as strong a scent here in this country and they wilted sooner. It was strange to go and look at the high bluffs that surrounded the town and that had not yet been given names. They protruded like big knees and shoulders that seemed to belong to nameless giants who were digging themselves down into the ground. Most of all he missed the light evenings in Norway—those remarkable summer nights when a person could stay up without getting sleepy.

He thought about his home and everything he was going to take along with him when he made the journey back—and Sophy, whom he was going to bring with him when he returned. He continued to receive joy from her name, and could hardly understand how a fellow like Omley could have come up with such a beautiful name. There was such a quality of distinction to this name, and it was just as fine whether it was pronounced or it was spelled out. He had tried it both ways. It gave him such pleasure just to repeat it half out loud when he puttered around alone.

Summer came and with it vacations, and these in turn brought Sophy and Mabel home from college. They had also been at home for the Christmas holidays, but since these coincided with the slack period when Lars was not at the workshop he had not seen either of them. He had, for that matter, dressed up and gone out on the streets where he thought they might possibly come, but it was very cold during Christmas and he couldn't just go out and freeze. So he didn't get to see her. He hadn't had any real Christmas either.

Lars's heart worked like an eagerly clenched fist beneath his oil-coated painting clothes when he saw her for the first time after her homecoming. She had grown taller and paler, but her face was even finer than before, and she was so good to him that she greeted him with the joyful exclamation, *"O gee!—how you scared me!"* when he rose up with great determination in order to greet her. He had begun to stir the contents of a paint can and had his back toward her when she came in. He had to find something to be dawdling with before he dared to turn around and face her. Then they had an opportunity to talk together and she told him about the school and all the fun they had had there and wasn't the least bit proud or put on, he thought.

The days to follow were happy ones for him, for they could go out together. The vexing thing about it was that Mabel always came along, and then they spoke only English and kept talking about things from school which were so funny that the two of them laughed incessantly. Lars didn't think they were so funny, but he had to laugh a little too. He had enough upbringing to know that he had to laugh some when they laughed. Then it occurred to him to invite Henry along when they were going somewhere, and in that way he was halfway free of the other—but only halfway, because Mabel was determined not to let the distance between the two couples become too great.

But days and even whole weeks went by when he didn't see her. The girls had an outside world—friends from school and girlfriends and interests that were foreign to him, and this, their world, was not open to Lars.

In August she went away with Mabel to spend some time at a lake where they had arranged a camping party. It cut Lars to the marrow to see how eagerly they looked forward to this. His greatest comfort was that he at least had had the company of a couple of young ladies who "had spent an extended amount of time at a summer resort," and his greatest chagrin was that he had no one to tell this to who could really understand the "fineness" of it. It reminded him of how the very finest people in Norway lived. They should just know back home that he had such acquaintances over here. He couldn't help thinking of Karoline. Karoline in summer residence at a resort? It sounded so absurd that he almost had to laugh.

The days were dreary while they were gone. When he came home in the evening and cleaned up, it was as though he was still hungry even when he had just eaten. Then he got dressed and went into town just to avoid having to sit inside on those warm evenings. It was unbearable also out on the steps.

He strolled along the main street looking at people, and he was out of sorts and critical. Nothing was the way it should be. There was a stream of young people on the main street—or more correctly, two, because there was one coming and one going. It struck him as somehow unfitting that all the young girls appeared to be of the better class. He knew some of the girls whose parents were Norwegian. If the parents were poor, no one could tell it by looking at the daughters as they flitted up and down the street in flocks, giggling and happy. They had white shoes and white stockings and fine light dresses of sheer fabric so he could see their bare arms, and there was much embroidery and decoration. Many had the kind of low-necked dresses which he knew were worn at fine parties in higher circles. They were almost always bareheaded and most of them had fine curled hair with silk ribbons. He remembered he had read in a mission paper that certain kinds of heathens, when their daughters reached adulthood, decorated them with all kinds of finery and went off with them to the slave markets to sell them to other heathens to be their wives.

He wondered if it was the intention of these ordinary Norwegians to get their daughters disposed of or married to rich men when they decorated them like this and let them out on the street as though they were on display—or if these girls, like those in olden times who were consecrated to the idols, decorated themselves before meeting their terrible fate.

He also thought that he saw buyers. Outside the hotels on hot summer evenings there sat traveling salesmen and other fine gentlemen with their hats back on their heads and their thumbs stuck in the armholes of their vests, spectacles on their noses, and cigars in the corner of their mouths. They sat there and inspected these flocks of girls like experienced horse-traders, with one eye half-closed, while their gazes wandered across the slim bodies of the girls with a look as though they had only to choose. Others—and they were young men—stood suspicious-looking by stairways and nooks, on the corners or in the doorways of the billiard parlors. They were young men whose shoulders were shrugged almost up to their ears, their hands in their pockets and caps pulled down over their eyes. They stood leaning forward as though ready to run; but they never ran. They almost never moved from the spot where they were standing. They just tried to look smart and dashing, and it happened that one or another of these fellows sometimes succeeded in receiving some encouragement from the girls with an admiring, *"My—but doesn't he look tough!"* Then he would outdo himself and spit straight across the sidewalk without even having to take aim.

Judging from appearances, one could believe that they had committed ten terrible murders and were planning the eleventh, they looked so depraved and dangerous. But no one was afraid of them, because there was no evil to be found in them. If one looked more closely, he noticed they had low shoes and embroidered stockings like the women. These were young men who still could not afford to buy a wife. But since they had to think about getting married sometime, they were interested in seeing what the homes of the town had to offer in the way of marriageable daughters.

It was the newcomer boys like himself who hung around the streets to watch the radiant flocks of girls that passed by. These boys were well dressed and earned money; but they moved carefully aside for these girls, girls from another world who were far above them—especially with regard to breeding and refinement. Their thoughts wandered from these girls to the newcomer girls who worked as maidservants. Each of the homes in the finer residential area had their own girl up there in the kitchen, but it was only on Thursday and Sunday evenings that one could count on them. The boys thought they were pretty in their own way, too, but the best thing about them was that they were not so expensive and within the reach of a simple laborer.

These girls were also aware that they were not so fine as those who had gone to high school and business school and the like, but they had their lives ahead of them. Fineness was something they could make up for when they married, and make up for it they did—many of them.

It was along these lines that Lars's thoughts moved as he wandered about feeling annoyed that there was such an overabundance of fine folk in America—to a degree that it wasn't anything much to be fine.

This quality among the youth was something he had noticed from the beginning and it was most obvious in the relationship between parents and children. The children were so polished and refined that it was as though their Norwegian parents were ashamed to be seen with them so as not to bring them any offense because of their own coarseness and lack of upbringing. On the other hand, the young people put up with their parents' lack of refinement at home, but away from home they couldn't be expected to endure everything from their parents. There have to be limits to everything. The parents sensed a boundary to their children's patience and wouldn't take any chances.

Among people of other immigrant races, conflicts often arose between the grown children and their parents when the latter did not live up to the demands of the children, or when the parents themselves made demands. But Norwegian parents, for the most part, behaved themselves so well and showed the children such respect that they could keep them at home so long as they refrained from making any demands.

This was generally the impression Lars had received when during the winter he had visited homes where there were young people. He had sat in the living rooms where there was a piano, fine rocking chairs, and carpets on the floors, and portraits in *crayon* of Father and Mother, in gilded frames, on the wall. Here he was introduced to the portraits on the wall: *"This is ma! This is dad!"* But he was not introduced to the parents themselves, who, as a rule, considerately remained out in the kitchen when the children had a party or guests, and were not nearly so fine in reality as they were on the wall behind glass.

Sometimes he could catch a glimpse of the mother when she shyly came with the coffee tray. She was perhaps both large-limbed and awkward and did not resemble her daughters in the least, which she knew, and therefore never put herself forward. It impressed Lars to see wives with such agreeable and modest manners and he felt kindness toward such a mother. The daughters would also look at him with eyes that questioned triumphantly: "Don't we have a well-behaved mother?"

Lars couldn't help thinking of this good relationship and the difference between the older and the younger generations as he strolled down the street on those warm summer evenings, and saw all the attractive young people.

Among the girls who passed by in their finery and drew attention, Lars recognized Mrs. Dale's advanced daughter, Gertie. Apparently no one could tell by looking at her that she was only the daughter of an ordinary laborer and that she had been born and raised in Norway.

IX.

I F HENRY NELSON had any thoughts whatsoever concerning the future, he kept them to himself. He had not made any more demands on life than life had made on him. When his mother would say during a spell of bad humor that now he had to find something to do, about the only effect it had was to make him realize that she was in a bad mood and this was her way of letting off steam. If he didn't earn anything, he didn't use anything. He would gladly say yes to an amusement if Lars or someone else paid. But it didn't cost him a great deal of self-denial to say no either.

Like an overgrown child he existed through the four seasons without it ever occurring to him that a year of his life had gone by.

His mother understood well enough that there was something wrong about this, but she was still very afraid of losing him. It was common for boys Henry's age to go out west to make ends meet as best they could, or, in dire necessity, to enlist. In either case she would have been without him. If life were thereby to be given some meaning for him, it would lose all meaning for her. And Henry had no bad habits. There must be some sort of way out, she thought. But there was none, and there was certainly no serious attempt to find one either.

Later on that summer something happened which was to be very important in Henry's life. One day as he was walking through the park he came across Edith Perkins and her younger brother. He had met the girl in high school. She had begun later than he, and had finished before. Now she attended a college for young ladies and had just come home for summer vacation. The family had returned early from the coast that year. Henry knew that Edith was the daughter of one of the town's wealthiest real-estate brokers, but what he didn't know was that Edith, from the time she was in high school, had had many daydreams in which the noble-looking football captain was the hero. He didn't know that when he was leading his troops on the sports field he was the greatest hero in the world, at least in the eyes of a young girl who was not only the prettiest but also the richest girl in the whole school.

It was a bad blow to Edith that he had to stay on from term to term, but, in the first place, he was not the only one, and in the second, it was not his wisdom that had caught her fancy to begin with. But it was too bad for the sake of others that he didn't get anywhere.

She had known so many people and had been pampered and flattered so much that, in a way, his image had become veiled. This chance meeting again brought him to the fore. Henry, for his part, remembered her only as a pale, thin little girl with a pair of eyes that were much too big, but as she stood before him now a fully developed young woman just as pretty as a picture, he nearly lost his composure. This was so obvious that Edith completely lost her head and stammeringly expressed her joy at having met him. Then he lost whatever remained of his composure and asked her where she had been all this time. That neither of them had their wits about them was clear since they had never spoken to each other before.

Her brother, who had just started high school, was of course familiar with Henry's triumphs from football seasons when he was growing up. He rose on his thin legs, stuck out his chest and spit, and asked in a professional-sounding tone what Henry thought of the new football team— and how it would do against the Ochochee school team. This was a great relief, because Henry could explain many things about football to the boy, and his words were obviously falling on good soil.

They seated themselves on a bench and talked football with feverish enthusiasm. They talked about nothing else, but in those occasional glances which Henry and Edith sent each other across the enthusiastic young boy's slender figure could be read something far more complex than football. They talked only about football, but in reality they were telling each other how inexpressibly precious it was to hear each other's voices.

The boy was enthralled when they parted. He felt he was as well qualified as anyone in the whole school to have a correct grasp of the game in the upcoming season.

"It was really nice of him to explain all this to me, wasn't it?" he said to his sister when they had gone some distance. "Yes, it was nice of him," she answered absentmindedly. "He's big and strong, isn't he?" the boy questioned further. "Yes, I guess he is," she answered, as though in a dream. "I wonder if he would train with me for the football team so I could be a substitute player this fall?" the boy spoke again. Then she gave a start and said almost angrily, "Ask him about it then, you fool. Why didn't you ask him about it?"

This accidental meeting had great significance for Henry in that it got him started thinking. He no longer lived a dreamless existence. He began to build air castles—but big clumsy ones like those the bright boys in the fourth grade at the public school build. He was going to be a powerful man, maybe governor or something like that—or he was going to be enormously rich. Or he would go to war, if there should be one, and distinguish himself, or at great risk to his own life he would rescue Edith from drowning—if she, for example, fell into the water—or he could save her in some other fashion, say, for instance, if the horses should run wild or if she were attacked by robbers. Or he could journey out west and become a genuine cowboy and come back and present himself to Edith and her brother in full costume with a belt, six-shooters, a broad-brimmed hat, and a red bandanna around his neck. These cowboy daydreams were really the ones that appealed to him most and he even walked as if he imagined himself gloriously reappearing from a rugged life rich in perils out in the Wild West.

The dreams also had another effect on him—he began to sing, or more correctly, to hum. They were off-key, braying sounds, because he had neither a singing voice nor an ear for music. Love songs that he had heard and which had seemed too sentimental and dumb to him had left some bits and refrains in his memory. They now came back to him crammed with meaning and he hummed them from a full and simple heart. His mother understood that something new had taken hold of him, but to her he said nothing. He was sheer goodness, but he no longer liked to fetch and deliver laundry in the light of day.

W. W. Perkins, real-estate broker and capitalist, and his respectable and somewhat sickly wife saw with astonishment that their daughter Edith began to take a greater interest in domestic duties while she took less and less interest in tennis and music. She liked to watch George practice football out on the tennis field with a big fellow who could kick the ball over the tall elm tree. W. W. Perkins and his respectable, sickly wife could add two and two together. They thought well of the boy, but didn't think much of the way he got his daily bread. They talked about him to their daughter, but very carefully, because she was not to be fooled with. They had to admit that in many respects Henry was an exemplary youth, who neither drank, smoked, nor cursed. Further than this they never got, and further than this they thought it was not advisable to go either, because she was not to be fooled with. W. W. Perkins and his respectable, sickly wife began to be anxious, and their anxiety gave rise to many plans.

If the man had been able to follow his natural inclinations he would simply have grabbed Henry by the seat of his pants and set him on the other side of the front gate and bidden him farewell with a good swift kick. But Henry was big and strong, and Perkins was well past his prime, and in his business he had learned the art of self-control. In this instance, though, it wasn't all that easy for him to keep control of himself. Here came a big slovenly lout of a poor boy and fixed his dumb calf-eyes on his daughter—a daughter who had cost him over three thousand in education and music besides everything else in just the last two years. A son of a Norwegian laundry woman—a fellow who couldn't support himself and who was naive enough to think that people don't have to work when they have a mother who can do laundry for people.

The two of them made plans. With good united effort they ought to succeed in getting him out of the house. They tried to be very cool toward him, but it had the same effect as water running off a duck's back. They had to try something else, something more forceful. He was a big brute and had to be treated as such. Perkins thought he could handle it.

He showed himself to be more friendly toward Henry and was often an observer when the boys played ball. He became even more friendly as he prepared to wield the death-blow in an unmistakable and effective manner.

Henry was invited to the Perkins' for tea. Not just inside the fence to play ball with George, but inside the house itself. Mrs. Nelson steamed and pressed Henry's now worn graduation suit and made a nice crease on his trousers. She carefully mended the frayed edges and gave him fifty cents for a new tie. It flattered her vanity that the boy was invited to such a fine home—one of the best in town. But she thought that it was not so unreasonable. He had gone to school and conducted himself as well as anyone. It was quite natural that he should be among better people and she viewed him with near religious reverence when he stood before her all dressed up. She looked at him and then at herself and her eyes were drawn down to her apron. She looked at her rough, worn hands and remembered her crooked body and her wrinkled face and her almost tooth-less mouth. Was it really true that this big, noble-looking, fine young man was her son? She felt almost unworthy of being his mother, but that's the way it was. God had been good to her to give her such a son. She was nothing and not to be heeded, but her son they had just better pay a mind to. And when he turned to leave, she saw the same good childlike face she had always seen—the same trusting eyes of a child that seem always to be looking for mother. These eyes were just the same as she remem-bered them from the time she had them at her breast—they had followed her when as an infant he lay and watched her in the kitchen where she worked for strangers. He had been so smart and had understood so well that he mustn't cry when they were with strangers.

Her sight was obscured by tears, but they were tears of pride and joy which now filled her old eyes to the brim as she saw her elegant big boy move so confidently along the street.

Henry walked with head held high. It positively sang within him—something indefinite that struggled to make its way out to get air—a feel-ing which up to now had been foreign to him and which he hardly grasped—something in the process of being born in him—not in pain but with an inexplicable sense of well-being.

This increased when he sat on the enclosed porch of the Perkins' ele-gant house. He felt like an honored and admired guest. He had never heard anything other than that he was an exemplary young man and since no one had ever reproached him about anything he never felt any self-reproach either. He was a prince among princes and did not have to look up to anyone with his trusting Norwegian eyes of a child.

Perkins and his respectable and somewhat sickly wife were the personification of amiability itself—that somewhat tense amiability which doctors always show their patients who are about to be chloroformed before a necessary operation.

Perkins began very diplomatically by asking if his mother had much to do and to this Henry could reply that she had more than she could manage. "Wasn't it difficult for her to work like that?" Henry couldn't come up with an answer to this because he had never thought about it. But to say something he said it probably wasn't so easy for her. To which Perkins responded. "Yes, she undoubtedly has to work hard if she is going to earn enough doing that kind of thing. But she does have a grown son who ought to be able to provide for her, doesn't she?"

Henry turned red and shamefaced and didn't answer. Perkins had raised himself up and posed for effect. His voice quivered with suppressed and righteous anger: "Just what would you do if your mother were to become sick or die on you?" Henry couldn't answer that. He had certainly never thought about what he would do if his mother were to get sick or die. Perkins continued with rising anger: "You can't earn enough money to buy a pair of shoes, or even repair their soles, but you can go running after the girls? Yes, that you can do!" Henry was not just red; he felt burning hot throughout his whole body and there was a buzzing in his ears. He sank down on his chair utterly speechless. It was as though a feeling of languor had taken hold of every limb. Edith, weeping, with a handkerchief up to her eyes, had fled into the living room, and George, distraught, whisked through and in and out incessantly. He started out saying, "*Cut it out*" and then he was gone; then his voice was heard again and more timorously from the living room, "*Cut it out!*" Thereupon was heard a brave "*Cut it out*" from the stairs, and finally an angry "*Cut it out!*" from the lowest step of the stairs.

But Perkins did not quit. Like a rampaging elephant he stood there stamping his feet in anger in front of Henry, who sat and made himself small in his chair. The respectable and somewhat sickly wife now thought she had to do something to restrain her husband a little since it surely was not good for him to be so agitated. So she took the floor and addressed Henry in a motherly tone of voice: "Couldn't you," she said, "who are so big and strong find yourself some sort of employment with which you not only could provide for your mother but also get yourself a higher education and be a great blessing here in the world and not only help yourself and your mother but also all others who need help—here in this world?"

Henry did not answer but sat stooped and speechless in his chair.

This stirred up Perkins even more, putting him into a complete rage. This strong young man who sat hunched together like a washrag made the blood boil in his veins. "What he needs is a good sound drubbing," he hissed and stamped his foot. "A drubbing is what he should have! See that you get out of here, and be quick about it!"

He took a couple of steps toward Henry and seized him by the arm. This physical contact with the boy had the effect of an electric shock on him. He jumped up like a steel spring, and the action was so violent that Perkins took a bump on his shoulder that sent him flying backward across a footstool. He ended up sitting perplexed in front of his beloved and somewhat sickly wife's feet in complete bewilderment as to whether he had been struck or had fallen as the result of carelessness.

But Henry grabbed his hat and headed off. He felt his knees shaking beneath him and he did not look back. Nor did he stop before he reached the park and there he sat down on a bench to catch his breath and—weep— it seemed to him the natural thing to do, and that was what he was going to do. But strangely enough, nothing came of it. He began to think instead.

What would he do were his mother to die? But they could have said it like decent, rational, civilized people. It was true that he ought to have a good, well-paid job, but where was he going to get it? It was true he had been promised a place as clerk at Willum's, but he knew well enough that Willum didn't want to have him as a clerk. An office job was out of the question. There were plenty of efficient girls with business-school training to be had for four or even three dollars a week. To become a teacher— that required a degree from a normal school, and besides, that was just for women. The factories would just as soon have boys fifteen or sixteen years old because they could be employed more cheaply. He couldn't think of any work that he could get.

But behind and beneath or alongside all this was born a new feeling of power such as he had experienced mightily within himself during the football games when the opponents had pulled their wily tricks. He realized that the Perkins couple had done this because they didn't like him to keep company with their daughter. They had taken him off guard—*played foul*. They wanted to keep their daughter, but he would show them. He got a dangerous gleam in his eye. If that was the way it was, then he was going to show them that he was not the person they had thought him to be.

He said nothing to his mother about what had taken place. It was so difficult for him to explain anything to her since she was even worse in English than he was in Norwegian, and this was decidedly an English matter.

Perkins remained sitting long enough at his loving and somewhat sickly wife's feet to see Henry's broad back disappear through the door. Then he got up and rubbed his sore shoulder and his anger left him completely.

"Maybe there is something to that boy after all," he said with an indescribably perplexed glance at his dear wife.

And later on that evening whenever he sat down or got up and felt pain in his shoulder and hip, then these thoughts returned: There was maybe something to the boy—basically, he liked the boy. Maybe he had been too hard on him.

X.

I *WISH I KNEW a trade*." Henry repeated this again and again when he discussed with Lars the possibility of finding something to do. He had now tried several places, but there was no one who had any use for him, since he hadn't learned anything at all in high school that factory owners, craftsmen, or merchants had any use for. It seemed strange to him that he, who had gone to school for so long, should be in a poorer position than newcomers. All of them got work, while the town's own sons, who were born and raised there, went around just like himself or they sold something or had to be agents for something. The sons of well-to-do people went from high school to the university and came back as physicians, lawyers, or engineers or something like that, but the others hung around home until the parents chased them out west or got them jobs in stores owned by relatives or something else out of pity. He was totally envious of those clumsy newcomers for their ability to get ahead.

It is often the case that when something goes wrong, other bad things follow. This was one of Mrs. Nelson's theories and it was a part of Henry's upbringing. It was confirmed for him when just barely a week after his visit to the Perkins' his mother fell on the cellar stairs and scraped her shinbone. She didn't pay much attention to it in the beginning, but then it became infected. Her foot swelled up and a doctor had to be sent for; Mrs. Nelson had to go to bed, and it looked as though it might be for some time.

When Mrs. Nelson got sick, then it first became really apparent to Lars how helpless Henry was. He could barely cut himself a slice of bread, much less manage to do the necessary housework. Lars helped him a little and showed him how this or that should be done, but under the circumstances he could not continue to live there, so for the time being he moved in with another family. The neighbor women were kind and came and helped Mrs. Nelson and her helpless son to the best of their ability.

The third or fourth day following his mother's accident, Henry chanced to cross a street where a group of workers were digging a deep ditch for putting down sewer pipes. He heard the men speaking Norwegian among themselves and took note of how they filled their shovels with gravel and hurled it up. Then the thought occurred to him that he should be able to do the same thing. It looked quite easy. He went to the foreman who stood nearby and asked as matter-of-factly as he could if he needed men. The foreman sized him up and said, "Get yourself a pair of overalls and come tomorrow at 7 o'clock." Henry was not slow to take him up on the offer. He even forgot to ask what kind of wages they paid.

The next day he stood in the ditch in brand-new overalls and dug along with the others, and it was with a feeling of manly fortitude that he threw the dirt unnecessarily far and high.

It was fun in the beginning. He was strong as an ox. But he hadn't carried on for very long before his arms, wrists, and neck began to ache, and he sweated more than the others. He had taken a clean handkerchief with him that morning and took along a couple the next day. Later he discovered that a good-sized rag or a shirtsleeve served the purpose. Toward evening the first day his hands were sore and full of blisters, but he noted with some satisfaction that the pain he felt didn't get any worse.

The men he worked with were all Norwegian but one, and he was a Swede. They were all mature adults and Henry felt himself a real grown-up now when he stood in the ranks with other men and did a man's work. It was a new feeling and it tickled his vanity and made up for his sore hands.

In the evening he came home dead tired and after he had eaten he sat down on the steps and enjoyed a rest. His back ached long after he had gone to bed, but when he woke up the next morning both the aching and the fatigue were gone. The only thing was that he felt stiff. This was just during the first days. He noticed that the other men took short rests off and on and that they didn't work as hard as he did. He noticed especially the little bowlegged Swede, who seemed to throw the dirt up without effort. He took careful notice of the way he held the shovel and the position of his body. He wasn't nearly as tired the second evening as he was the first. And then he began to get acquainted. When the others spoke Norwegian he had to follow suit. Here it was not necessary to weigh what was said. They dug and worked and talked the whole time. Henry learned a good deal from them because they talked about everything under the sun and it amazed him how much more they knew about all manner of things than he did. He learned about the difference between the Republicans and the Democrats. They talked about Lars Skrefsrud,* fishing in Lofoten, Wall Street, Napoleon, Krupp guns, remedies for different ailments, and conditions on the West Coast. Henry thought he learned a great deal every single day.

His proudest moment, though, was payday, when he discovered they had paid him two dollars a day just like the others. When he went home with his first wages, which included a brand-new ten-dollar gold piece, then he wasn't a boy anymore but a real grown man who did a grown man's work. This was something different than having to sit squeezed into a school desk. Now his back didn't ache anymore either and his hands began to get used to it. He just waited for Monday to come so he could start anew, and made an agreement with a neighbor woman to come in and see to his mother. He attempted to do a few things in the house and no longer had the troublesome feeling that he was all thumbs.

The men he worked with were pleasant, kind fellows who, just like Lars, seemed to know something about everything, and since he heard and spoke only Norwegian he became much more proficient in the language and could carry on whole conversations with his mother in Norwegian. Before, he hadn't had a whole lot to talk about to her, but now the evening was hardly long enough for him to tell her everything as she sat up in bed with blood poisoning in her foot. And each conversation usually ended on the note that now there was going to be an end to her doing laundry.

A couple of weeks or so had gone by when Perkins and other passengers had to get off the streetcar and go on foot a little way where the tracks had been removed and the street dug up. He recognized Henry, who

---

* Lars Skrefsrud (1840-1910), missionary and linguist, served mostly the Santals in India and translated religious literature into their language.

stood there digging with the others, and went over to the edge to see if it really was him. Henry recognized him at once and threw a shovelful of dirt right at him without looking up. Perkins calmly brushed himself and went on as though nothing had happened or this was the most natural thing that could have happened.

"You're in for it now," one of his friends told him. "The man who got all that nice muck all over him was the rich man Perkins, one of the directors in the company we're working for."

When Perkins came home there was almost a tone of self-reproach in his voice when he repeated what he had said earlier, "Maybe we were mistaken about that boy after all."

XI.

L ARS FOUND temporary housing with the Skare family, who lived nearby. The man was employed as manager of one of the big stores in the town. It was a good family and one that people spoke well of. Most of the children were grown and had had a good education. The two eldest daughters both took "lessons"—the one in guitar playing and the other in pyrography. The one who now took instruction in guitar playing had earlier taken lessons in elocution, and the one who learned pyrography had gone through a course in which she had learned to paint porcelain. A younger sister, who had also finished high school, worked without pay in a hat shop in order to learn about millinery. It was a great joy for both parents and brothers and sisters to hear her make plans about all she was going to buy and do when she was fully trained and would earn eighteen dollars a week. Next came the oldest son, who went to high school. There were two children, a boy and a girl, who had not yet finished public school, and then there was a little fellow five years old, who had not yet started school, so it was a large family. It was a home where everyone was engaged in something or other. When the oldest daughter sat and strummed on the guitar without let-up, and her sister used an instrument to burn amusing figures on pieces of wood, and the one who was learning millinery practiced on her own hats, then the mother was almost always standing and ironing blouses for her daughters.

When Lars told the plumber that he was going to move to the Skares', the plumber gave him what he said was a piece of good advice. He should always go straight to the bank with his money every time he had any and never go around with loose cash. He should complain that he had to support his old parents, or that he had copper shares and had to pay out everything he earned so as not to lose his prospects of regaining what he had invested, or something like that. But those people were experts and he would have to lie wisely or it would be to no avail. Mr. Skare had a good position and always had his nose to the grindstone, but he still borrowed from everybody who appeared to be a likely candidate for that purpose.

Lars had not lived there long, either, before he saw that this was excellent advice. The eldest son was after him the very next day to lend him a dollar, and the next to the eldest tested him for a quarter. Skare himself waited until the week was at an end before he suggested that Lars accept his note for fifty dollars at eight percent interest. Lars felt sorry for the man who was surrounded every day by his children demanding this thing and that. Skare was proud of his pretty daughters and an inveterate optimist: he could begin to pay back all his many loans with interest when one of the daughters began to give lessons on the guitar and the other in pyrography and the third earned her eighteen dollars a week in the millinery store, and the son got a good position in the bank.

And he could well be proud of his daughters. Their faces were smooth and without a wrinkle. Worries and thinking give early wrinkles, but here there were none. Their eyes were clear and pure as though they were never used and the tears which now and then welled up in them when they "didn't have a thing to wear" only helped to keep them bright.

Clothes were the most important thing. It was mostly clothes that were talked about. Fine clothes, modern clothes—clothes that were becoming and clothes that were not. Probably not a girl in that house would not have considered selling her immortal soul for clothes, Lars thought; they had heaps of them, but there was the constant complaint that they had nothing to wear. This he thought very odd since he never saw the girls dressed in the same outfit two days in a row. They used, for example, different clothes for cloudy weather than under sunny skies and the two eldest made a terrible uproar when the one wore something that belonged to the other. They also talked as though the whole town was deeply concerned over whether they put on a brown or a blue skirt and they always discussed the matter of clothing from that point of view: What will people say if we wear this or that?

In this house the young people spoke only English, and when Lars spoke Norwegian the one stared helplessly at the other. The boy who tried to borrow a quarter the second day Lars lived there came back later and tried to soften Lars's heart by speaking Norwegian. He stretched forth his hand and said: *"Laana Kvart kan du? Pœa dœ bak nekste Vikku."**

Lars felt sorry for the wife who couldn't even properly communicate with her own children. Mr. Skare had already been in this country over ten years when he made a trip to Norway and got engaged and married. He was a widower with two little girls. His wife therefore had to begin keeping house as soon as she came over to America. The two young girls spoke only English and their father translated for her when there was something they wanted. Otherwise they had to manage together as best as they could, and Mrs. Skare spent most of her time in the kitchen. When she had two children of her own it was the two older children who played with them and spoke to them and Mrs. Skare had more and more to do in the kitchen and less in the parlor as the family increased. Then the children were in school. She washed them and cooked food for them and got them ready and sent them off. When they returned they wanted to go out into the street and play. Mrs. Skare had to wash the dishes, wash the clothes, wash the floors, and much else. The children noticed quite early that Mother did not understand them so they conversed with each other. Mother

---

* The boy uses a bad mixture of Norwegian and English to say: "Can you loan me a quarter? I'll pay you back next week."

became like a piece of household furniture—the most useful in the whole house, essential and incomprehensible—something that existed like a fact and neither needed nor required any explanation. Whenever Mrs. Skare had tried to patch together some sentence in English, the others had great fun at her expense—not only the children, but also her husband. In the children's fun there was a strong element of surprise, like that one feels on hearing parrots the first time they utter whole sentences. Mrs. Skare brought one child after the other into the world without being able to speak understandably to them. She could make agreeable sounds and speak Norwegian to them while they were small and lay at her breast, but when they began to speak themselves it was their sisters' tongue they spoke, and she was embarrassed to speak Norwegian to them when they were old enough to understand. The worst thing for Lars was when the family sat up to the table to eat and he heard the mother ask continually: *"Haa sier'n Andrew?—Haa sier'o*, Andrew?—*Si te'n det, du*, Andrew,"* etc. The father was always the interpreter when he was at home. When he was out they used gestures or some language which was produced there in the house and which the mother understood when it was accompanied with gestures. When the young boy opened his mouth and made a smacking noise with his tongue and said *"ita*," then he was given something to eat. His mother understood that he was hungry. When one of the girls took up a blouse from the basket with sprinkled clothes and held it up to the mother and said, *"Ut, otteklok, Mama*," then she realized it had to be ironed before eight o'clock and answered *"alreit"* in English.

At such moments, and when the mother showed a better than usual ability to comprehend, then she would be rewarded with happy and surprised looks which the children sent each other, looks which affirmed that the mother had understood almost everything they had said to her.

It was like the pride one has in a well-trained dog that sometimes can display near-human intelligence.

It cut Lars to the marrow to see this speechless mother. When the father was at home, he kept company with the grown children and Lars and

---

* "What is he saying, Andrew? What is she saying, Andrew? Tell him, Andrew."

laughed and had the greatest fun, while Mrs. Skare, with a dispirited look on her face, kept on with the endless ironing out in the kitchen. The little boy would come running, radiantly happy, into the kitchen, bubbling over with something he wanted to tell, and stop abruptly in front of her as though going to say it. But then he would immediately gather his wits and stand there as he caught his breath and then run off without saying anything at all.

But what made Lars feel worst of all was to hear her stand and talk to herself. His room was a little bedroom just off the kitchen. There was no stove in his room, and when the days and nights got cold they would leave the door standing open a little so that the heat from the kitchen could come in. Mrs. Skare was up early on the morning she was going to wash, and then he would hear long monologues that she would deliver to herself while the family members slept. When, for example, she would pick up one of that endless number of blouses, she would begin to rebuke her daughter with motherly strictness: "You should really be ashamed of yourself, Emma, that a girl your age can't wash or iron your own clothes, even, or help your mother in the least. You see how much I have to do, how I slave and toil from morning till evening without a bit of help from girls as big as you are. You should be ashamed—really be ashamed—and you, too, Milje, you're not one bit better yourself. You can just get angry, but it's the truth all the same—and I, as your mother, have to declare the truth to you before God and man. You're heading straight to ruin the way you run out every evening to have fun. When I was your age I had to go out and work to help my parents and my sister Kristiane, who was sickly, with money for clothes and the doctor. You never think about your parents, and now both your father and I are soon worn out and they keep coming to us with bills and more bills, morning, noon, and night."

And then she would begin to add up all they owed and Lars listened, horrified. He could not imagine that it was possible for an individual family to be indebted to so many people at one time. When Mrs. Skare got hold of a stocking which belonged to the little boy she would sometimes mutter to it with great tenderness in her voice: "No, no, my dear boy, how have you got that big hole in your stocking? I wonder if the other one has got a hole in it, too? Then Mama will mend them for her boy, oh—they're the same in the knees, too. Mother doesn't want her boy to go with anything like that, no. But you should have come and told me before the holes got as big as these, 'cause you're Mama's boy, aren't you? Of course you are, *sure thing* you are. Mama's *baby boy* isn't going to go around with holes in his stockings!"

That was the way she would carry on and Lars thought it was terrible to hear.

But there was one good thing. Mrs. Skare was a well-dressed woman. The reason was that she could always use her daughters' discarded dresses by making a few alterations. She also got their discarded shoes. So when she hobbled off to a Ladies' Aid meeting or an afternoon visit on a pair of high-heeled tan shoes worn down on one side, and with a blouse which showed the tanness of her thin arms, then she was even the object of a crumb of envy.

XII.

AFTER A COUPLE of months had passed, Lars was happy to be able to move back with Mrs. Nelson and Henry. Winter was approaching, and it was good to get back to his cozy old room again. But things were different now. Henry came home in the evenings like any other laborer and washed and changed clothes. He had coarse hands and a rough red neck like a regular worker. Because Henry worked all day with Norwegians and spoke Norwegian, he also liked to speak it at home. He was always in a good mood and wanted to talk about everything possible. Instead of plopping himself down in a chair with a newspaper, he would rather talk about politics, or town affairs, or the men with whom he worked. He had also begun to read a Norwegian newspaper, which Lars subscribed to, and had become a completely different person. But it didn't appear as though his mother was totally happy with this change. Before, she had had a fine son, whom she could look up to with pride and respect. The son she had now wasn't much different from those who had come right from Norway. She limped around now on her bad foot and was cross and irritable. She no longer did laundry for others. Henry had threatened to wreck the first washtub in which he found clothing from strangers. Lars had to admit that he also thought Henry had become more commonplace, so he no longer could be as proud of living with him as before. But, on the other hand, he could not side with the mother either when she gave him long sermons about what was fitting for a person with his education and what was not. Henry took it all good-naturedly. "All this advice is good, isn't it?" he was accustomed to say to Lars. "I didn't think Mother was so smart that she knew everything. If we could live by it all, we'd be all right, wouldn't we, Lars?"

Mrs. Nelson couldn't help feeling a little crestfallen when she was with the other women because her son was doing such ordinary labor; but then again, her boy was providing for her now. There was a thorn in it, all the same. She yielded to her fate. It was undoubtedly not the will of God that her son should be an exceptionally fine man and therefore he had sent her this affliction with the bad leg.

It was quite obvious that Sophy had grown when she came home for the Christmas holidays. Lars had a feeling she had grown much taller than he.

But at the same time he had also become more of a man. He already had a couple of hundred dollars in the bank and had sent quite a bit of money to his parents in Norway. He had good clothes and had had a photograph taken of himself. When he looked at this picture he couldn't avoid seeing that he looked like a very fine young man. He felt he was almost irreplaceable at the workshop now, and he was no longer afraid of losing his job.

He had not had much opportunity to see or speak with Sophy. When autumn came, she had gone off to school again. But the little he had seen of her was encouraging and his hopes were kept alive. He had, for example, noticed that she didn't like it if he talked too much with Mabel. He kept himself on good footing with her brothers and always gave them something when they came to beg him for money, which they often did.

Otherwise everything was just as usual at the Omleys'. The wife worked in the kitchen, as was customary, and her husband worked out both early and late. He got some work as a result of telling his customers that he could accept contracts for much less because he worked himself— or that he could deliver better work because he was on the job himself. He could probably have done business on a bigger scale, but he was so accustomed to emphasizing the advantages of his personal work that he dared not let go of it. He secretly invested his money in mortgage-bonds. People often needed money when they were going to build, and if Omley could provide them with a loan he could count on doing the painting for them and could also charge more. But these loans were also arranged in the greatest secrecy. If it should be known that he was putting a good deal of money aside it could hurt his business, for he got jobs by talking about his difficult situation and the expensive school attended by his daughter. This was an especially effective procedure among his own countrymen.

His children were his pride. And it was the thought of them that drove him out an hour earlier than the others every morning, and it was this that sustained his wife in her daily toil. No matter what they did to assert themselves, they discovered that others knew this art still better. It was easy to see that their children were finer than the children of the other Norwegians, and they believed that others must be able to see this. They had had their dreams about journeying back to Norway in order to shine there themselves, but now it was the children who should shine here instead.

It awakened no little concern therefore that Sophy had been both to a concert and to the theatre with Lars, and in addition, to a basket social in the church basement. They knew that Mabel had also been along and they first nourished the thought that it was at her that Lars had aimed his attention; but when they later learned that Lars and Sophy had exchanged letters and that Lars had sent her his photograph, they became apprehensive. He was just a common Norwegian, and barely more than a newcomer at that.

Omley then let Lars understand, in a gentlemanly fashion, what a huge gap there was between a newcomer and a young lady with a college education and music lessons that cost seventy-five cents a time. Sophy was not mentioned; but from his own experience Omley could cite several examples of ordinary newcomers who made sheep's eyes at young ladies with a good education and were miserably put to shame—ladies who were later married to attorneys, traveling salesmen, insurance agents, and other fine persons.

Lars made no reply to this, but just pushed ahead that much harder. When he became sufficiently fluent in English it wouldn't be so difficult to find a different and better job which could make him more worthy of a young lady of quality. It helped a great deal to level the differences between them, however, when he came to the full realization that Sophy's parents were not much finer than his own.

Christmas had come and Sophy had come home for the holidays. Lars had prepared for her arrival by growing a little mustache, like those he had seen on fine merchant clerks and office workers in Norway. It was to be very little, and that is just what it was. As Christmas approached it was just long enough for him to hold the ends of it between his fingers and give them a tiny little twist. Omley observed this mustache with increasing concern. It didn't take long before these newcomers began to get above themselves and follow the latest fashions. He had been in the country several years before he grew a mustache himself, and then it was one with ends pointing modestly downward. To his way of thinking, a mustache that pointed downward inspired more confidence—there was something more serious about it, much more suited to a genuine man of the church. He was a regular churchgoer and one of the pillars of the congregation. Lars's mustache irritated him and it even occurred to him that in some way or another it might hurt business; he feared it most for his daughter's sake. Lars knew what he was doing.

It was a big event for Lars when he received an invitation from Overhus to spend Christmas with them, because Sophy would be there too. He went to the barber and requested everything he had to offer, and the hair artist clipped, shaved, shampooed, massaged, and carried on for over an hour.

Everything at the Overhuses' had been arranged on a grand scale. Mrs. Overhus had undergone great changes during the course of the past year. She had come in contact with real Americans through a mattress-manu-facturing family—a man with whom Overhus had business connections and who lived in grand style. Here Mrs. Overhus had had occasion to observe American customs that she now aspired to practice on her more uninitiated fellow Norwegians. She stood now in the hallway in a modest low-necked gown and received her guests. Her full gray hair was dressed according to all the rules of the art, and a little powder gave her face some of the aristocratic, floury touch that suited the wife of the mattress manufacturer so well. Mrs. Overhus raised her arm very high when she shook hands. This was one of the trumps she used. The guests entered the parlor one after the other with the same vain upper-class ges-ture. Mrs. Stenson, who had been out among fine people before, could not refrain from telling Mrs. Overhus that they had always used this method of greeting at the Rutherford Vincents' where she had been employed for so many years.

Instead of serving an entire evening meal, only coffee and hot choco-late were served, in very small cups, and some tiny pieces of cake together with a wafer. Mabel came later with a plate on which there were pieces of chocolate candy, and each took one. It was truly a dignified, solemn occasion, and the plumber, who got in everywhere because of his wife's English background, said that it was about like going to Communion.

The guests seemed also somewhat overwhelmed by the great demands that in such a place were put on their upbringing. The Overhus people were no longer to be considered as ordinary Norwegian folk. Mrs. Overhus spoke English almost exclusively, and said, *"Dear me"* and *"I declare."* Who could have believed that the Overhus people could have risen up like that? Mrs. Hill sat there positively aching to get home so that she could try out that fine high-arm greeting on her next-door-neighbor lady, who still lived in a state of innocence when it came to shaking hands. The very next morning she would make it a point to go there on some errand or other. She could actually feel the muscles in her right arm play with exultant desire.

One who did not give the impression of being content was Overhus himself. He was silent, to begin with, and quite aloof. One of the reasons was that he had to wear a suit coat. He was so accustomed to going around the house in his shirtsleeves that the coat bothered him. But he set himself down in a former bedroom that Mabel had turned into "*Papa's Den*," and furnished with many things made according to directions in the Sunday papers for the beautification of the home. A pretty embroidered footstool held a very prominent position on a little table; there was a blanket with a Norwegian and an American flag; and on a fine silk ribbon which hung on the wall were his initials in elegant three-inch-high letters. Pennants were placed around the room, together with pictures and nice things made by ladies that had to do with smoking. There were objects for storing cigars, matches, and pipes, along with mother-of-pearl ashtrays, and a writing desk fresh from the store.

Here Overhus sat down with some of the older men. The plumber looked around in vain for a spittoon. When Overhus procured one he made a sour apology that it didn't have pearl trimming like everything else. After a time, when the discomfort of all the decoration had settled a little, the conversation got under way.

The conversation centered mainly on the congregation. There had long been talk of a church building. And then the perpetual topic: the children and their future.

"We have to build for the sake of the young, I suppose," Stenson said. "The English have fine, big churches, and if we don't put up something just as fine, then the young people will go where it is finest."

The men all concurred in this.

Stenson developed further what had to be done for the young. A place ought to be set up in the church basement where they could have a little fun and play billiards or something else of a permissible nature. Something had to be done to keep the young away from other churches.

The plumber thought that in that case a saloon or a pool hall with a bowling alley would be the very best. There was nothing better to keep the young away from churches, if that was the intention.

Stenson did not understand the sarcasm and developed further how it had first been thought that it was the lack of English services which had kept the young people away. Now this lack had been remedied, but they still didn't come to church. Over half of them never came back to church after they were confirmed.

They sat a long while, puzzled, pondering this difficult problem, and returned to the church building as the only solution.

"I can't understand what it is that is wrong with the young people," said Overhus at last. "When I came here, then we were almost all new-comers, we were young and we were poor. We worked hard, and most of us had had very little schooling. But we started a reading club, we had a big male chorus, and there was even a Norwegian band here. We organized our own health insurance, and we would pool our resources once in a while and get some well-known person to come and give a lecture for us. We had discussions about everything possible and we even put on the play 'Til Sæters' here, and it wasn't so bad, either.* But we were then only simple working boys and servant girls, almost all of us. The young people now never get anything going. They go to school until they are adults. They seem never to have anything to do, yet they seem to be more tired when evening comes than we were who toiled with heavy labor."

"Yes, it seems to be the same everywhere," said Newhouse. "The big Y.M.C.A. we have was built by the older folks. They gathered funds and built it and furnished it with swimming facilities, gymnastic equipment, basketball courts, bowling lanes, billiard tables, and the like, and they still have to set up prizes and use many kinds of contrivances to get the young to come; it's quite a struggle to make it work."

"Maybe it's the times we're in," Overhus uttered philosophically. "I have a grown-up boy myself," he added. "He's a fine boy, and he's like the others, but something seems to be lacking. He's a good boy, but

---

* A popular play by C.P. Riis with folk songs and a strong nationalistic emphasis.

it's as though it's only his body that grows. He is so childish and simple-hearted—there is something foreign about him so I have to stop sometimes and ask myself, is that really your boy there? When he looks at me it's just the same way he looks at other people who come into the store—as if he wonders a little bit who I am." Overhus paused a moment and suddenly made an about-face and with a happy smile continued: "I'll never forget that boy when he was little. I used to have him on my lap and I'd ask him, *'Who's your pa, Johnnie?'* And he'd take hold of my beard with those little fingers of his and he'd say, *'You is my pa, ain't you?'* and then I'd say, *'Co'se I is your pa, Johnnie,'* and then he'd say, *'Co'se you are.'* We could carry on like that a long time—and my wife would say that Johnnie and I sounded just like we had been born in this country."

"I thought you spoke Norwegian to your children when they were small," the plumber cut him off.

"Yes, we did with Mabel, who was the first," Overhus said almost apologetically. "With the boy it was mostly English. Neither my wife nor I could speak much English when Mabel was little. When the boy got a little bigger there wasn't so much talk. They're pretty sharp, those little ones—and suddenly he was correcting things I had said, and telling me it shouldn't have been said like that and that I should have said this—and all that. It isn't much fun for a father to be corrected by a little toddler, and so I kept quiet instead—and I suppose then it was his mother and his sister he talked to most."

"He got to know who his father was anyway. There are those who grow up among us here who don't even get that much stamped into their heads," said the plumber.

Overhus didn't notice his mockery.

A bit of the happy smile remained that had been summoned by the memory of the boy when he was little, and his eyes did not see clearly, otherwise he would have caught sight of the ironic smile which played on the plumber's mouth as he spoke.

This evening became a significant one for Lars. Mr. and Mrs. Omley left very early since they had got wind that this was the fine thing to do by observing the Stensons, who broke up early. Omley had another reason for being in a hurry—he was hungry. This was possibly what also drove the Stensons off; but everyone knew, of course, that it was the custom among "better people" to leave early.

The young ones, however, did not adhere to that custom. They had taken over the big sitting room. Their entertainment consisted of everyone begging an individual to play and this individual said that she didn't have music with her and that there were others who played much better. When she finished playing her piece they all applauded and asked each other if they didn't think the piece was just beautiful and answered each other that they thought it was just beautiful. Then they tried to get someone else to come forward who reluctantly could play another absolutely beautiful piece. In addition, they looked at photographs and views. When the conversation was completely carried on in English, Lars took little part in it. He sat rigidly on his chair wondering if it was all right to sit with one leg crossed over the other. There were a couple of other young men present and the one did it and not the other. The greatest pleasure for him was to sit and think about what a fine party it was. Father and Mother and the rest of them back home should see him here in such a fine salon with the most expensive furniture, and only English spoken around him.

Overhus's son John went to high school. He didn't speak to anyone but went around with a stern expression on his face and wore a sweater. It was obvious that he belonged in another sphere. He felt, however, attracted to Lars, who was very big, and wanted to know how much he could lift. Lars couldn't tell him this, but to do something in that regard he took hold of the crosspiece of a chair with both hands and stretched them out and lifted it up with taut arms. This interested the boy greatly, who then showed him various things, among them a tomahawk. Lars also had occasion to see the bookcase, which was very handsome, but with the exception of a few religious books, *Earth, Sea, and Sky,* and *McKinley's Biography,* most of the works were scientific, English books, which the boy explained had come all the way from Washington from their local congressman. The boy explained that there were also many books in his father's store.

But what gave the day its great value was that Lars got to walk Sophy home that evening. She was so pretty in her new mink furs that Lars nearly lost his breath at the thought of being able to walk beside her.

They did not say much. Sophy was not a little downcast to think how fine things had become in Mabel's home. But it was a great comfort that Mabel now knew that Lars was walking her home alone. She walked with slow steps and seemed to be in no great hurry to get home.

As he walked, Lars shivered at the thought that this evening he ought to let her know how much he cared for her. He didn't exactly have to propose to her, but he could ask her to wait for him until he had been able to save a certain sum of money. But, should he say it in Norwegian or in English? He would begin by saying that it was dumb and foolish of him who was only a simple newcomer to say to her, who had gone to schools of higher learning and knew music and in whom much money had been invested, that he cared for her so unspeakably much and if she would just not promise herself to anyone else, then he would show that he could both work and save money so as to be worthy of her.

He would say something like that. He would begin by saying it was dumb of him, etc. He chewed this over and over. It was maybe best to say it in English; he could certainly manage that much. And today he also had on his best clothes and had got fixed up for almost a dollar at the barber's, and besides he had come from a party. It seemed to him most appropriate to broach such a subject after a party, when he was finely dressed. Yes, the more he thought about it the more he shivered—even though it wasn't particularly cold and Sophy appeared as though she was much too warm. He hardly dared look to the side where she was.

When they got to the gate, the two of them remained standing there indecisively and Sophy said something about thinking they had all gone to bed and she said this in English. Lars then said that he also thought they had gone to bed and there was again a long pause. Then she made a movement as if to open the gate and Lars at once made a big decision—he would just have to try his luck in English:

"*I feel like a fool,*" he began, shaking with excitement.

"So do I," she broke in and threw herself suddenly around his neck and gave him a quick little kiss on his little mustache, and with that she ran. Lars stood perplexed a moment as he turned to leave, but when he turned around he saw her there on the steps, tall and slender, and she waved to him with the glove which she held in her hand. Lars walked backward into a lamppost as he waved back to her with his cap. This was the most curious courtship he had ever heard or read about. And he had even wondered if it was proper to kiss the hand of so fine a lady when proposing marriage.

Lars did not sleep much that night. He just lay in bed and thought and thought—and he built house after house—the one finer than the other, and he did all the paintwork in these houses himself. Nothing was good enough for a lady as fine as Sophy.

XIII.

H ENRY NELSON had had remarkably good fortune since he began as a road construction worker. Not long after he threw a shovelful of dirt in rich Perkins's lap, he was offered the job of timekeeper. It was certainly nice work—just to go from place to place and shuffle his feet and make notations in a book. But when his salary proved to be the same as before, Henry preferred to work like the others. Maybe they thought he wasn't strong enough to use a pick and shovel? Then he would show them. He had seen Edith just one time since that day out on the porch and that was while he was digging and she rode by in the family's new landau with someone else. Just then his head and shoulders were up over the edge of the ditch and he recognized her, and a resounding "Prrrr—!" as the vehicle passed by told him that she had forgotten neither him nor the way high school girls gave a signal. He then answered, also with a high school shout, which the little Swede asserted was "awful and not at all Christian sounding."

After this the lumps of clay flew up out of the ditch as though a volcano had become active.

He met many people in his work, among them an older man who had known his father. Yes, he knew Hank Nelson well and had worked with him in the woods and could tell Henry a great deal about him. Henry learned that his father was from Odalen in Norway and that he had done his time in the military and gone to a school for non-commissioned officers and was good at writing and arithmetic. He also learned that his father was considered to be the strongest man in the lumbering camp and that he could bend a horseshoe. All this was of tremendous interest to Henry. The man also told how "Hank"—he never called him anything else—had got his arm broken by a falling tree and how he had had it set and put in a splint by the cook, who was handy with such things because he had studied to become a doctor before drink got the upper hand, and then Hank had continued to work and saw with the one arm in a sling because he didn't think that as a recently married man he could afford to be laid up and not earn anything, now that there would be an addition to the family before spring. When the man told about this, Henry didn't get much more work done. He leaned on the shovel and thought about how great it would be if his father were still alive and he thought it was so strange that his mother had not told him any of this.

When he heard about how Hank had lifted up a tree trunk that had knocked an Irishman to the ground, or about the time when a bear had got into the cooking shanty and Hank grabbed it by one of its back legs, Henry's eyes beamed. This he had to tell his mother.

When he got home he would ask all kinds of questions about his father, what he had been like, how big he had been, etc. His mother answered him curtly and sourly when he asked such questions. She had the impression that her son was becoming more and more ordinary and more like the other people she knew and had had around her. He was no longer his old self—he who earlier had conducted himself so nicely and spoken English and talked about the teachers at the high school, and about things which had taken place among the most prominent people of the town.

But good fortune continued to follow him.

When the ground froze that winter and most of the workers were dismissed, Henry was given work in the office. When he had time left over, he was given the task of copying plan drawings of various kinds and calculating numbers and the like. He had, of course, learned to do some of this in school, and now it was being put to good use. The engineer who worked there full-time took an interest in him. Henry plugged away as best he could and was glad to be employed.

When spring came he was made foreman of a work team. This did not force him to quit working with the others, while it gave him the advantage of being able to choose what he wanted to do. And he was strong and willing and did the heaviest jobs himself. This gave him the advantage that he never had any trouble with the ten men who made up his team. He did not have the maturity for his position, and most of the workers understood more than he what had to be done; for that very reason commands did not have to be given and the team worked so well that Henry was praised for having the best work team in the company. But the best of all was payday. Twenty dollars a week was a great deal of money—he could barely understand how he and his mother could have use for so much. The amount he earned was the only reason he was glad for his promotion. He liked to dig in the earth, he liked the smell of the damp sand and soil. He could pick up handful after handful just to let the dirt slip through his fingers. When he got rich he would buy himself a farm. He felt as much at home among the people who stood in a row and dug as a soldier did in formation. Here he was just as good as anyone else, and then some, and here he filled a decent and strong man's place. It occurred to him that here was the only place where he had ever had this feeling. At his school desk he had always felt that the lowest in the class was better than he, and he had gone to his examinations like a criminal who had to rely solely upon the mercy of the judge.

Edith Perkins was not to be fooled with and was used to getting her way. The lectures she gave to her parents were both sharp and forceful. Her mother took this calmly because she gave lectures herself on occasion and knew that her daughter had inherited this propensity from her.

Perkins did not have a good conscience at all with regard to Henry. Basically, he liked the boy now that he had found himself a job. Here was a boy who looked after his mother—and that was good—Perkins had done that himself; one who was not afraid of soot because it was black and was not afraid of hard work—that had never been his lot, but he had nothing but the greatest respect for those whose lot it was. There was yet another thing he liked: the boy stayed away from his house and from his daughter and seemed to take it all as a reasonable man should under such circumstances, when there was nothing else to be done. The thought came to him that he ought to make a man out of this big, foolish boy. It flattered his vanity that he had understood the boy in just the right manner, and when he had got the shovelful of dirt in his lap he knew that his daughter would feel no pressure from that direction. "The boy is simple, and that is no vice; but he's no *sucker* either, and that is a great virtue," thought Perkins, because he had an aptitude for philosophy. And so he put in a word for Henry with the manager that carried some weight.

Thus it happened that good fortune followed Henry right from the first day he took hold of the shovel.

That autumn he was given responsibility for an independent project, because the man who was supposed to be in charge became ill. A road and a little bridge were to be built through a marsh. It was not exactly difficult work, but difficult enough for him who hardly understood the drawings and specifications which he had been given. He had a dozen men with him, most of whom were Norwegians and old work comrades. When they had pitched their tents and were to begin, Henry hardly knew in from out, but a beginning was made and he worked and toiled alongside the others and there were great discussions and consultations. It surprised him that the workers themselves seemed to understand what it was that should be done. They argued and discussed among themselves every time there were difficulties to be overcome, and the one who knew least of all was the one who was to lead the work. The little bowlegged Swede and the man who had known his father were both in the crew, and he stayed close to them. The Swede constantly reassured him, saying, "It'll turn out O.K.," and the man who was a big talker spent long evening hours explaining to him what had to be done the next day. Henry tackled the heaviest work while the others argued among themselves, quibbling and cursing their way forward to the solution of one task after another. The end of it all was that the work got finished, but not quite according to the calculations and directions of the engineers. The crew had built the road where it ought to be, but where the engineers had said it was not possible to build it. There were a lot of materials left over, and the work was accomplished in less time than planned. The county inspectors were extremely well satisfied because the road was built where they had said it ought to be all along. The company was not only satisfied but awarded the crew a hundred and fifty dollars as an extra bonus. Henry divided this among them so they all got an equal share.

When he was asked to explain how they had accomplished this work, Henry was at a loss for words; but the manager was greatly impressed by the young man's capabilities.

There wasn't a happier man in the whole town than Henry when he returned from this assignment. This was something quite different than going around knocking on kitchen doors peddling soap and perfume and the like. To have had a hand in building a road across a marsh—that was something more suited to grown men. He began to dream about becoming a man like the Swede, who had understood how the work should be done from the very first day, or like the man who had known his father, who had waded back and forth in the marsh and had found a way where it was believed there was none. Work which presented a challenge which had to be overcome—even if it was only a big stone in the ground—that stirred him. It filled him with the same intense exhilaration he had experienced when he played football. He was learning something the whole time, and was never in doubt about what to do in a situation he had been through before. He had never had feelings like this toward books and lessons. Those were not real jobs—they were more like finding one's way through a fog. His brain seemed to be distributed throughout his whole body, and if his whole body was not engaged, he was not interested.

All was going well at home. His mother now had plenty of everything, and one of her washtubs leaked and had fallen apart. For a long time she had kept filling it with water, expecting that if something should happen she would again have use for it. She still had two tubs in good condition for their own laundry, which she continued to do herself. She would not hear of giving up this aspect of her work. Actually, she was very well-off. She, who previously had seldom conversed much with her son, could speak with him as much as she wished because now they could understand each other, and he liked to speak Norwegian. It had even become the most natural for him, he said. This his mother could not comprehend, and disappointedly shook her graying head. Here was Lars, who had just come from Norway, becoming finer and finer with each day, and even beginning to speak English, while her son—"that Henry of mine," as she often referred to him—became simpler with each day and would soon be speaking nothing but Norwegian. Everybody else would soon be getting ahead of her and her boy. Mrs. Dale had stopped by and told about her precocious daughter who now "went with" or was as good as engaged to a distinguished American, who was called Jim but signed his name James, and had a brother who was a lawyer and another who was an alderman. He would become an alderman or a lawyer himself. He studied at his brother's office and had sent her daughter letters typed on a typewriter which looked as if they were printed.

Mrs. Nelson had little with which to retaliate. Once she would have been able to tell about invitations her boy had from some of the finest families, but that was in the past.

It was as though her efforts to make a big fine man out of her son were a total failure, and all his education thrown out the window. She liked the fact that he went to church with her whenever there was a Norwegian service, but she would have liked it better if he had gone to the English service that the prominent young people attended. But she took comfort from the fact that he was considerate, and neither drank nor smoked nor swore. She would have to accept it as God's will that he should be nothing more than a common laborer.

Out of the blue she asked him worriedly if he wasn't forgetting how to speak the English language and reminded him that he must remember what he had been taught when he went to high school. But Henry, poor fellow, could hardly remember a thing he had learned in high school.

XIV.

I F THERE WAS ANYTHING the rich W. W. Perkins was leery about, it was those penniless counts and barons from the countries of Europe who came to America in order to marry themselves off to wealthy heiresses. He could work himself into a rage just by hearing someone mention such words as "count" or "baron." He had never seen any with his own two eyes, but he had seen drawings of them in the Sunday editions of the newspapers and read about them in popular magazines.

With the coming of winter, the whole family traveled to Florida for the sake of his wife's health. The boy was sent to an academy, and Perkins himself went with his wife and daughter to one of the most fashionable winter resorts on Florida's west coast. Here they checked into one of the most exclusive hotels, adequately suited to rich people, and it did not take long before Edith had a whole swarm of admirers.

Perkins was sitting on pins and needles. For every new acquaintance he asked himself: I wonder if this is a count? When he calmed down, he sat with his wife and daughter, spoke ill of counts, wrung his hands, turned red in the face, and searched his memory for all the examples of bad marriages he had read about in which these counts played the role of villain. They were decadent, immoral, and incapable of earning a red cent, any of them. Edith, who had not been able to forget her childhood hero from school days—she was, of course, an adult now—sought to remind him that he had chased away from the house one who was neither decadent nor immoral, and only because he was poor.

"But he was lazy, my dear daughter!"

"If you call standing in a ditch shoveling dirt all day long being lazy, then I don't know what laziness is, dear Papa."

"He was an imbecile—had no brains, no thought for the future."

To this Edith responded quite sourly that she could not understand what a person needed so many brains for when he had the money he needed anyway. If, for instance, everyone who wasn't over-endowed with brains were to be chased away from this hotel, then only the waiters would be left, and not all of them either.

To this there was little to be said because Perkins had had similar thoughts himself about most of the hotel's prominent guests, and he was absolutely honest.

He lived in constant uneasiness. Every time he saw a really disgusting, overdressed fellow, he thought: This has got to be another of those confounded count-scamps from Europe, and he could not free himself from the thought that they had come precisely with the intent of capturing his idolized daughter.

Edith was not to be sneezed at. Nor did it take very long before a fellow was flirting with her who, among the many examples of decadent gentlemen, came as close to her father's notion of a really rakish count as it was possible to imagine. Mr. Perkins eyed him with ever increasing anxiety. It was perhaps best not to say anything yet—not to let on; but he began to lose his appetite and did not sleep well at night. When he saw this skinny, baldheaded man arrive in his patent leather shoes, with a bouquet of flowers in his gloved hands, he sought refuge in a remote corner where he found comfort in swearing to himself.

Sleepless nights are long nights, and long nights beget gloomy thoughts. There were times when he would gladly have given his only daughter to a ditchdigger, if it meant being free of a son-in-law like this creature who came striding along the garden walk on his two beanstalk legs with a bouquet of flowers. They were flowers for Perkins's coffin—for the burial of his happiness.

At such moments he thought of the boy he had chased away from the house. To work was no shame—he had not done much physical labor himself; but he knew many good people who in their youth had worked with their hands and now were proud of it. He could have paid for the boy and provided for his education—to become an engineer, at any rate. He had tried to make a man of him anyway, and that had gone quite well. It would not be such a dumb thing to make a decent man for his daughter out of this big simple boy, and get him to the point where he might turn out to be useful to him.

He began occasionally to speak well of Henry. The story about the road-building job, which the supervisor had reported to him, that was good, he thought. He did not tire of speaking about it, and even added a little. He told how Henry, ten days ahead of schedule, had reported that everything was already finished with the construction job except for the drawings and the plans, and he would bring those as soon as they came from the office.

Edith listened to this with seeming indifference. It was obvious that her thoughts were now occupied with another, and Perkins kept on saying good things about Henry until his forehead was shiny with sweat. It was nervous sweat, too. Maybe he was already too late.

When Edith was in her own room she could sit for a long time and delight in thinking about her own shrewdness and laugh contentedly at her own image in the mirror, tap her white, well-manicured finger on her forehead and say something like: "You've got quite a head on your shoulders, Edith my girl. The most remarkable thing about it is that you must have been born with it on your own, because it doesn't run in the family. Papa makes progress every day in the consciousness of his sins, even if it comes too late for a man of his age. He has no idea what a smart daughter he has—and she's not even nineteen yet—a whole book could be written about this"—and she laughed until there were tears in her eyes, pinched her ear, and said: "You should have a spanking, you naughty child, making such a fool of your father—and when it comes down to it, that may be a sin too—you must also remember, my girl, that you have a mother who is not well." And then she laughed again as she stood before the mirror making faces she thought might be fitting when, contritely, she would explain everything to him; but that would probably not be before—yes, well—so she went to bed and slept sweetly on her misdeeds, which

naughty and self-willed children always do, while their parents lie awake
pondering and wrestling with dark thoughts about their future.

Henry had not been as fortunate this winter as he had been during the
previous one. When the ground froze, work was unsteady; but he kept on
as long as he could, and when there was nothing else to do, he found something to keep him busy around the house. But close to Christmas word
was sent to him and he was given a job at the office, just like the winter
before. It was pure strange luck, he thought, because he could not comprehend what possible good he could do there. But the pay would come
in handy, since he had bought the little house they were living in on
monthly installments. He was again given drawings to copy and estimates
on which to test his ability to figure. The work was tiring and boring,
almost as boring as school; but he stuck with it and waited for the arrival
of spring when he could again find some real work.

XV.

SOPHY WAS NOT sent to college the following winter.
Mr. Omley and his wife felt that Sophy already had both
knowledge and education enough to be a wife for some-
one like Lars. Had Omley guessed at the possibility of there ever being
anything between her and Lars, he would certainly never have spent as
much money on her as he had; she had been fine enough for an ordinary,
simple Norwegian just as she was without additional expense.

He almost began to feel dislike for Lars, as though, in some under-
handed way or another, he had cheated him out of the considerable sum
which he had spent on his daughter. Mrs. Omley shared this resentment
and disgustedly banged all manner of dishes in the kitchen when Lars came
on one of his all too frequent visits. The others would really have something to gloat about when Sophy couldn't do any better than the likes of

him. They had had big plans for her, but no one has any control over such things. But they were not going to throw any more money away on her, and she would have to learn to "pitch in" like any others who were going to become ordinary working men's wives. When you make your bed, you have to lie in it too. Sophy was put to doing quite a bit of housework, which they had considered too simple for her, and when she objected she always heard: "You better get used to it. You know Lars doesn't have any money, and if you're going to marry him, then you're just going to have to learn to do all your work yourself."

Whenever she wanted to have something new to wear, they told her: "You're plenty good enough for Lars." Just to mock him they continued to call him Lars, even though he had long since taken the name Louis. Mrs. Omley had never before had the courage to act with any sternness toward her daughter, but now that the daughter was reduced to being the fiancée of a laboring man with a wage of two and a half dollars a day, there was something in this situation which gave her strength and courage to tell her daughter many unpleasant truths.

Nor was Mr. Omley inactive. When he realized the kind of relationship which existed between Lars and Sophy, his unfailing business sense told him that he could now keep Lars for the same low daily wage without giving him a raise. He knew that Lars could well have received fifty cents more a day now if there had been a chance of him going to work for someone else, but Lars would not very likely go elsewhere as things now stood. He was almost sorry that he had twice raised his pay a quarter, but he had no idea things would take this kind of a turn. It was not until summer vacation, when Lars and Sophy began to be off on their own, that he realized what was going on, and then it was too late, because he had already given him a raise in pay.

Little by little, Lars began to understand the situation. He understood that the five hundred dollars he had saved and his two and a half dollars a day counted for very little. But he was happy anyway. Hadn't all these Norwegians begun with much less than this—some even with debts? But when he saw how beautiful and fine Sophy was and thought about all the money that had been spent on her—over eight hundred dollars, Omley had said, and that didn't include all her clothes—then he was often seized with despondency at the thought of how difficult it would be to create a home she would want to claim as her own. When winter came, this feeling got stronger.

Omley kept him working through the winter primarily because he had taken on work which only Lars was capable of doing—sign painting, decorative work, and the like. Omley began to grow accustomed to the thought that all Sophy's education was money down the drain and that it was only right that he should be able to squeeze out of Lars at least a part of it by letting him work for less pay. Besides, he took comfort from the boys—one of them had already started confirmation instruction—who were turning out better, and one of the signs was that they did not show the slightest desire to do physical labor. They both did well in school and the one planned to be a doctor and the other a lawyer. It was really fun to listen to them argue between themselves about which of these professions was the more highly regarded and the best paid. When they finished confirmation, they were both going to go to high school.

They were very gifted boys, especially when it came to throwing things. There was almost no limit to their throwing talents. The one who was going to become a doctor hit Lars right in the neck with a snowball just as he was knocking on the front door one Sunday afternoon. This snowball was so well made and struck with such force that Lars was dazed by it and just about stumbled across the threshold. Then Omley had to smile. This land was America, and here such things could happen. The young here were not so cowed as in Norway and other European monarchies. Even Sophy had to smile. And in this smile there lay some family pride. Without being able to say why, she laughed together with the others. This snowball was the better and more respected family's protest against Lars, who was a simple man—it came as a message from a different, more spacious, and more energetic world than the one in which Lars felt at home. And that's why Omley and his wife chuckled. What they had not been able to put into works had been crystalized by their boys in a snowball, and it said with a thud what Omley and his wife had been thinking for several months. It released a tension in the depths of their souls which needed to be unleashed and it gave them relief—yes, a comfort which set their laughing muscles in vigorous motion.

Lars did not like this mirthfulness. He thought, however, that he too had to appear cheerful, though his neck hurt and was beginning to get stiff. One of the boys—the one who was going to be a doctor—had come in through the kitchen and joined the merriment with gleaming eyes and smiling face.

Lars did not stay seated very long, and when he left he was lucky enough to see the future doctor sneak out ahead of him. When he bent over to open the gate, another snowball whizzed right by him. He quickly turned around and saw the aspiring lawyer about ready to throw yet a third. With a few swift paces he was beside the boy, who had fled up the steps, and grabbed him by the neck and gave him a couple of slaps, after which he headed homeward as though in a daze.

Lars had viewed these two boys, one of whom was to become a doctor and the other a lawyer, with a certain amount of secret awe. In letters home he had even referred to them as young men who were to be educated to this end, and now he had laid his hand on one of the untouchables. But when he thought about all the money these boys had begged from him, and his stiff neck, and the laughter, then he was glad he had given one of the boys a boxing on the ears after all, and even began to make plans as to how he was going to warm the ears of the other.

Unable to sleep, he lay awake the whole night. Anger and pain alternated in his troubled mind, anger over the bad treatment he had received and pain at the thought of Sophy, whom he now might not get to see anymore.

Was this the end to all his dreams about a fine wife who could play the piano and have a maid? What was going to happen to his connections with upper-class families—doctors and lawyers who spoke only English and moved about only in higher circles of society?

The few hundred dollars he had in the bank were his greatest comfort. He should maybe show them that he was too good a fellow to be their fool. Basically they were just simple people too, and in Norway they would not be regarded as upper-class at all.

In his thoughts he wrote not just one but several letters to Sophy break-ing off their engagement. In his thoughts he went to the house not just once but several times to receive her assurance that she still loved him very deeply, that she could not live without him, and he forgave them all and was so noble that there were tears in his sleepless eyes as he consid-ered how good he really was. But the anger returned with greater inten-sity. Hadn't Omley taken unfair advantage of him, keeping him with too little pay the whole time? Hadn't he remained there like a fool? Wasn't he just as good as any of them?

But the next day he did none of these things. He did not do anything and did not return to his job. Omley was furious. Hadn't he, just out of compassion and helpfulness, taken this newcomer under his wing and made a man out of him? It cut him to the quick to think of the several hundred dollars Lars had saved up—this was money which once had been his own, and which he still did not feel he could let go. The ungrateful fellow had received all this money from him. Where would he have been without him? This was his thanks. Never again would he help any new-comer. As soon as one learned how to manage on his own, then it was goodbye. Omley ground his teeth at the thought of how good he had been to Lars.

Lars heard a couple of weeks later that Sophy had gone back to school. He started several letters to her, but he never mailed them. If he hadn't stopped to consider what he was doing before, he did so at the mailbox. This solid iron box deterred him. Once the letter was put inside, Lars's destiny would be set. He heard nothing from her. He was certain that she was terribly sorry, and that caused him anguish; but the Old Adam was also on the prowl and whispered into his ear that it served her right.

He had had his plans for his own house, and it was a fine house with a piano and expensive furniture. These plans lay in ruins, but up out of the ruins there arose a picture of another home—simpler, but with stronger roots in reality. Into this home stepped Karoline Huseby. She would be wide-eyed at a capital of over two thousand crowns. She would look up to him—look up to him to the degree that he tingled inside thinking about it. He would certainly not be too simple for her—here it was more a question whether he was not too fine. She could bake, cook, and wash, and make her own dresses besides. He could start his house without having to take anything out of the bank. And the best part of it all was that he could now show the folks back home that he was faithful and did not reject a girl just because she was poor or because he could marry someone better.

The end result was that he wrote to Karoline Huseby and promised to send her a ticket if she would come over to marry him. Nor did he conceal the fact that his employer's daughter, who was a very fine lady with great learning, especially in geometry, physiognomy, and piano playing, had been so much after him that he had had to seek another position to be rid of her importunity. It did him good to get this letter in the mail.

Lars got work thoughout the remainder of the winter in Overhus's furniture store. He was a handy fellow and could repair damaged furniture so it looked as good as new. Overhus also took old furniture in trade and this part of the business had grown to considerable proportions. Here Lars's skills proved very useful. He also worked as a clerk in this department and had a way of gaining the customer's confidence which was especially effective in the used-furniture section.

He liked working there. The pay was not great, but it meant he didn't have to be without a job; when spring came, Overhus offered him a steady job and Lars accepted. When he didn't have anything else to do he slapped together some cheap landscape paintings of the kind which are sold in furniture stores. He had seen some which Overhus got from Chicago, and his first thought was that he could do paintings like that himself. Overhus may possibly have had similar thoughts, but it was Lars, who was a painter, who put the thought into practice. He also learned how to make frames. There was no end to his skills. He was as industrious as an ant, and just as dependable as the seasons.

It looked as though there was going to be a snag as far as Karoline was concerned. She did not write to express her great joy and gratitude over the fact that Lars would have her; in fact, she made it clear that it might perhaps be best for him if he took that fine daughter of his employer, since she was herself as good as engaged to someone else, whom she had grown to honor and hold in high regard. Since Lars had not written to her for such a long time, she had taken it to mean that he had found another girl for whom he felt greater affection, because there were undoubtedly a good many over there who would be more suited as wives for someone like him who rubbed shoulders with upper-class people every day.

This letter caused Lars some annoyance and not a little vexation besides. After he had written, he had counted the days for the arrival of the awaited reply. Months had passed before it came. He knew, however, from his sister's letters that she had made constant inquiries about him, and that she had faithfully helped his sister care for his mother when the old woman was ill and near death. This, to which he had not attached any particular significance earlier, suddenly took on great importance for him and became a kind of counterweight against the "other" whom she had told about in the letter and who had caused him concern. He wrote again and told her that he loved her for both time and eternity and that he would be boundlessly unhappy for the rest of his life if she should pledge herself to another. He may not have meant to state it quite that strongly, but in the book *Letters for Lovers* these expressions were recommended in situations where one had reason to believe that his fiancée's love was beginning to cool. He also wrote that he was now a clerk in a large store and was, in a way, manager of one of its more important sections. To this letter he received the answer that she was just an ordinary girl and did not have the learning or the education befitting the wife of a man who would frequent upper-class circles.

This letter hit Lars where it hurt. He wanted to show that he did not let rank and position stand in the way and wrote back that those fine folk here were basically just simple folk like the two of them, but they had money and became fine in that they could buy many things with which to dress up their homes. But otherwise they talked just like simple folk in Norway except when they spoke English, which they almost always did. He was certain that she was fine enough for him, if he could just be a good husband for her, and that he would sincerely try to be. He was very touched when he wrote this. If anyone thought that he was one of those vain people, then they were shamefully mistaken. He would send her a ticket if she would only come.

This letter seemed to be the deciding factor for Karoline, because she now wrote that she would come next spring, but that she would provide her own ticket.

Now Lars sent her a photograph of himself with a mustache and wrote that he would await her arrival with longing and joy.

During the following spring Lars had to move. Henry was going off to the state university to be educated as a civil engineer. That came about in great haste. Mr. Perkins would provide the money. Henry did not care at all about going off to school, and said time and again that he hated books and school. But his mother wept and chided him because he wouldn't take advantage of such an opportunity—and the worst of it was, she had already told the women in the Ladies' Aid that her son was going to college. He then gave in to her as he usually did. Actually, it was not so unusual for a wealthy man to help a poor boy get an education. But Mrs. Nelson had her thoughts, and they were of the sort that could not be contained and something slipped out. Yes—Indeed! Henry would surely do great things.

Since Lars was going to get married in the autumn anyway, it was arranged that he would stay with Overhus for the time being. He was, of course, considered a friend of the family.

XVI.

I T DID NOT TAKE LONG for Lars to discover that this attractive family was not really a happy one. After Mrs. Overhus, assisted by the wife of the mattress-factory owner, had entered what she believed was a better level of society, she changed a great deal. She pointed her nose in the air as she walked and constantly looked insulted, because the wife of the mattress-factory owner always looked insulted. And Mrs. Overhus had also taken on a strange floury appearance, because she had bought powder and a powder puff like the others, and it was a shame to be stingy with anything as cheap as powder. She therefore applied it thickly. Lars could hardly recognize her. She had also learned to raise her eyebrows and say "*dear me*" when she was being critical. She found especially many faults in her husband, who really, "*dear me*," just brought shame on the whole family.

On the other hand, however, she also thought her husband was as he ought to be, because all the other select wives had husbands who lacked breeding and were of simple origin. She just committed the tactical error of speaking about it both at home and away, while the others only spoke of it when they were away.

Lars would probably have liked best to move back to the Skares' where he had stayed when Mrs. Nelson was sick. But much was different in the Skare family now. Mrs. Skare had been taken to the county mental asylum. The doctors were of the opinion that she would get better, since her case was not so severe. She would have crying spells and hallucinations. She usually got these after she went to bed in the evening, and then she would have to get up. She claimed that she heard the children in the stairway—the pitter-patter of the small, bare feet of toddlers. She thought they had got up out of their little beds to look for her, their mother. It was something others could laugh at, because the children were now quite big, even the youngest. But Mrs. Skare herself wept over it. She had brought them into the world, these children, and if she hadn't understood everything they said unless her husband translated it into Norwegian for her, she had understood them when they were little and in the dark of night had come toddling in to find their mother, because it was she and no one else who was their mother, she said. Then she had squeezed them to her breast and told them about God and his guardian angel who was always keeping watch over them, and the little ones had at least then understood that she was their mother, and in her presence they were not afraid of any of those bad things which lurk around children who are alone in the dark.

Now she had grown much older and had a great deal of gray hair around her temples and the children had grown up. The tragedy was that the years in between had passed out of her memory as if they didn't exist. She remembered everything relating to the children up until they started school. That was the dividing line for each child, and so it continued until she now thought she had the whole flock the same age. Apart from this, she appeared to be normal. She helped with the washing and ironing at the asylum and worked as diligently as she had done all her life. The habit of standing and talking to oneself and to what one has in one's hands— that is not uncommon even among people who are well.

There could no longer be any home for Lars at the Skares' with those helpless grown-up daughters.

The plumber was always very sarcastic when he spoke with Lars about the Skare family. "There go four grown-up daughters who laze about and are too fine to do anything," he often said, "while their father works at the risk of losing his health and their mother has already lost hers. Now they take turns crying over the washtub and over their rough hands, or they stand sniffling over the ironing board. Maybe now they miss their mother."

And then he would hold forth about rearing children. This was his hobbyhorse even though he didn't have any children of his own. The parents ended up getting it the way they deserved it, he said. Children who were brought up to be dependent on their parents for food and clothing became permanently dependent on others and their labor. Children learn to eat off their parents as long as they last, and later they have to eat off others. Norwegian parents were so dumb as to think it was splendid to be devoured by their children. It has always been fine to live off others—at one time fine people kept slaves, but that was forbidden, and then it was fine to live off laborers and hired help. But poor young folk who wanted to be fine had to live off their parents, because fine they had to be. The parents reckoned that when the children were given fine clothes, ample learning, abundant food, and a good house and never had to do anything then they would be very fond of their parents, because that was the way Norwegian cotters had imagined the kingdom of heaven. But they end up sitting in their big houses alone with arthritis and debts while the kids go off in different directions, because it dawns on these fine young people that their parents are by and large too simple to give them what they want and that they have to get out and be on their own. Schoolteaching provided work for many of the girls, and those who didn't get schools used their waiting for one as an excuse not to do anything else. The boys were not unwilling to work when they just found work that was fun. They often took a job and kept it only as long as they found it enjoyable. But, thank God, they did not feel compelled to do anything that was not.

In one way it was a bleak summer for Lars. Even though he now exchanged letters with a girl in Norway and had pledged himself to her, he was far from happy. He had suffered a defeat—that was one side of the matter; but there was something else that hurt, and it was that he had been so in love with Sophy. Her fine bearing had attracted him first; but there was also something else about her which had made an even deeper impression on his soul, and that was her helplessness—that purely luxurious quality about her. It was as though she had been created and raised to be an adornment for her husband, something to show off—something one had great honor in possessing. But at the same time he understood of course that it would be very expensive to keep such a wife, and his practical instincts whispered into his ear many desirable things he could acquire for himself for what such a wife would cost; but he still wept inwardly when he thought how willingly he would have borne all the necessary costs. And yet—how long could he have kept it up? Hadn't Sophy said herself that her winter coat cost close to fifty dollars, and her hat last summer cost four and a half and that she had to have three hats because she had three different dresses and she had to have a special hat for each dress? When he had resigned himself to staying with Karoline, it was with the feeling that she was really all he could afford to have in the way of a spouse. One shouldn't end up in the poor house just to make conditions suitable for a fine wife. And with regard to Karoline, it was out of a sense of duty that he now turned to her. It was only when he first understood that she could very well live without him that he decided he could not very well live without her.

But it was always as though a shock went through him when he went for evening strolls down on the main street and saw Sophy saunter past, laughing and chatting with other young people. Then he would head in a direction away from the strongly lit main street and walk at random though residential areas to get rid of the feeling of being suffocated.

It was on such an occasion that he stopped in front of the house where the Dale family lived. A swarm of people had gathered outside because loud, long howls from within the house pierced the night air. They closely resembled the howling of dogs—those unpleasant howls which are often believed to be a foreboding of someone's death in the neighborhood. It was Mrs. Dale who wept over her precocious daughter who, in spite of the fact that she had been in this country such a short time, had still become so advanced. Now she had left home, and her mother didn't know where she was. Mrs. Dale had gone to the man who had led her astray, and he had said he didn't know what it was she wanted. She had gone to his brothers and they had turned her away. She had even been to a Norwegian attorney who had shrugged his shoulders, and to the minister who did not know what to advise her, and now she vented her anguish with prolonged, resonant, mournful howls.

Neighbors and others who stood in a cluster out by the fence discussed the situation with vehemence. She was not the first girl to be in circumstances like these—on this all were in agreement. One incident after another was mentioned in whispers. There was no indemnity for poor folk when things like this happened. The scoundrel's family had influence and no one had any desire to fall out with them. The district attorney was a candidate for reelection and his popularity was founded more on all that he had not done than on what he had done.

The seducer should be forced to pay a considerable sum. He should not get by easily. There should be a law against this sort of thing, the neighbors said, and shook their heads sympathetically.

As though the woman inside could read their thoughts, she continued her awful wailing that could be heard so clearly out in the dark night.

Thus Mrs. Dale lamented over her precocious daughter.

This made a strong impression on Lars, because he remembered how radiantly happy Mrs. Dale had been over this daughter who so quickly had forgotten the Norwegian language and had surpassed her father and mother and the others in the family to the point that she felt embarrassed by them. Now, it appeared, they would have to feel embarrassment because of her.

He also recalled having seen her on the street—but then he saw Sophy's image before him and the feeling of suffocation returned and he could readily have mixed some of his own wailing with what he heard from within the low green house.

So he struggled through a winter and a spring, and the summer came and went. Karoline's trip had again been postponed—there was always someone who needed her at home.

XVII.

IT GOT TO BE LATE autumn before Karoline Huseby came. Lars had awaited her arrival with great excitement. As the time for her arrival grew closer, he began to make his plans. They were not going to do things in a grand way, but have a quiet wedding and begin on a small scale. Much could be saved that way, and she was of course a newcomer and would not make big demands. They would rent a modest apartment to begin with—he had already noted several pieces of used furniture in Overhus's storeroom which he could get cheaply. He wanted to be able to start his own home without touching any of the money he had in the bank. If he knew Karoline, she had provided herself with clothing back home, where it was a good deal cheaper.

For his part, he wanted her to understand right from the start what a man he had become. He had already bought a pair of fine patent leather shoes and a winter coat with plush lining and a fur collar. He wanted to be finely dressed when he came to the station to meet her—he would get her baggage checks and turn to a porter and give his orders in English in a confident manner; he even practiced what he was going to say so it would come out quickly and fluently. Then he was going to take her to one of the finest restaurants and order something good to eat in English. He could get quite warm and happy thinking of the look of amazement in her eyes and the impression all this would make on her.

At last the big day arrived and Lars put on his finest attire. It was late November, and unfortunately it rained that day. All the same, Lars put on his new coat that was lined with expensive plush and had a fine collar and cuffs made of soft fur. He also put on his new patent leather shoes. He would not put on galoshes—it was important to make a good impression. He had long dreamed about this, and this was the way it had to be. The streets were muddy, and in spite of his carefulness his shoes did not give the appearance he meant they should when he arrived at the station. He went into a corner and wiped them off with his handkerchief and rubbed them as shiny as was possible. It helped, too, because they got back much of their original splendor.

The train finally came. There were no other immigrants who got off the train, so far as he could see—and there—there she was in person on the station platform. His heart pounded wildly. Was this young woman in the neat dark blue traveling outfit really Karoline? His fur coat with the expensive plush lining was too warm and he felt so sweaty that he had to dry his face with his handkerchief as he momentarily pondered what would appear best: should he run right to her and embrace her, or with deportment walk over and present himself as Louis Olson who had come to meet his betrothed at the station in America? When it came down to it, he did a little of each, and all went well. Karoline was ecstatic; it was as though she wanted both to laugh and to cry and Lars found it difficult to bear himself with the kind of deportment which might be expected from one who had been among finer folk. He took her around the waist and laughed and lifted and swung her. When the initial joy of meeting had subsided a bit, Lars remembered his English, got her baggage checks, and together they went to a baggageman at the station. Lars gave his orders with an expression which was intended more to impress the girl than to inform the man. All this went just the way he had planned it, but how amazed he was when Karoline jokingly threatened the baggageman with the handle of her umbrella and said, "Remember to handle with care—I'm not to be trifled with." Lars just about sunk into the ground. "How on earth are you able to speak English, Karoline?" he asked, utterly bewildered. "Oh, I had to try and learn a little before I left, since I was going to America," she said, "but what I just said to this baggageman was something I learned on the way from a redheaded English woman who said it every time we switched trains. We traveled together the whole time. I also learned something else," she added, "but I'm afraid it may be swearing."

"And what was that?"

"Well, it was 'shucks,' and 'oh shucks!' "

Lars was relieved. "That isn't swearing," he said, "that just means, 'aw, cut it out,' or something like that."

"Oh shucks!" laughed Karoline.

He wanted to know if she was tired. No, she wasn't tired in the least. "But here we are standing in the rain, and your feet are getting wet. Don't you have any galoshes?"—"We hardly ever use anything like that over here," he said.—"But isn't that being careless?" she asked.

The whole time they were on their way to town Karoline acted as though she had something on her heart, and time after time it seemed as if she was trying to suppress laughter. "What on earth is going on?" he asked. "Are you laughing? I don't see anything to laugh at."—"No, but I do, because your face is terribly black," she said.

When Lars reached for his handkerchief, he remembered he had used it to shine his shoes and had later used it to wipe his face. Then he had to laugh, too, and she laughed and said it was about time he had someone to look after him. Then she took her handkerchief and held it where water ran down an awning and Lars scrubbed the black away. Then she laughed even more and said that not until now could she recognize him—now he looked so handsome. Lars had forgotten both his shoes and his dignified appearance and only thought about how different she was from Sophy and Mabel and those fine girls he had been associating with. She spoke loudly, and laughed loudly too—the others only smiled when they laughed. He took her into a restaurant, but not the one he had originally intended, where he knew one of the waiters. Everyone could see right away that Karoline was a newcomer. But he would take her to that other restaurant some time after she had been in the country awhile and had become more like the other girls.

He had not believed there would be such a big difference between her and the others as there actually was. At first he thought she was very beautiful; but after a while he thought to himself that there was something wrong with that rosy color on her cheeks. People didn't usually look like that—he couldn't think of a single member of the church choir who was so red. It occurred to him that she would draw attention to herself—and to him as well, and people would think they were both newcomers. To rectify this he used many English words and even whole English sentences as they walked and talked together on their way to the temporary lodgings he had secured for her.

Lars had a sleepless night with much pondering and speculating. Now she was here, and she apparently expected they should go right ahead and get married at once. And he would no doubt have to make good his word, because he would not let anyone down. But he realized that there was a considerable difference between young ladies and Norwegian girls. He could have made a better choice and got someone whom he could have taken anywhere, to church and to concerts and to parties and everything under the sun.

There was something of martyrdom in this and he was willing to be a martyr—but he was still young and he had to fix things so it didn't happen just yet. If she had only been a little more like Sophy—or even Mabel, or just about any of the young ladies who sang in the church choir.

He wanted to explain to her in a nice, gentle way how beneficial it was for a newcomer girl to learn the customs of the country and that one learned them best by taking a position in a fine family for three or four dollars a week. In that way she would learn the language and earn money and learn the customs and manners of better folk so that she would be at home in the best circles when she got married and had a house and family of her own.

This thought was so reasonable that he slept on it until the crack of dawn, and when he had slept on it, it seemed to him to be absolutely the best and only way in which to proceed.

Karoline agreed that maybe this was for the best. Lars would help her find a good position; but she very decidedly turned down his offer of assistance, and the next he heard was that she had obtained a good position, which she liked very much. Nor did it take long before she got the same pay as other girls more familiar with American working conditions.

America was a disappointment to her—she had loved Lars ever since they had been in confirmation class together, and even during those years when he did not write letters but simply sent greetings she had been a good support to his aged parents and had visited them and helped them in many ways. The only pay she received was to read the letters from Lars. They had not always given her joy. But she was always happy to hear that things were going well for him. When he began to write to her, it was difficult for her to believe that he was serious, but when she understood that he was in earnest, she worked hard to get ready for the journey. She had worked during the day and done sewing during the evenings. He would not have any expenses on her account, not for the time being anyway. She had attempted to learn English so that she could get along, and she had struggled bravely and denied herself many, many things in order to be ready.

And now the drudgery was to begin again here among strangers. Sometimes she was nearly on the verge of tears; but she defiantly held them back and acted as though everything was as it should be. She thought well of Lars, but if he really had a mind to put things off, she would let him wait until he tired of waiting.

The days were endurable because she could always find something to do, but Thursday and Sunday afternoons were the worst, because then she was free. She would not admit that she had nowhere to go, but dressed up like the other girls and pretended to be happy. But when she stood out on the street wearing her new coat, she didn't know what to do with herself.

She had promised her parents that she would go to church regularly, and she always attended Sunday evening services. But the worship services lasted only an hour, and if Lars didn't come to walk her home, then she stood out on the street again. He almost always did, and that was good of him. She liked the worship services. She heard the same hymns and scripture texts as back home and she liked the minister and it was almost as though she forgot she was in America when she could sit and listen to him. She attended Sunday after Sunday and began to recognize the different faces she saw there, but no one spoke to her and she didn't get to know anyone. When there were English services she went to the other church. She did not like the churchgoers so well, even though she knew they were Norwegian and Lars had told her that many of them were rich and had large stores and were prominent in every respect. She thought that all of them looked as though they were keeping an eye on each other, and that all of them looked offended because they were being watched.

It was from a Good Templar lodge back home in Norway that both Lars and Karoline had their fondest memories. Lars always warmed up when they spoke about it and all the pleasant times they had had there. They spoke about this so much that they finally began to consider the possibility of starting a similar lodge in town. Karoline had a very good singing voice and would gladly have joined the church choir, but it consisted of what was called the "congregation's youth," among whom there were no maidservants so far as she could tell. She had also been to a meeting of the youth organization, but everything there was in English. The young people were all well dressed and conducted themselves in an exemplary fashion. All of them seemed to know each other and had all kinds of fun among themselves, so it was certainly cozy company for those who were born in the town; but Karoline came and went as a stranger. Nor did Lars know so very many.

By the time spring approached, she had come to know several Norwegian girls who worked in the same neighborhood as she did. A couple of them had also been Good Templars in Norway, and Lars knew several young men who wanted to join. There was great enthusiasm about it, and Lars wrote for regulations and rituals. In a short time ten of them met in the home of a family where one of the men stayed, and it was there that the lodge was founded. They rented a little hall, and now they knew where to go on Thursday evenings. Karoline could hardly wait for these Thursday evenings to come around, and she was not the only one for whom this became the important event of the week. When they met each other, it was always the lodge they talked about, and they thought about it during the day.

They enjoyed singing and readings; they had a handwritten newsletter and much more besides. And afterward they played Norwegian games and it was almost impossible to quit until close to midnight.

And the young people attended. Here it was that Karoline got acquainted with Norwegian-American farm girls and boys who had come to town to find work. Some of them, especially among the girls, spoke Norwegian so fluently that Karoline thought they were newcomers, and she could hardly believe it when they told her they were born here in this country—and in some cases also their parents. These and the young people from Norway hit it off especially well together and there was no difference between them.

Gradually, city-born Norwegians also began to attend, especially the open part of the meetings when the entertainment began. Whenever games were played they sat stiffly and at a loss without taking part. Karoline tried to get them involved, but she soon made the discovery that they did not know how to play games. Nor did they seem particularly interested in the program when it was presented. If there was something funny, they did not laugh—they only smiled. That was also true of the girls when they were asked about something. But after a while they joined in as well, and then no one seemed to have as much fun as they did. It also became apparent that many of them could handle Norwegian quite well when they realized it was not shameful to be able to speak two languages. It even became fashionable to speak Norwegian in the lodge. A choir was started which sang only Norwegian songs. When the lodge had parties, there were always many people who attended. The young people came to understand that Norwegian was more than just the catechism and crudeness.

The minister began to view this activity with concern, as did some of the older members of the congregation. As long as "our own" had stayed away, they reasoned that the new immigrants could do as they pleased, but this business of "our own" young people was becoming a problem.

The matter was even brought up at a meeting of the congregation, but there was not much to be done about it. It was concluded that the lodge was better than the public dance halls and it kept many of the young away from drinking. But in one way it was painful that they should go after other amusements than the monthly meeting in the church basement, where there were talks on missions and other tasks of the congregation, plus songs and many educational lectures by some of the outstanding men of the church.

That there was a need for even more entertainment was yet another sign of the depravity of the times was the opinion of many of the older members when the subject happened to come up at Finstad's saloon, where such things were readily discussed, since Finstad was himself a member of the congregation and was interested in the welfare of its youth both for time and for eternity.

He was also interested in his own welfare and not a few of the young men of the congregation had become good customers.

After a time, the problem concerning "our own" youth seemed to solve itself and in quite a natural manner.

It came to light that young men whose parents were determined they should become professors, architects, civil engineers, employees of fine office firms, and such had accompanied some of the servant girls home from the lodge—and—oh, horrors—girls who took music lessons and could play both this and that had allowed themselves to be accompanied home by some newcomer boy who worked at the sawmill or in one of the factories.

Mother, who had herself been a maid, told her son once and for all the difference between ordinary girls and fine girls, and father, who himself bore the marks of hard labor, took courage and explained to his heedless daughter what she owed her position.

And not only did the sorely resentful parents fight for their children's futures. They fought also for the beer pail which the boy refused to carry and which the girl could not tolerate seeing even when it was empty.

There are limits to what youth can endure. When the boy who was intended to become something important here in this world was suspected of being in love with a servant girl, that was the limit. And when the girl who could play both this and that on the piano was accused of being in love with a newcomer boy who worked at hard labor, that was also the limit.

One must not forget all the cost and the position one had attained after all this money had been spent.

And so, one by one, the young men went their own way.

Fifteen years later, women who remained single could still be heard to brush aside the terrible accusation that they had been in love with this or that newcomer boy, who once had worked at the sawmill but was now a well-to-do man. So one could of course understand how unkind and offensive such an accusation was.

XVIII.

KAROLINE SOON ADJUSTED to her place. The wife, her husband, and the two little girls were all very friendly toward her. They were also very wealthy people and often gave parties, so Karoline had good opportunity to learn the customs of the country. There were two other servant girls besides herself. The cook's name was Kate. She was from Alsace, and could speak fluent French and German in addition to English. The other girl was Irish, and she was kind and pleasant. The master of the house was a district judge and was very well respected. The family was a leader of fashion in the town and lived in a large, splendid house, which stood all by itself just like a little palace with a large lawn in front and a garden in the back. A wide asphalt drive led up to the house. A grown son was at home and another studied at a university back east. There was no loudness in this house. The man was a New Englander of the old school and did not like noise. The doors swung silently on their hinges, thick carpets absorbed the sound of footsteps, and no one was in a hurry. What amazed Karoline most was that she did not have the feeling of being a servant. The rooms she was to keep in order were described as being hers. The Irish girl had others. And the kitchen was Kate's. There was never any scolding in this house. If any girl was incapable or slovenly, she was dismissed but not reprimanded.

For Karoline, Judge Highbee was the epitome of righteousness, and that made her feel secure here in this foreign house.

They gave a party when the son was home from the university. Wine was never served in the house, but good humor was not lacking at the table. Karoline and the Irish girl served. The conversation turned to Europe and a trip which the family had made to France, Germany, and Italy. The elder son showed a large old beer stein which had been bought in Germany on this journey, and there was an inscription on it which no one could read. It was passed from person to person and at last the elder son handed it to Karoline and said, "You who are German, or maybe something worse, you can probably read these hieroglyphics, because no Christians can." Karoline did not understand the joke and, helpful as she was, she was on her way out to the kitchen with the stein before anyone could stop her. Kate, who had a high-school education in her own country, turned it back and forth, and in just a few moments Karoline stood radiant before the gathering with the stein: "Kate says it is not German but some sort of ancient Latin and that it says, 'Come, let us drink together,'" she eagerly explained in her poor English.

The young man blushed all the way up his forehead and for once Judge Highbee laughed out loud and the others joined him. But it was not to be denied that there lay an ominous embarrassment behind the laughter. "That was one on you," said the younger son to his brother in triumph. He only saw the humor in it. Karoline realized that she had acted foolishly. The judge was still laughing. "Yes, that was a good one," he said. "Here sit half a dozen people with a university or college education, and when an academic question is to be answered we turn to our cook." The embarrassment was vented in general amusement. "There must be something wrong either with us or with our schools," the judge said at last. "We study Latin, too, both in high school and the university, but there are few of us who can read the diploma we received when we graduated. We study languages, too, but when we go to Europe we have to have interpreters, every single one of us."

"Maybe we don't have those kinds of abilities, Father," said the younger son.

"It is rather that our school system is set up to be the way the pupils like it best," the judge said thoughtfully. "If Kate's school had been suited to her own wishes when she was young, then maybe she would have been just as dumb as we are to decipher old inscriptions. And you, Carrie," he said, addressing Karoline, "I suppose you also know many living and dead languages, if you just want to come out with it?"

"No, Mr. Highbee, I just know Norwegian," she said with a curtsy, which she had not yet become accustomed to.

"God bless you for that," said the judge. "You will not embarrass us by exposing our ignorance, will you?"

"No, never," answered Karoline flustered, with a new curtsy.

Another outburst of laughter and now it was Karoline who felt embarrassed.

It was on the Seventeenth of May that they had some strangers for tea. Karoline had decorated herself with a big Norwegian Seventeenth of May ribbon which she had worn at the festivities at home the year before. One of the ladies present took notice of it as Karoline served and asked what it meant. "It is the Seventeenth of May," said Karoline simply, and looked puzzled.

"Of course, I know that," the woman answered forbearingly, "but what does the date have to do with that ribbon?"

"The Seventeenth of May is the same in Norway as the Fourth of July is here in this country," said Karoline.

"Oh, yes, I understand, but you're not in Norway now, you are in America."

"Yes, but I am still Norwegian all the same," the girl said shyly. "If I were an American and were in Norway on the Fourth of July, I would do something to show it. There are several at home who have been in America, and they fly the American flag on the Fourth of July."

"Well, that's different, of course."

"I can't see any difference."

The woman tossed her head back and turned to the others. "There ought to be a law against such a thing," she said. "Daughters of the Revolution and Women's Relief Corps should take up this matter. When people come here from lands where they have been oppressed and can take advantage of all the freedom our people have fought and suffered for, then they should be forbidden to go here and wave the colors of other countries right in our faces. If this land isn't good enough then they can just stay where they are until they learn to appreciate freedom."

At first Karoline did not know what she should say and fumbled, at a loss for words, with the tri-colored ribbon. The worst of it was that she didn't know if she could formulate her thoughts well enough when she spoke English. But she had to say something: "Excuse me, ma'am," she said, "Norway is not an oppressed country and I do not have one more bit of freedom here than I had in Norway—and in Norway I could have voted in elections. I thought of waiting to travel to America until I had had one opportunity to vote in my life because I knew that here women are not considered much better than mental patients and criminals are regarded in Norway—and if I didn't get a chance to vote once there, then I knew I would never have a chance because here women have no such rights—"

This came out in sobs and broken sentences, but when she finished, Judge Highbee stood up and he was clearly so moved that it made her almost fearful.

"Don't bother yourself about this, Carrie," he said as though struggling to suppress his emotion. "You will have an opportunity to vote here too. We will no doubt have to revise our ideas about foreign people and foreign lands. In certain things they are further ahead than we are—in some very vital areas they are ahead of us. The day will come, and it is not so far off, when our American women will have the same rights as the Norwegian women. Until that happens, you are doing the right thing in wearing your ribbon. But," he raised a threatening finger toward her, "if I find you on the Fourth of July without an American ribbon—well, you know what the results will be."

"Maybe I can use the same one, because it is red, white, and blue," she said quickly. He laughed. "You are smarter than I thought," he said. "They are the old freedom colors, and they do not belong to us alone."

And Mrs. Highbee touched Karoline's arm lightly as she turned to go. "Is that ribbon all the way from your home—in Norway?"

"Yes."

"May I clip a little piece from it and wear it in honor of the land which does not consider women to be idiots or dumb animals?"

"Oh! Take the whole ribbon, ma'am—please take the whole thing."

"No—I couldn't do that."

"Take enough so I can have a little piece too," said another of the ladies.

"Me too," said a third.

Karoline was red and embarrassed and stood curtsying with moist eyes as the scissors clipped and her ribbon, bit by bit, went to the ladies. As though in a dream she heard Judge Highbee's voice in the speaking tube which went out to the stableboy's room: "Dennis, put two of our flags by the front steps—one on each side. It's Norway's independence day and we want to celebrate."

When Karoline went out she was stopped by Mrs. Highbee in the vestibule. "Don't pay any attention to Mrs. Smith," she said. "She's not an American—she's some kind of Scandinavian as they call them, but she doesn't want to admit it. Come and take tea with us. Kate can bring it in."

But this was too much for Karoline. She broke out in weeping. "You are so good—so terribly good to me," she sniffled, "but I can't do this."

"As you wish, Carrie," Mrs. Highbee answered kindly.

When Karoline came into the kitchen she ran right over to Kate and threw her arms around her and told her as well as she could what had happened. Never had she believed there could be such kind and good people in the world. Never had she thought that anyone could be so good.

Kate was older and wise.

"We'll drink tea by ourselves," she said, "and celebrate out here." And she found something good to go with the tea. She knew about everything good in that house when it was something to eat.

XIX.

T IME PASSED. Karoline had been with the Highbee family for over two years and liked it there very much, and she was not at all eager to make any changes. There was also another reason: she thought she was earning good money. She had parents and brothers and sisters back home in Norway who needed help. Almost every letter she received contained a hint about something they badly needed. Karoline was very fond of Lars, but she dreaded the day when she would be forced to ask him sweetly for a few cents so she could help her people.

And she could not get used to the idea that she would remain in this country for good. There was so much she missed. And there was something about Lars that remained foreign to her.

She remembered how in Norway, as poor as both of them were, they always had so terribly much to talk about. They had gone for long walks together, because it didn't cost anything to walk, and the cheapest thing two young people could do was to go for a walk. And how interested they were in everything they saw when they were out together. He was just a house painter and she had just been confirmed. He almost always wore clothes that had become too small for him, and she wore clothes that were too big which her sister had outgrown. He wore a stiff, round-crowned hat, in which he had made a nice crease to hide a hole in the crown, and she had also had a hat—she had to blush when she thought about that hat and the rose which was the only decoration on it. She had never really known for sure which was the back and which was the front of that peculiar hat; but they had walked and talked about books and everything under the sun, and who was the best poet, Bjørnson or Ibsen, and she told about the subject matter of books which she had read, and he retold the contents of books which he had read. They had even sat, each with a pencil and a piece of paper and each on a stone down by the shore, and written verse after verse about the waves and such.

That was then. Now they both dressed in fine attire and they had their own bankbooks and Lars talked about his old boss and his new boss and about the store and someone who had been there and bought something and someone who had been there and didn't buy anything and what they had said to him and what he had said to them and what he had thought to say but didn't, and what he had said which he hadn't planned to say, and what Overhus had said when he did say something, what they had said, etc., etc., and what a necessary person he was in the store and how much better he understood several things than did the boss, etc. And she wanted to tell him the names of some of the people whom she had served and describe a cup which a cat had knocked down from the table and what she had done with the pieces and about the thrashing the cat had been given, etc., etc. That was what Highbee called "talking shop." If she started to tell other people about books she had read or to speak about home and parents and things like that which were close to her heart, then the young people started to tease her and the older people would send a concerned look her way and say, "Will you listen to her? She doesn't feel at home in this country, the poor thing," and that was worst of all, because she had come among such kind people that she was positive the likes of them could not be found in all of Norway, so it was not that that was the matter.

So then it was best to talk shop, shop, shop—I said that, and then he said, and then I said this when he said that—buzz, buzz, buzz, like a little bee.

She often longed for her home with the view out over the fjord and the pleasant trips out among the islets during the light summer nights. Lars was not like he once had been. He was now Overhus's right hand in the store and he talked a lot of business and was very careful about not having any particular opinions about anything. He even stayed away much of the time from the Good Templar lodge, but always wanted to be there. She had the impression that he felt his participation would harm "bisnissen," while her participation would benefit it. He got smarter and smarter and after a time it struck him that it could also hurt business that she went there so much, since people knew they were engaged. By "people" he meant some church people and saloon people who both for their own reasons were upset about the lodge.

Then she told him that if he had any "bisnis" which was of greater importance to him than the "bisnis" of being engaged to her, then he would have to be man enough to sacrifice whatever it was he prized least for whatever it was he prized most.

But, oh, how she had loved Lars! She had never told him about those unbearable years when he didn't write—she had never told him how much his first letter had hurt her.

She would not give up the lodge. She had grown too fond of it to do that. The young Norwegians who had grown up in this town were in many ways behind the youth in Norway, but in other ways they were ahead. They were not quarrelsome, they never said bad things about each other, they never said indecent words. The boys seldom broke their promises, and the girls never broke theirs. She also soon learned that when any of these girls had gone astray it was not the young men of Norwegian background who were the guilty ones, but those of another nationality—or Norwegian newcomers. And how interested many of them became in stories and such from Norway. Many of them also began to speak Norwegian, as best they could. But the worst of it was that the majority so quickly lost interest in the lodge and went away. Several of them, though, got so good in Norwegian that that was almost all they spoke when they were together, and they thought it was splendid to be able to do it.

With Lars it went in the opposite direction. When they were out walking together, he did not like to speak Norwegian if other people could hear it. She had even found him out on the steps once reading *Decorah-Posten* with the *Chronicle* on the outside so it appeared as though he was reading an English newspaper.

For his part, Lars was quite content with the way things were going. He still lived with Overhus and had his own room in the basement, but he was also a tolerated guest in the rooms above.

Mabel had been away at school almost the whole time, and when she came home she avoided him. As long as Sophy had shown an interest in him, then she could also, with a shred of decency, pay attention to him. But that was over and now he worked for her father and was something of a servant who stayed in the basement and with newcomers and the like and no one to be concerned much about anymore. That he was engaged to a maidservant was quite natural, and that was what Sophy had also said.

Lars had never liked Mabel. She was not remarkable as far as beauty was concerned. She didn't even come close to Karoline in that respect, but her high-flown stiffness impressed him. He had to think of the finest ladies when he saw her, and tremors of respect went through him when she passed and looked down at him as if from a high mountain. Mrs. Overhus had also become much finer and had, as it were, grown several inches taller since the first time he had seen her at the Omleys. Everyone could see that these were prominent people.

The boy would soon finish high school. He would often look up Lars in the basement or at the store and talk about his future plans. He wanted to get a ranch somewhere out west, where it was really wild and where they rode broncos. He explained for Lars many of the tricks used for taming broncos, and how they had to be handled. He already had some of the necessary equipment. He had a lasso which he practiced throwing in the back yard. He was already so accomplished that he could stand on the steps and lasso Lars over by the woodshed. He also had revolvers and a big hat with brass buttons on it. Lars learned that the boy always slept with a revolver under his pillow so as to be in readiness to fight off robbers if any should break in. Lars and Overhus also came across him once as he sat in his room looking at himself in the mirror with a revolver in each hand, a red bandanna around his neck, and the hat with the brass buttons hanging behind his back. He had a tough expression on his face.

Overhus had shaken his head.

The remarkable thing about Overhus was that he seemed to get more and more ordinary as the others became finer. He complained about expenses for this and that, and it seemed as though he cut down on his own requirements while the others increased theirs. There were continual clashes, and most often when they sat down to the table to eat. Mrs. Overhus had learned how to speak with a tear-choked voice when she pointed out to her husband the great injustice he committed against them all in being unwillng to buy a set of china, which they needed so badly, and a player piano, which they could not be without. It was even worse when it came to clothes for mother and daughter. Then Overhus could flare up into a rage and tell them what he paid out during the year in clothing for them and what he got himself and that he now wore a hat that was a year old, a suit that was two years old, and a coat that was six years old, while they had to have something new every month. Then Mabel wept and her mother said with a quivering voice that it would undoubtedly be for the best if they could just die and that with regard to herself she would be happy to be able to leave, while the boy sat ghostly pale with clenched fists and scowled at his father with hate-filled eyes.

Lars always sat in silence while these storms raged. When Mrs. Overhus was especially distraught she sobbed, "Oh dear, oh dear, oh dear!" so fast that it was just possible to say it, and Lars got the feeling that he positively sat in one of the finest American homes a person could imagine.

Mrs. Overhus had her ambitions. One of them was to have a maidservant. When the other women in the circle of which she was now a part talked about their maids and about their deeds and accomplishments, Mrs. Overhus sat silent and out of spirits. And the others would ask her: "Do you really do your own work—and four in the family—how can you do it?" Then she felt like a martyr and it cost her great effort to state once again the often repeated lie that Overhus was so exacting about everything that only she could do the work to his satisfaction. Servant girls nowadays could no longer be trusted—they cut corners everywhere, but pay they wanted to have. Thus Mrs. Overhus lied and smiled when she was with the others, but she wept in her kitchen. The air of superiority which she had put on was also four-fifths wasted when she didn't have any servant to impress.

Mabel, too, had her dreams, and they were of another sort and went back several years. She had read an account of a wedding in one of the town's finest families. She had read many, in fact, but there was one sentence which had stuck in her little head and would not go away. It was this: "The bride descended the stairway." She had in her imagination seen how the bride in her splendid gown of white silk net with a train and a veil and flowers in her hair had appeared on the uppermost step and glided downward while the guests stood solemn and the groom waited at the foot of the stairs.

She could imagine herself as the bride, she could imagine several as the groom—but a wedding in this old-fashioned house without a decent stairway that led down into a spacious entrance hall—that she couldn't imagine. When she was younger it had not seemed so important, it was such a long way off. But now that she was in her twenties, the question was much more pertinent. How could she get engaged to a man under these conditions? True, no one had asked her, but if anyone had, what could she answer the way their house was arranged?

Just like her mother she took on the expression of stoic calm that martyrs have who know that a day of reckoning will eventually come.

In the meantime, Lars became more and more established both in the family and in the store.

But his marriage plans dragged on. He had also had his dreams. Karoline was of his own rank and position, but the worst of it was that everyone could tell just by looking at her that she had not been in America very long. Nor did it appear that she was terribly anxious to get married herself.

XX.

I T WAS IN THE THIRD year following Karoline's arrival that Lars heard that Sophy was engaged and was going to be married to one of the most highly esteemed young men in town. His father was a Scotsman and quite wealthy. The young man had a university education and held the position of assistant cashier in one of the town banks, with a promising future ahead of him. He was always very generous with money and was also such a courteous and genial young man that Mrs. Omley was nearly choked with excitement when he asked her about something or simply said something to her.

Omley himself thought he was quite different from the impoverished Lars. Both he and his wife used all their might to be as charming as they could for their fine son-in-law-to-be, who, on top of the bargain, was *engelsk*—really the man for Sophy, in whom so much had been invested. Mrs. Omley curtsied him both in and out of the house and Omley himself was so careful regarding the young man that he put *Skandinaven* out of sight, removed the plug of tobacco from under his lip, and lit a cigar instead whenever the suitor made a call. He listened with gaping mouth as the talented young man told about astronomical prices earned on the grain market or by the purchase or sale of stocks. This was a new world for Omley. What were his own paltry trade and hard-earned, scraped-together thousands against the sums that this young wizard could tell about and that others had earned just by signing their names on some papers.

And this man was going to be Omley's son-in-law—Omley's own son-in-law who was assistant cashier in a bank—a person whom he could address by his first name and to whom he could say what he wanted.

Omley did not want to rebuild or add on to his house the way many others did. It did not pay to do that. He wanted to build a new house and rent out the old one. The wedding could be held in the new house.

A building frenzy had come over the Norwegians in town. They built, and they built big. It was always out of consideration for their children that they did it. They always said apologetically that as far as they were concerned the old house was good enough—but it was for the children who had grown up. In one way or another they felt as though the children were slipping or had slipped away from them. The children had learning, the children had refined manners, a different language, other interests. They had perhaps already distanced themselves so far from their parents that they had nothing to discuss with them apart from food and clothing. When the parents went to church one place, the children went another. When father read his church paper or about politics, the boy read detective stories or sports results. When mother sought edification, the daughter attended dancing school. When father came home with aching limbs after a hard day's work, the son came home even more exhausted after playing baseball. When mother, with her aching back, looked forward to resting in the easy chair, she found her grown-up daughter sitting in it even more tired than she was herself. And all of it was so natural. The parents were ordinary people who were destined to do hard work. The children were of better stuff, and it was well known that fine folk got tired more quickly than simple folk.

But behind it all lay the fear that the parents would lose their children —that in the end it would just be too simple for them at home. The bonds were loosened or cut and there was little to tie them to their homes. These fears produced thoughts of a big house that would be worthy of the children. When such a house arose on the old lot, the children would be proud of their parents and honor them. If they had not grown attached to their parents, maybe they would feel attachment to a big house with many rooms.

And the one wanted to outdo the other, the one always had finer children than the other.

Later that summer, work was begun on Omley's new house. It was to be totally modern, big and roomy. The more rooms the better. There was to be a veranda with pillars and a tower on one corner of the house. Others had built large, expensive houses, but none of them had a tower on one corner.

The future son-in-law advised against this large expense. If a man had the cash it could be put to much better use by purchasing stock which was certain to increase in price or land where the railroad would be built and where towns would be established.

But Omley just smiled. He would clearly not be without funds if he built a decent house for his family.

The boys were now sent to high school to get an education. It was the shortest way to the university. Sophy's education was now mainly for adornment, but the boys' education would pay off with interest, because it was understood that both of them, when they had attained good positions, would pay back whatever their education had cost.

Omley's house rose with a tower and a veranda, and it was a great day when the family moved into the grand, cold house at the end of November.

One bad thing was that it cost so much to heat it. The central furnace consumed coal in shocking quantities. Omley had spared no cost in building the house, but heating it filled him with anxiety. The one was like an operation—when it was done it was done—but the heating was a sneaking and chronic illness. He developed a mania for saving coal. When anyone complained that it was too cold, he went into the cellar to throw a shovel of coal on the fire. He begrudgingly took a full shovel—and if he had to take several, he felt as though it was a part of himself which was hurled in to be devoured in the insatiable chasm. And here he could save money. The cellar was outside of civilized order. When he sat in good company in his new living room, then he was an American and a hundred dollars more or less was of no consequence. But down in the cellar he was Norwegian to the very marrow of his bones and grieved over the coal that was never enough.

The wedding took place close to Christmas, and it was an event which awakened justifiable attention. The *Daily Chronicle* carried half a column about it. The bridal gown was described in detail, nor were the bridesmaids overlooked. The floral decorations received special attention—the colors were pink and white, which were now the most fashionable. The wedding march from *Lohengrin* had been played and the bride had carried pink roses, which were suited to her complexion. It was just like reading the society columns of the Chicago newspapers, and even the sentence "the groom was dressed in the conventional black" was used. Nothing was lacking except photographs of the bride and groom, but for this the newspaper wanted extra money. The newlyweds left on their honeymoon for Florida where the bridegroom had an aunt.

The newlyweds also lived in style. This was nothing unusual, because most Norwegian-American young people did the same thing when they got married—according to their ability.

They rented an expensive modern house. Mr. Omley hoped that the young couple might live in the old house, which he planned to rent out anyway. He also suggested it in an indirect manner, but soon realized that this proposal brought him only shame and embarrassment; he understood right away that he had been dumb—the future son-in-law's condescending, distant smile and the injured expression in his daughter's eyes had told him that he was not only dumb but also inconsiderate and brutal. So he gave up the idea. There was deepest within him some genuine Norwegianness which now and then played the trick of suddenly appearing as good logic—the Old Adam that was not quite dead and lay in hiding not only in the cellar but also in the parlor.

The newlyweds also got a maid. Mrs. Omley could not understand why they really needed a maid, because the Old Norwegian Adam had not quite succumbed in her either. She knew very well that Sophy was not strong enough to do any heavy work—very few of the young girls on whom much money had been spent were strong enough for that, but she was herself, in spite of her gray hairs, quite active—and she had also been thinking of a plan—that she could do the washing for her daughter and help her now and then with a little cleaning and such. Just as bravely but more wisely than her mate she had turned to her daughter alone with a proposal concerning the matter and had at least not been told no—it was possible that the maid would need help. When Mrs. Omley heard that Sophy was going to have a maid anyway, she reasoned thus: Then let the maid do it—a maidservant doesn't overtax herself. And Mrs. Omley's plan was just as fully wrecked in coastal waters as Omley's had been wrecked on the open sea.

Mr. Omley could not understand how two newlyweds could not get by on a hundred and fifty a month. He and his wife and the whole family had managed on fifty dollars. But it became apparent one day that the young couple could not manage to pay their grocery bills. In this respect they were no different from many other newlyweds with good upbringing who could not pay their bills either. The merchant would, in a friendly manner, ask Omley if the young folks were all right. And then Omley could not very well say anything different than that they were all right. This meant in turn that the merchant, in a friendly manner, held him responsible for what the young people ate—which Omley then in a friendly manner paid for.

Omley had placed a great deal of confidence in his son-in-law's father, whom he knew to be a prosperous and respected man. He would certainly bear his part of the burden regarding the young couple. But the father said straight out that he had spent too much on the son as it was and had already helped him out of a couple of tight situations before he got married. He had trusted that the boy should have learned better economy since he had married a girl who had grown up in poorer conditions and who, at any rate, ought to be expected to be more economical.

So—that was what he got there.

Omley had thought himself that Sophy would have become more careful when she had married a man who was employed in a bank. They were all so careful and counted money so precisely.

But a man who lives in a house with a tower can't very well say: "I can't afford it." He was again an American and shelled out the money; but deepest within him sat the not yet dead Norwegian Adam who complained and cursed and fought to come up through Omley's throat.

He had at any rate acquired an amiable son-in-law; Sophy and her new husband often came to visit and they always had something new to show. The young couple often gave parties to which they invited other young folk; they didn't invite their in-laws to these parties, but they did invite them afterward, since there were always many leftovers after a fine party. As unaccustomed as the parents were to being in better circles, they would have just felt uncomfortable anyway. The young couple were then so considerate as not to invite them when they were giving a party.

The young man could not help feeling that he owed a debt of gratitude to his father-in-law, who had done more for him than his own father would do. The only way in which he could show his gratitude was to make his father-in-law aware of good opportunities to earn money, by, for example, helping him in *on the ground floor*, when a new joint-stock company was to be formed. This opportunity presented itself when the

Imperial Copper Mining Company in Arizona was to be capitalized. Stock with a face value of one hundred dollars could be had for twenty cents a share. This was done in a cunning way so that those who were *on the ground floor* would have the shares when the stock came up to par and over and there would be a great run on it. Omley even got to go to the club with his son-in-law to meet the smart men who stood behind this venture and look at drawings and blueprints that showed where the copper lay down in the earth. The initial money was to be used to secure this valuable land before its owners learned its real worth.

Omley did not understand much of this, but a man who lives in a house with a tower can not let on that he does not understand. Omley had never been with such fine men and they sat by themselves in a little room where a waiter in a black tailcoat came every time someone pressed a button. They had champagne and cigars at three for fifty cents. Omley had never dreamed that he would be looked upon as *the main one* among such fine people. At the outset the old Norwegian Adam made some objections and said, "Don't get mixed up in anything you don't understand"—and Omley was ill at ease. But when Omley had had more champagne and the finest of the men had slapped him on the shoulder, then it did not feel at all as though the old Norwegian Adam wanted to come up through his throat, but rather that he wanted to come out another way. He was also given a precise calculation of the price of pure and impure ore. Lists covering exports, domestic consumption—yes, they were even shown samples of this ore and there was no doubt that it contained copper. So he purchased ten thousand shares of the stock and rose up from the table like a prosperous man. Spring had come and the weather was quite mild, but now he hurled a great deal of coal onto the fire. It occurred to him that he had frozen throughout the entire winter. When this stock came up to its full value then he would be a very rich man.

But that did not happen. Quite the contrary, the police came during the month of May to search for the man who had actually been the leading spirit in this venture in the town. It was revealed that he had also been in other towns and that he had vanished into thin air. Omley's two thousand was thrown out the window. The only consolation was that it could have been worse, but—true as this was—it was a far from adequate cause for comfort. The son-in-law really took the news quite calmly. When a person speculated, he had to take his chances—it was like a lottery. But now the still far-from-dead Norwegian Adam became so strong in Omley that he gained the strength to call his son-in-law a scamp, one who was determined to ruin him just as he had attempted to ruin his own father. To this the young man could say nothing, because he was an educated man and understood that it must be vexatious to be cheated like this. Sophy, on the other hand, understood that the transaction had been made in good faith as far as her husband was concerned. Had they not had many pleasant moments talking about all they would do when Papa had earned a hundred thousand from his stock? Didn't anyone think about their disappointment—everything they now had to forget about? Was it their fault that things had gone as they had? No one had thought more about making use of the profits than they.

Following this blow, Omley was very silent and disheartened, and the Norwegian Adam regained the upper hand. After a time he rented out the big house and moved back into the old one. Both Sophy and her husband thought he could very well have let them live in the new house since they were going to make do with the old one anyway, but that was not the way things were arranged, with the result that a very cool relationship came into being between the young and the old, and Omley sent the bills, which continued to come, to the son-in-law's father, and so the relationship also became cooler on that side.

Omley began again to be busy as before and set the alarm for five o'clock each morning. But he had been dealt a blow and was not the same. He was very tired during the evenings and a cold, which had begun in the new house, hung on, so there was always something wrong with him. That autumn he had to take to his bed. His only joy was little Melvin Clarence. He held long conversations with him in Norwegian, because here there was no one to make him feel ashamed. Melvin was to have the whole shop with all the paint supplies and the ladders and handcart and everything and be a painter like his father. Omley even had time to teach him the letters and the first pages in a Norwegian reader. When he got well and felt good again he would teach him more. He also told Melvin many things that he had not told others—he depicted for him how it had been for him when he was a little boy, that he had herded sheep in the mountains and once built a millpond in a little brook, with two wheels that went around and around.

The boy had large, sad-looking eyes, which, however, were given life and sparkle when his father talked about these things. And Omley, who felt his own life's candle burning down in the candlestick, thought he saw it lighted anew in the boy's big, innocent eyes.

The time came when Mrs. Omley had to send for the minister. He could not come that evening because it was raining, but he came the next day.

Omley spoke wildly. He fancied that he was in Norway and had Melvin with him and was showing him everything in his childhood home. He held the boy's hand in his and smiled and squinted at the sun as he pointed with his other hand: "There is the brook which I told you about," he said. "Right by that big stone, there is my mill—it stands there yet— you shall have it. Over there by the wall I have a big barn with eighteen cows and four horses and many sheep—you are going to have those too. Up in the old pine tree there is a nest with eggs in it—shhh! Don't frighten the birds!" He raised himself halfway up in bed and shaded his eyes and looked up.

Mrs. Omley wept. "He is *bughouse* now all right," she sobbed. In spite of the seriousness of the moment, the minister could not hold back a smile, the expression *bughouse* struck him as being so comical.

As afternoon approached Omley was rational again and the minister spoke and prayed with him and gave him Communion. When the minister asked him if he had any other wishes, Omley said that he wanted the boy to learn his catechism in Norwegian. "Then he will forget neither his Maker nor his father—in this country it is so easy to forget them both."

When evening came he felt better and thought that he could sleep. His cough had also subsided. Mrs. Omley, who was exhausted with watching, fell asleep in her chair in the kitchen as she sat wondering if she shouldn't go to bed.

Early in the morning she was awakened by the ringing of the alarm clock and she jumped up in a daze. At the same time she heard noise in the sickroom that she could not explain.

When she entered she found Omley face down on the floor and the clock still ringing. She stopped it and with great effort she got her husband up onto the bed and leaned over him. With difficulty he put his arm around her neck, and her head fell down toward his breast. She shouted, "Lars, Lars!" But in her agitation she clearly heard her husband's heart working unevenly like a machine that is broken—weak, then strong. A long breath and a short—then a little shudder—and then it was completely quiet.

Then she gently freed his arm and pressed a kiss against the dead man's cold, damp forehead.

She remained kneeling for a time at the side of the bed. Everything was gone now. In spite of the children, the house and everything, she felt herself poor and desolate. Two arms, two legs—an aching head and eyes that could hardly see. That was all she knew she had when with difficulty she raised herself up.

The alarm clock showed a few minutes past five. Without thinking and from force of habit she must have set it like that during the evening, and when Omley, also from force of habit, was trying to get up, he had fallen forward.

The funeral was held with many people in attendance. It was a beautiful autumn day and Lewis Omley lay in his coffin in the living room, which was full of flowers and sorrowing friends. Mrs. Omley sat dressed in mourning with Melvin on her lap. Sophy looked very nice in her soft black crepe dress, which so becomingly accentuated her light hair and violet-blue eyes. She busied herself with arranging flowers here and there. They were waiting for the minister, because the body was to be taken from the house of mourning to the church, from which the burial would take place. The black hearse with the horses draped in black had already arrived. Carriage after carriage came and released its passengers by the gate and afterward drove to a side street to wait. The minister came and the rooms were filled with people.

The two grown-up boys had come home from school and wandered despondently around the house, at a loss as to what to do. Everything was so oppressive inside. They were out by the outbuildings and over by the woodshed. There one of them found an old ball, which their father had taken down from the eaves trough and left there. The younger boy threw it to the older one and he tossed it back to his brother. Then he threw it again and in a while they were completely caught up in throwing it. They got into position and the ball whizzed back and forth as in bygone days. But then the singing of a hymn started, and the plumber, who was also present, came out to them and asked if they didn't think it would be more fun to play football. In that case he would provide them with their father's old hat that still hung in the hallway and they could see how far they could kick it. Then they realized that what they were doing was not fitting and they silently followed him into the house and stayed in the kitchen until the body was carried out and they were to go with Mother, Melvin, Sophy, and her husband into the black carriage which was to follow immediately behind the hearse.

Lars also had rented a carriage and attended the funeral with Karoline. It was a large and splendid funeral, because Omley was a highly respected man who had done very well for himself the years he had been in the country.

When the funeral was over Lars also went back to the Omleys' to see if there was anything he could do to be of help. He was, of course, an old friend of the family.

Right after the funeral, a reporter came from the *Daily Chronicle* and wanted to know about this and that concerning the deceased. He addressed himself to Sophy and the boys with questions about where their father had been born. "In Norway." "Yes, but where?" The children knew nothing about this. How old was he? Sophy went to ask her mother. "When had he come to America?" No one could provide any information about this. "When was he married, and where?" Again, someone had to go and ask Mother.

Lars felt in a melancholy mood following this funeral. It was expensive, and there was nothing to be said against it in that regard. All people have to die. But there was a feeling here that Omley had been dead a long time. There was indescribably much oppressive feeling, but no real sorrow.

Or it was like when a soldier falls in battle in a foreign country. There is so little time to stop and reflect. The next time maybe it would be one's self—yet, no—many, many others first. So one recovers one's self, looks straight ahead, and tramps along on his journey in the foreign land.

XXI.

THE SAME NEWSPAPER that published the notice about Omley's death also printed the news of a great victory for the university's football team, and Henry Nelson's picture was displayed together with a half-dozen of the leading players from both teams. But the difference was that the obituary notice was given a modest place among the local news items while the news of the football victory was on the front page under a headline with inch-tall letters that extended over several columns.

Henry had suddenly become a famous young man. The article told about his muscles of steel and his weight—unusual for a boy his age. He must have boasted of his work as a ditchdigger, because it was specifically mentioned that he was a boy of lesser means who by hard work with pick and shovel had obtained the money for his education. He was referred to as an example of a sound soul in a sound body and much of his ability as a football player was attributed to his ancestry in a direct line from the old Vikings, whose courage, strength, and presence of mind turned defeat into victory. Their well-known berserk fury was not a kind of combat blindness, but the result of cold-blooded calculation. Just when the opponents thought they had won the battle they grew lax. That was the psychological moment for the Vikings to send all their reserve forces into a violent and irresistible attack.

With this tactic from Henry's team the odds were 3 to 1 in favor of the university. It was he who in the second half of the game had taken the lead and turned defeat into victory.

The news nowhere stirred greater attention than in Henry's own town. Lucky was the person who could say he knew Henry. There was a great contest as to who knew him best. Out-of-town newspapers were bought and read as never before and high school boys with the unavoidable accompaniment of high school girls walked through the streets and shouted: "Rah, rah, rah!" and "What's the matter with Henry!" and "Henry's all right!"

Perkins, with his wife, son, and daughter, had attended the big football game. The old man had become young again and had bellowed and shouted in competition with the boy. His sickly wife's nerves had undergone a serious test, but she had come through it quite well and Edith glowed with excitement.

The only thing she had not liked was that hundreds of young ladies had surrounded Henry and the other players afterward. She thought that all of them were especially interested in Henry. It almost appeared as though in the initial intoxication of victory he had forgotten the ones who had spent so much money to get him to the university.

But these notions vanished when she later had him all to herself. It was like a great festival when in the evening they could celebrate with such a hero at one of the town's best hotels.

Edith was a practical girl. She always thought in straight lines. When she and the others returned home, Henry would again be surrounded by these hundreds of young girls and have no one to defend him.

Old Perkins was also a practical soul. "How is it going with his studies?" he asked one of the teachers who he knew could tell him. The teacher sadly shook his handsome gray head. It was not going at all well with his studies. The boy did not work. It could be he had the ability, but he did not work. In such a situation, where he was so indispensable to the football team, one was accustomed to looking through one's fingers—it was out of the question that someone like him could be let go—they were agreed they would have to be lenient. When a person had done so much for the university, it would have to be reciprocated.

This appeared to be fully satisfactory to the professor, but it was not quite so to old Perkins. He liked to see the state's football team win, but he did not like to pay for it if no one knew about it. And when the professor concluded his remarks with the hope that they would be able to keep Henry as long as possible, Perkins said, "I wish so too," but in his heart he said, "*Not on your tintype*."

He knew about a college in one of the states farther east where everyone could receive a diploma in a relatively short time. It cost; but then again one saved in other ways. Edith was basically correct when she said that when a person had money he didn't need so many brains. The most important thing was that he didn't have any expensive habits. The boy would still be a cheap son-in-law for him, and when he owed them what he was, they had the assurance that he would be compliant. He was a thousand times better than that decadent aristocratic rubbish from Europe. There was the advantage with Henry that they could deal with him as they wished.

And here both father's and daughter's thoughts met at one point—namely, that they could be married in a couple of years.

It was seldom that father's and daughter's thoughts met at any point at all, but when it happened, results followed.

In this case it was decided, without any sign of opposition from Henry's side, that he should leave the university at the end of the football season and travel to another place and get a degree as a civil engineer and be finished by the end of the next spring term.

Old Mrs. Nelson had not attended the big football game or the festivities that followed. But the waves caused by her son's reputation also reached up to her where she sat and knitted in the little apartment where she and her son lived. She lived only for her son—had always lived only for him. She comprehended little of what was taking place, but she understood that it was something big and that she, who was the mother, had judged rightly when she recognized that her boy was created for something better than being just a simple laborer. In her naive mother's heart she thanked God for everything.

The days had not been happy ones for her here in the big city, where she had no acquaintances and where she was afraid to go out. For the most part, she sat at home and knitted. She had first knitted all thinkable things for her son that could be knitted, and then she had begun to knit for others. It was so nice to have some money which she had earned herself, especially for the church. Of course she knew that her son only accepted Perkins's money as a loan that would be paid back with interest when he had finished his education and could earn an enormous amount of money, but all the same, only with difficulty could she touch any of that money for herself. She managed the household and kept accounts with the little she had saved and earned, so she could believe that only her son, and not she herself, made use of the money that came regularly each month and that Henry turned over to her. She already had a neat little sum put aside—her own unused portion.

When Henry went away she got herself a position back in her own town keeping house for a widower with a couple of children. She thus earned her own living and two or three dollars a week in addition. From these she added something regularly to what she called the Perkins-money. They would not have expenses because of her. She would show these fine folk that Henry's old mother, even if she was poor, would not place a burden on anyone. They would not be able to say, "We had to help your mother, too." It was different as far as the boy was concerned—they couldn't do enough for him—he was worth more than all their money put together.

The work was quite hard for the aging woman, but she was happy just the same because her son could get ahead. This was something quite different for him than to have to go to hard labor as his father had done. She asked right out if the other women had seen the picture of "my Henry" in the paper. And then they said, "Gee, yes, Mrs. Nelson—everyone saw it—everybody saw Henry in the papers."

The Perkins folk were kind, fine people. They had understood what a boy Henry was. She could never thank them fully for what they had done for him. The only thing she could do was at least to pay back the money they had put out for her. They would be happy when they saw that Henry's mother could do something to lighten their expenses. When the widower was grumpy and the children impossible, this thought kept up her humor and her desire to work, and for every week that passed she was three dollars richer.

She also understood well enough that it was not fitting for her, who was Henry's mother, to come poorly dressed to the fine Perkins folk. She would be pretty so Henry would have no shame on her account. Mrs. Dale went with her to the milliner's shop to buy a new hat. Hardly anyone used bonnets nowadays. Several of the Norwegian women had hats with ostrich feathers. If she could find a hat like the one Mrs. Stenson got a couple of years earlier, she would like that best. She knew it was a fine hat, and Mrs. Stenson was from the same place in Norway and the same age as her.

It was not easy to find what she wanted. But the woman who waited on her found a hat with quite a long feather which had cost nine dollars and fifty cents. She could have it for eight. Mrs. Nelson almost got dizzy. Eight dollars for a hat! Mrs. Dale tugged her arm and said, "Come on, let's go somewhere else." But then the owner of the store came and said they could have it for seven and followed them to the door and went down to six and pulled them in again after they were well outside and said it was the only one she had like it, so they could have it for five dollars. Then Mrs. Dale and Mrs. Nelson weakened in their determination to go elsewhere and Mrs. Nelson got that fine hat for four dollars and fifty cents.

The two women hurried home with their bargain.

You may be sure that Mrs. Nelson thought a lot about her wardrobe. She had to have a white ruff on her black dress and something white on the cuffs. She searched out her old silver brooch and polished it—the watch Henry had given her when he worked, that she had to have too—then they would see at any rate that she had a watch. She even rubbed her thin gold ring—the only ring she had ever owned—the remembrance from her short marriage. If only her husband were alive now so he could see what a man Henry had become. She combed and smoothed her hair and got it to lie nice and flat behind her ears—wet her finger so as to flatten a couple of stubborn hairs that wanted to stick out on their own. And then she put on her hat. Now they would see that Henry's mother was not the poor woman they might have thought. She would show them she had money to pay her debts and to buy decent clothes.

She went off with light steps. It could not be a sin to dress oneself up like this when it was not done out of vanity but because of circumstances, and a person had to dress up for one's children. She had not yet seen Henry's fiancée and she was supposed to be such a fine young lady, one of the finest in town some of the women had said who knew about such things.

But she was not without a little vanity when she felt the feather touch her neck every time she took a step—

There was not a little commotion when the maid came and announced that there was a woman out in the kitchen who wanted to speak to Mr. Perkins and said that she was Henry Nelson's mother. A feeling of anxiety came over them. They knew well enough that he had a mother—at one time they had been very interested in her, and Henry had often spoken about his mother. But they had not seen her—for that matter, they had not thought about her either, except as a possible regular expense item when Henry and Edith got married. Therefore the fact struck them as something new, something they were not prepared for, that she was the mother and that she now with a mother's eternal right had put in her appearance and was even at that moment out in the kitchen to hold them to account because they were trying to take her boy away from her.

"She's probably come to get money," thought Perkins, and decided to meet every reasonable claim. "She has probably come to rebuke us," thought Mrs. Perkins, and made ready to bear herself with dignity suitable to the occasion. Edith had turned bright red. Her relationship to Henry had always, in spite of the fact that she loved him so, been accompanied by something that resembled a bad conscience—something she had defied—something that was against all reason—in the midst of the knowledge of being loved and loving there was always something that said: What a fool you are, Edith, to throw yourself away like this! She could read it in her father's eyes, it was written in her mother's tired and forbearing smile, it stood out in every corner of the house, the trees whispered about it in the garden, the light steps of the maidservants proclaimed it—it lay spread out over expensive carpets and pieces of furniture. It confronted her everywhere.

Mrs. Nelson had first gone to the main entrance, but her courage had failed her and she went to the kitchen door. She wore a big smile as she sat and waited in the big, fine kitchen.

She wore a big smile when she was led in. Why shouldn't she be happy and smile—they had been so good to her Henry and helped him get ahead.

The gloomy atmosphere in the Perkinses' large and grand living room underwent a sudden change when the little elderly woman, dressed in black with a cheerful, smiling face and a big brown feathered hat, entered the room. Not only did her smile reveal several missing front teeth, but her excitement had brought forth tears as well, so it looked as though she wanted to laugh and cry at the same time.

Perkins had a cold cigar in one corner of his mouth and it began to dance round and round and moved by itself over to the other corner of his mouth and then back and forth, while he moved forward to offer her a chair. Mrs. Perkins was going to ask her to remove her wraps but was not able to produce a single word and had to turn around to hold back an outburst of laughter. The maid, who had come in with Mrs. Nelson, remained standing by the door and fought against an attack of the same nature as that about to choke Mrs. Perkins. But Mrs. Nelson saw none of this. She saw almost nothing—her eyes were filled with tears—here she was among these fine folk who had been so good to her Henry.

But she knew, of course, why she had come. She opened her handbag and took a clean handkerchief out of it in order to dry her eyes and clean her glasses. Next she took out her purse and out of it came a wad of bills that she began to count out loud until she reached one hundred, and then she walked over and laid them on the table with a triumphant expression on her face as she explained in her poor English that they should have this in return for what they had spent on Henry. She knew, she said, that what they had spent was much, much more; but this was something, and not so bad either.

Perkins extended his hand in protest—he would not accept a penny. That money she had to keep herself—not one cent. The man's determined refusal also brought Mrs. Perkins back to her senses and she took on an injured look. Did this washerwoman think that they needed her money? But Mrs. Nelson was prepared that they would be determined not to accept it. She expected this of such fine folk and it was her prerogative now to insist that they should take the money and she was already moving backward toward the door where the snickering maid was still standing.

Should she leave without any of them even extending her their hand? Edith sprang forward to the table. "Take the money, Papa," she said. "It is honest money, which the woman has worked for, and I think I know what she means, if you two don't. It is a hundred dollars more than Mother and I have earned together in our entire lives."

The old woman could not leave like that. Edith went out in the hallway to fetch her and saw that she was still smiling and put her arms around her and kissed her: "So you are my Henry's mother, are you not?" "Yes, of course, I'm his mother all right," said Mrs. Nelson, beaming, and patted her hand and said, "God bless you," in Norwegian when she left Edith on the stairway.

It was difficult for her on the steps. Her eyes were watery again so she could not see where she put her feet.

She wept with joy when she got home also. How beautiful the young lady was who was going to have Henry. How good she was. She had even kissed her on the mouth. And the others had also been so reasonable and polite and had invited her to sit down and everything. She thought everything had worked out so well and, naive as she was, she thanked God for everything.

The first thing Edith did was to give the snickering maid a box on the ear as she passed by her. The other was to tell both her father and her mother that they had conducted themselves so churlishly that she respected Henry's mother a hundred times more than them. And the third thing she did was to fly into her room and throw herself across the bed where she burst into violent weeping.

—If she had just not smiled so much—and those grimaces—and that hat—and the way she talked—and—and—

There was that voice again which said, "How dumb you are, Edith!"

But—oh, how she loved Henry! She twisted her fingers in despair when she thought how much she loved him.

XXII.

THORE OVERHUS did not keep up with the times. Somehow or other this had become established knowledge among the Norwegians in town. They could say among themselves that Overhus had once carried the best, most up-to-date items in the whole town—but that was earlier. Now he was too old-fashioned, and too expensive besides. Nor did it help that Lars, when this came to his ears, could say that Overhus represented the same well-known firms, and that they were the land's best and most solid. It didn't even help that he still counted the town's best families among his best customers—the common opinion was that he had become old-fashioned and no longer had what was in style.

Farther up the street a little dark-haired Jew had opened a store, and he was up-to-date. Everyone could tell that just by looking at him when he nicely, and smilingly, and with white collar and diamond pin on his breast bowed and rubbed his hands together and personally followed his customers to the door and bowed them out.

He was not only modern but he was also cheap. It was possible to bargain with him. Overhus never gave any discounts. He had his set prices and they were marked with ordinary numbers which everyone could read. Overhus often appeared in his shirtsleeves and almost never had a white collar and almost never went with his customers to the door. Consequently, many of his countrymen went to the Jew to shop, especially when they had cash. If they needed credit, then they went rather to Overhus, because the Jew had the fault that he sold only for cash. But for the most part, things began to go downhill for Overhus. He was often in difficulty when large payments fell due.

It was not easy to keep up since Overhus had got the reputation that he did not keep up with the times. His wife and daughter felt this perhaps more than anyone, and when they entertained they never failed to discuss Papa's lack of ability to keep up with the times when they made excuses for the old-fashioned furnishings and the many improvements which could have been made, but which Papa always opposed.

It had come to the point that everything he undertook was done exactly the wrong way. It was not only in the store that he had his shortcomings. He did not walk right, either, and did not eat right and did not behave right. He could, for example, not sit right in a chair, and he had no comprehension of how he ought to dress. The mother and the daughter, on the other hand, did, and expostulated with him about his various faults both early and late and especially when people were present. It was one of the signs that they moved in other circles than he, that they had their eyes open for such things. But Overhus did not change—only, as time went on, he became more unreasonable and bitter, he whose kindness had once known no limits.

The gap widened. When the mother and the children looked forward to a big new house with a tower like the Omleys' and a garden with a tennis court and a wide stairway leading down to a large entrance hall—a stairway which would be suitable for Mabel to descend as a bride—then Overhus's thoughts went back in time to their happier days when they had had only two rooms down in Chicago and where they held onto a ten-cent piece without being able to decide whether they should use it for food or for fuel—that time when they had striven together and his wife stood ready to receive him on the old stairway, and they walked together through a narrow hallway with their arms around each other and he had bounced Mabel on his knee and they had encouraged each other to eat, because the one didn't think the other had had enough. When he was in a good mood he would tell Lars about this, so often that Lars was quite bored by it. It was not easy to be Lars either, because everyone in the family confided in him. Overhus never spoke ill of his wife or his children, but it was apparent that he thought his best days were behind him. The mother and children, on the other hand, spoke as though their only hope for happiness was connected with the future, and the only one who stood in the way of their happiness was Father, who did not keep up with the times. When they spoke only English, then he went over to speaking mostly Norwegian—to his wife, at any rate. And she spoke only Norwegian when she got very angry or had a crying spell and wished that Our Lord would soon release her and those children she had carried beneath her heart—and this was soon the only thing which she could wish for herself in Norwegian.

Lars seemed to be created to be everyone's confidant, because he never took sides. Nonetheless, he understood of course that the mother and children were far ahead of Overhus when it came to refinement.

But bitterness grew on the one side and callousness on the other. At last, Overhus did not bother about his wife's tears and just went his way followed by his children's hate-filled eyes.

The situation improved somewhat when the boy was sent to the university. He made a short farewell to his father and was accompanied by his mother and sister to the station. He did not have nearly as much equipment with him as he should have had. His suits were purchased ready-made. His mother and sister had provided him with a smoking jacket out of their own pocket money, because in all the pictures they had seen in the illustrated periodicals there were students wearing smoking jackets as they studied their lessons. He did not have a bathrobe, nor did he have pajamas—regular nightshirts were good enough for him. His father had had his trunk driven up by the store's own conveyance—as though there were no expressman in town—there was, in short, no end to his pettiness.

The boy wrote regularly to his mother and sister. His father could at times, when the women were in good spirits, ask how the boy was; but then they always became distressed and answered as is fitting and proper that, poor fellow, he would have to make ends meet like other poor students with what little he had. Then Overhus would rise up in anger and say that the boy had everything he needed and more than was necessary and that he had investigated beforehand what others considered necessary and had also added to it—that the store brought in less than before and that he had to deny himself this and that—and many other unreasonable things which the women knew that he would not have said if he had not been so petty and old-fashioned.

He finally quit asking about the boy, and his wife and daughter wept bitter tears because of his baseness. They were of the opinion that he no longer cared about any of them. He also spent a good many of his evenings in the store after it was closed. He had an office in a corner, and during the day a man who kept the accounts and a woman who wrote on a type-writer were there. But during the evening no one was there but Overhus himself. He had much to take care of which only he knew anything about. Lars thought it was too bad that he should be there working alone so much and found excuses to go into the office. But then Overhus sat there with his head resting on his arm as though he were asleep. He especially found many things to do there when his wife gave a party. Then he could sit there far into the night and ponder. There was something wrong somewhere. His thoughts whirled restlessly like tired birds caught in a crevice. There was something wrong, something had failed, a foothold was missing. Was he slipping away from his own, or were they slipping away from him? They had drifted far apart; they had to shout loudly when they spoke to each other as though to emphasize the distance between them.

How had this come about? How had they become such strangers to each other? Why did he sit here after so many years of toil and hard work poorer than ever before? Of course, he had a home, but at the same time that he knew it was his home it was just as though it was not his home either. They had their kitchen thus and so because Jones had his kitchen thus and so. They had their living room the way it was because the Smiths had theirs that way. A chair of a definite type stood in a definite place and there it had to remain because the Camerons had a chair that stood thus. They said: Here is Papa's room and here is Papa's chair, but it was not him they meant. There was nothing in his room which was there because he needed it or wanted to have it, but it was there because a man whose name was Cameron or Smith or Jones or something like that—they wanted it that way in their rooms. He had himself from time to time hung up some pictures which he liked. They were portraits of his parents in crayon. They had to be taken down because one never saw anything like that on the walls of fine folk. Framed pictures of brothers and sisters had to come down because they were dressed differently than folks nowadays. A picture of Magnus Andersen and the *Viking* had to come down because Smith and Jones and Cameron did not have anything like that.* Instead they gave him Beethoven and Mozart, Thaddeus Kosciusko with drawn sword, and a number of Indian heads and tanned buckskin with branded figures and ornaments. He had splendid sofa pillows—one even said "God bless Father" on it; but if he tried to come near it, then his wife or his daughter was there immediately to take it away so it wouldn't get soiled. There was even a Papa's chair, but there was always someone else sitting in it. His own place was really out on the back steps—as far back in the house as it was possible to be, and then out the door. They did not come there to ask him to move, and there he could, when he was tired, lean against the railing.

If he came home and there were any guests, and they were having fun and laughing, then it got quiet when he came in. If he attempted to say anything, his wife or his daughter usually contradicted him. He didn't eat right either, and what he liked was always something which no one else liked. They were always painstakingly careful to be in fashion; but he could dress however he wanted. If he spoke Norwegian, they were offended, and if he spoke English they would correct his words and pronunciation.

It was not his home anymore. It was certainly not a genuine home—it was a counterfeit—a bungled copy of a number of other homes.

And his wife—God in heaven how much he had loved her—the way she once was. But she was also changed—she was no longer his wife but a floury and despondent imitation of Cameron's, Smith's, and Jones's wives. Why couldn't she be the way he wanted her to be? Smith and Jones and Cameron didn't care anything about her anyway. And there were the children. Certainly, they were his own, but at the same time there was

---

* Magnus Andersen was captain of the *Viking*, a replica of the tenth-century Gokstad ship, which sailed across the Atlantic to the Chicago World's Fair in 1893.

something totally foreign about them. They were also bungled copies of other people's children, with other upbringing, other presuppositions.

He looked at his hands which he held folded before him on the table. They were the same hands he had always had. There was the finger stump which Mabel could never stand to look at because she would throw up. He well remembered how he had worked day after day with that finger because he couldn't afford to go without those days' wages—and the doctor bills besides. And then it had to be taken off and then he went to work with the sore stump before it had mended. She was only three years old then, Mabel was, she could not remember it, but her mother ought not to have forgotten it.

Overhus was a strong man. But sometimes he could also be overcome—then he got a choking feeling. Then he opened a door to one of the cupboards and found a bottle of whiskey that stood there and took a good, long swig, and held the bottle up to the light to see how much was left. This bottle would probably not last as long as the previous one, and that had not lasted so long either.

It was clear that Overhus was often short of cash. So it was that Lars of late had had to leave a good part of his salary in the store and for this he was given legal notes which drew interest—double what the bank gave. Lars liked these papers. It was almost as though he walked with a part of the store—yes, a part of Overhus himself, in his pocket. When the notes fell due Overhus had to ask him please to leave them for another 30, 60, or 90 days—and Lars liked that. And he paid the interest, and Lars also liked that. To earn money he had not worked for—that gave him a feeling of individual pride. He was a businessman now, not just a simple laborer.

After a time, Overhus dismissed the typist and now Lars, as the youngest of the employees, was given the task of delivering the bills. This was also a side of business which he liked. Overhus would speak confidingly with him about this and that concerning the store. Lars Olson continued to gain respect. Before long, the oldest employee, who was a

German, quit. He was no doubt offered a better position with the Jew and took with him not a few of Overhus's old customers.

Lars now had to take over his place as well, and he showed himself to be capable. The best part of it was that that also brought him more honor and respect in the house. Both Mrs. Overhus and her daughter were good and considerate toward him. He felt himself flattered by the greater amount of attention now being shown him. In the beginning neither the mother nor the daughter had liked having him in the house as another lodger, but then he was willing and handy to take care of the furnace during the winter and cut the grass during the summer. Both mother and daughter liked to have someone like that in the house, and when they were out with other people then they could talk about how clever Lars was in such a way that people were led to understand they had servants around them. With his better position came also the fear that he would get married or move somewhere else, and in order to prevent this it was best to be pleasant to him. They always spoke Norwegian to him—it seemed more natural to speak Norwegian to him, and notwithstanding the fact that Lars now spoke creditable English, Mrs. Overhus held strictly to Norwegian with him. It was easy for newcomers to get the notion that they were just as good as everyone else—and that came with English.

Mabel also began flirting just a little with Lars. Things were not going so well for Mabel. She had no suitors. She was simply too far above the ordinary Norwegian boys. But at the same time, she did not quite reach up to the class which the well-to-do young men required. That Overhus was Norwegian could not be hidden, and everyone knew that he was no rich man. Mabel was not a part of the one circle, and could not enter the other. If circumstances should throw an acceptable young man her way, she had no means of capturing him. She could attempt to resemble the winsomeness of any one of the popular young ladies of the town, but somehow it always managed to misfire for her, and it made her angry whenever she thought about it. But she always came back to the stubborn notion that there was something wrong with the house or with her father, and that it was this that stood in the way of her happiness.

She began flirting with Lars by telling him what a change there had been in the store since he took charge and that there was now a different tempo, that he had naturally good taste, and such.

And Lars liked to hear this and it sidetracked him. She also said that his English was now so good that hardly anyone could tell that he had not been born in this country. Lars liked this too. She also had a complexion and a stylishness which made him think of the finest American ladies—even Sophy came second in that respect. Lars, for his part, had learned to cross his legs and rest his left hand flat on his hip while he supported his right elbow against something, and he could get his pencil to twirl around like a wheel between his fingers like one of the most elegant clerks. Mabel liked this. No one who saw Lars now would believe that he had once been a newcomer and a house painter.

There was one who did not like this change, and that was Karoline. With her bankbook and her irreproachable attire, she was still a maid. No matter what good manners she acquired, no matter what she earned, no matter how capable she was—there was still a wide chasm between her and a girl who did not have to work. Lars liked to talk about Mabel and what she had said and done—Karoline did not like to hear about Mabel and didn't care a fig about what she had said and done.

Clouds began to appear on the horizon.

Lars had become indispensable in the store and he proved himself capable. He spoke about the Jew in such a way that people unconsciously got the impression that they would be letting themselves be cheated by going there. But what proved most effective was when he told about the fine Americans who traded with Overhus, and he readily admitted that the Jew had the trade of the Norwegians and the Germans, because, for the most part, they were so constructed that they had to look for what was cheapest.

That helped. Many of the Norwegians did not want the blemish on them that they went after what was cheapest when such a blemish was pointed out to them. Trade began to take an upward turn again. Now it was Lars who did the talking from first to last. Overhus walked around despondent and at a loss about what to do and almost shy. When he sought comfort in the bottle then he became very agreeable and went along with everything. When he wanted to lower the prices, then Lars wanted to raise them. In that way he could knock something off the price for people, but the customers understood that he did this without Overhus's knowledge. They must not let it get out that he had given something to them cheaper. This was ingenious of Lars. People thought he cheated his employer for their benefit and they liked him and asked for him when they came in to trade. Lars fixed the place up. He was not a practiced painter for nothing, and he was busy as a beaver.

Overhus also began to lift up his head little by little as he could begin to fulfill some of his most pressing obligations. He was occasionally in a good mood and in a leisure moment would tell Lars the old story about their first years down in Chicago when Mabel was just a baby and they were so poor they sat and held onto a dime and pondered whether they should buy bread or fuel with it.

Afterward he would turn silent and stand a long time staring off into the distance—thoughts came and went, memories rose up before him and always with more clarity as his feelings became more painful—things which he could not tell Lars.

Maybe it was best in one way—it was hard work for a woman to be surrounded by a flock of children; but for him it was a source of grief that he could have had more—some smaller children who would have understood him—some with whom he could have played, who were not old enough to look down on him.

But such was not the custom here. That was one of the first things his wife had learned about, how she could prevent them from having more than just the two children—he thought with bitterness that he did not know how many of his children had been put to death unborn. He knew that he had aged fast when he no longer had any small children. He might possibly have had more of a home if there had been more—possibly the two he had would have been a little less spoiled and indulged—but that was the custom, and there was no custom which the Norwegian women adopted more quickly when they wanted to be like the *engelske*, which was their highest ambition.

He was not alone, that he knew. Here a good man like the plumber grieved over the fact that he had no children and everyone could sense the open wound which lay behind all the bitterness with which he attacked the yankee-fication of the youth and their shortcomings. Most of the other families had the children they had brought from Norway and maybe one or two more—they learned so fast. It was a shame to have many children— no fine folk had more than one or two children—and it was splendid to be among the fine—and then it was possible to give the children a much better education when there were only one or two—.

Yes, that was what was said.

But it was still a great joy to be poor and simple and have some children who came and met a man in the evening when he came home from work.

Well, that was life.

And then it happened that he would tell Lars again about the time when they lived in Chicago and were so poor that they sat and looked at a dime and didn't know if they should buy bread or fuel with it.

XXIII.

KAROLINE WAS STILL with the Highbees, and year after year had passed. She was given good wages and was nearly considered a member of the family. Kate had married and moved away, the Irish girl had gone ages ago—as far as co-workers were concerned she had worked together with a little bit of every-thing. The Highbees now had such confidence in Norwegian girls that they readily advertised that Norwegians were their preference, but it was dif-ficult to find anyone at all and no one remained long. There were farm girls who came to work and when they gained confidence in Karoline they would tell her with flowing tears about their heartless father who would not let them have the clothes they needed and who had said that they were old enough to buy their own clothing. When they had worked long enough to get themselves a new hat and a modern coat, some gloves and other things that they thought they needed, then off they went home. She was often astonished at their well-manicured hands, for being farm girls, and they didn't give her the impression of being accustomed to work. Others were very good, and spoke such good Norwegian that she was amazed. But, on the whole, they read nothing and knew little, so she could not talk with them about anything that wasn't at hand and their boyfriends—those who had had them or those who hoped for them.

Often, often—she longed for home. There was mostly English in the church, and when the minister preached once or twice a month in Norwegian he might use words that were absolutely wrong. She once had to work hard to keep from laughing when in a sermon on the text about the prodigal son he had used the word *"dagdrivere"* instead of *"daglønnere."**

Church attendance had also gone down. It had become more and more difficult for the congregation to manage financially, and they did it mostly with bazaars and such. Nor was it going well for the youth organization. There were so many demands on the young people, and the saddest thing was that so many joined other congregations. Love for Lutheranism seemed to a great extent to have fallen by the wayside—something which the minister could not comprehend. What he thought he comprehended was that it was the debate about the two languages which made the church no longer satisfying to either the younger or the older members. He had to proceed very cautiously in making the change to English and had now come down to two Norwegian services a month. He had begun to read from an English book at the Ladies Aid because it was so good and was not available in Norwegian, and looked forward hopefully to a time when everything would be in English, which of course was the language of the land.

Norwegian became more and more of an effort for him. He spoke English exclusively in his home, his reading was almost entirely in English,

---

* "dagdrivere" = idler, "daglønnere" = day laborer.

and it was the language of his prayer closet—his thoughts were always formed according to this language and it was difficult for him to preach in Norwegian.

But he thought the worst thing was when he was called to sickbeds and especially to older people who were close to death. He had all the words of comfort and promise and the Scripture texts prepared, but when he began to speak in English he almost always heard something like this: "Have you got your Norwegian Bible with you?" Or the sick person would answer him in Norwegian and the person's eyes would ask for Norwegian and he understood the silent request. They had spoken English so fluently while they were well and active, but this changed when they were on their sickbeds. They lay there and the remainder of their fleeing reason saved itself on their mother tongue like a raft that bore them and their distress signal up on a churning sea.

Then the minister felt fainthearted. He could not find words that seemed to hit home. He was there to help and to save. The foothold was secure, the will was good, the ability was not lacking—it was just his hopeless, distressful feeling that the lifeline was too short. It was hurled in the right direction, but it was as though it did not reach the poor person who was shipwrecked, whose hungry eyes did not let go of their expression of fear. The minister could not understand why English was not good enough for them when they were sick if it was good enough when they were well— or was there something stubborn about them? He remembered a joke from his seminary days that there were Norwegians who believed the Lord didn't understand anything but Norwegian.

But the day could not be far off when everything would have to be in English. It was, however, a sorrow to him to see that church attendance kept on decreasing. The newcomers went to the other congregation where the Norwegian language was used exclusively. He heard that attendance there had gone up.

Karoline often found her way to that church. It was simpler than the other, but seemed more homey. What had really given her the most pleasure until she found her way to this church had been the Good Templar lodge. It had had its ups and down, but a solid, if small, group had been formed that kept faithfully together. They sang Norwegian songs, read Norwegian pieces, and played Norwegian games, and it was there that she had found her best friends.

But she felt as though she did not have any really good friends. They were different here than at home. It was easy for her both to laugh and to cry. She was often ashamed that she could not keep from crying when she heard something about misfortunes and bad things striking other people. She had wept when a sad story was read in the lodge or the minister described the plight of the heathens or a visiting temperance speaker described misery and misfortune as the result of drink. Then the other young people had begun to smile and even snicker and Lars had had to poke her in the side, because people did not cry about something sad here the way they did in the Old Country. And she was ashamed of her tears, because one had to follow the customs of the land if possible. She could not, from all the years she now had been in America—and from all the meetings and services she had attended—remember that she had ever seen a young person cry about anything sad. Only a simple old woman here and there could do something like that.

The way things were now, she mostly kept company with some of the older women who lived down by the river, and who did not seem to live as well as those up in town.

There she had many a pleasant afternoon. The old women could tell about children whom they had lost, about sleepless nights and many tribulations and the most remarkable examples of answers to prayer when things were at their worst. And they liked the young woman with whom it was almost like speaking to an older person.

The people she visited most frequently were an elderly couple from Trøndelag named Morstuen. They had a son who called himself Morestew and who was something big in politics in the neighboring county. There were also four daughters who were married and lived far apart—one in Canada, two on the west coast, and one in Minneapolis. They were not even sure whether this last one was married. They liked to speak about their children, but liked most to speak about them when they were little. They had gone to good schools and got a good education and had probably all married well. The old-timers had been among the early settlers and from Norway there remained only the memory of their mountain district and the journey to America by way of the big city of Bergen from which they— first the one and then the other—had found their way by sailing ship to the new land. They had farmed in three different states and among different neighbors, and now at the sunset of their lives they had sold the farm where they sat alone and had moved into town where there were Norwegian congregations and where they could enjoy peace and quiet in their old age. They were both still active and the wife sometimes helped with the washing and such at the Highbees, while the husband could perform small jobs, keeping rich people's lawns and gardens in order. They did not have to do this, but unaccustomed as they were to sitting and not doing anything, they took what came along.

But they were not happy. The evenings were long and so were the days, and they did not sleep well at night. There were children somewhere in Canada and on the west coast of whom they were the grandparents, but they had no idea how many they were nor were they sure of their names. Seldom did they hear from them nor were they extended any invitations to come and visit them. And that was probably the way it was in such a big country—the young pulled out just as they had once pulled out, and now they sat alone as their own parents had also once been left sitting alone. That was undoubtedly the way it was to be and they did not complain.

But the wife had the strangest ideas. She told Karoline confidentially that there were all kinds of Indians around their house who were shooting outside their windows as they slept. They dressed up like high school boys so no one would recognize them, but they were angry because the house was standing on their property and because Morstuen had plowed down an Indian mound. The old people had never offended the Indians, but they always made a commotion around the doors.

Karoline had listened to this with an unbelieving smile. These were the strangest fancies she had ever heard and the man tried to contradict his wife, because he had never heard anything; but the wife would not give in. She had to believe her own ears. She had heard them whisper and talk and sneak around the house. And then she lay there and held her breath so they wouldn't hear her breathing, because that was what they were listening for.

Otherwise the old woman was quite normal and Karoline spent many a pleasant afternoon with her and there was always something good to go along with the coffee.

It was several months later that the husband, who was then working in Highbee's garden, took Karoline aside and said, "Mother was right after all, now I have heard it myself." And then he began to explain how they were shooting around the walls and that she would have to speak to Highbee about it because he could put a stop to it if he wanted to.

Karoline spoke about it to Highbee, but he seemed inclined to think that maybe someone was just making noise at night that the old people naturally exaggerated. But he advised her to stay over one night with the old folks to see what it was. It could be rats, he thought—and banging noises could often be heard in the walls of old wooden houses. But she should find some way to calm down the two old-timers.

Karoline was to sleep on the sofa in the living room. They went to bed late. It was a dark, nasty autumn night with cold rain. No one would want to be out on such a night as this. She tried to stay awake, but at last she dropped off to sleep.

After a time she was awakened by some loud talking. It took a while for her to realize where the sound was coming from, and then she got up and went out into the hallway. Out on the steps and in the cold rain, thinly clad and with only a shawl draped over her shoulders, stood old Mrs. Morstuen tall and straight and with her arms crossed over her breast talking out into the darkness:

"I know who you are. I've got the names of every one of you. Highbee is going to get your names. The girl is sleeping in the house and she is going to be a witness. I've found out who you are, and now there's going to be an end to it."

Then she turned around and went in and closed the door carefully behind her.

"I think that helped," she said proudly to her husband, who had sat in bed and listened.

There was no more sleep for Karoline that night. But the two old-timers seemed to sleep securely in the assurance that now "the Indians who appeared as high school boys" had been given such a scare that they would not bother them again for a long time.

Judge Highbee said that it was hallucinations—what astonished him most was that they had also infected the man. He had not thought that was possible.

Karoline should get them to move—maybe that would help. And the old-timers moved and moved again. Everything was fine for a while in a new house, but after a month or so the Indians would again find where they were and shoot along the walls and sneak around to whisper and listen to find out if the old-timers were still alive. A good remedy then was just to lie still and hold their breaths. Then they believed the old-timers were gone and it would get quiet.

Karoline often thought about these two lonely old people about whom it was said that they had lots and lots of money and she thought it was sad that they should be so unhappy in their old age when they had done so well here in this country in every way.

Although she often longed for her home back in Norway, her natural good humor sustained her. But she had many heavy moments when she thought of Lars slipping away from her. He was so involved with the store, even though it was not his own. He talked almost as though it was his own and no longer had an ear for anything other than to *"mæka monni"* * as he put it. He also dropped pointed remarks that Miss Overhus was no longer so uppity towards him—that she realized it was he and not her father who was the actual driving force behind the whole *"bisnissen"*—that she followed after him here and there and that she had said to him that now no one could tell by looking at him that he had not been born here in this country. Karoline would often respond to such comments with angry words that she later regretted and wept over. To her, it was as though he

---

*Norwegian American, meaning "make money."

gradually put himself at a distance and moved into something hazy and foreign—or that little by little he was being pulled into a whirlpool or onto some kind of grindstone that would pulverize her Lars into an unrecognizable and unrelated substance or make him disappear altogether.

All she could comprehend was that what was best in him—what she loved about him—was vanishing.

Was that the way it was with many of the Norwegians she knew? She remembered that from the beginning she had had the impression that the older people she had been with had lost something. It was as though they were preoccupied with something and yet searching—their eyes looked for something to which to attach themselves, the mouth searched for words, the face for an expression, the fingers for something to touch. They had an expression that people have who feel they have lost something but are not sure what it is.

Oof—that minister! He had stood and bungled the story about the birthright that Esau had sold. She could have given that much of a sermon herself. The Bible stated clearly enough that Esau was hairy and Esau was hungry and therefore he sold his birthright for food.

But the minister made it so that it was Lutheranism which was the birthright. Why not the rest of the Norwegian heritage as well? The Highbees were fond of Norwegian music and literature and the wife played Grieg and the husband read Henrik Ibsen, while in the Norwegian homes they busied themselves with ragtime and dime novels.

They had been hungry enough when they arrived. Hungry after wealth, hungry for prominence and honor, hungry to be something exceptionally grand. And thus it was that they gave up their birthright and their joy of living without knowing what they were doing, and in the end all that remained was the coarse hairiness.

XXIV.

I T WAS SOMETIME after Christmas that Lars came and told Karoline joyfully that the Jew had been after him and offered him a position with a higher salary and a percentage besides on all the sales he made. Lars explained how with such a commission, if he sold half as much as with Overhus, he would earn twenty-five or thirty dollars a week as sure as he now earned sixteen.

The worst thing was to solve the problem of how to get his money from Overhus now that he was going to quit working for him. It was true that the store had taken an upward turn recently, but it had gone poorly for a long time and the Jew had told him that Overhus owed a lot of money and that the best thing he could do was to pull out what he had coming to him there while he still could. He had said that he should require *secured notes* if he could not provide him with the money, but the best thing was to get the money in cash. If Overhus could not manage that, he could force his hand, because this was the salary he had coming to him, the Jew had said. He had even intimated that he could take his notes, if that was necessary, and give him cash.

"But wouldn't that destroy the store and all Overhus's business?" asked Karoline innocently.

Lars snapped his fingers with an air of superiority. Couldn't she see that that was the best thing that could happen, because then all the trade would come to him and he would earn twice as much. She was a silly woman if she couldn't understand that much about business. He could not hold back his laughter.

Karoline walked silently beside him and listened. She could not really make clear what was wrong with his plan; she just felt that it was terribly unjust of Lars to act in this manner.

"I think it would be a shabby thing to do," she said. "I would never have done it."

"You? No! But then you have to remember that you are rather new to this country, and business is precisely what you women are not able to comprehend. Haven't I worked fair and square for the money I have coming to me? Is it asking too much to get what I have worked for? Am I not free to go and work where I want when I can earn more? Should I go and work all my life for sixteen dollars when I can regularly earn eighteen and commission besides?" No, sir! Lars was not going to do that.

"But don't you think that Overhus would give you the same if you talked to him about it first?"

"Goodness, how dumb you are, Karoline! If I did that he would say yes, and then he would look around for someone else and one fine day I would be left standing there without any job and would maybe have to go back to painting again for a couple of dollars a day.

"And there's something else, too. Overhus is careless—he has big debts. Here just before Christmas he went to work and remodeled the inside of his house and it cost him several hundred dollars just to get a big *sitting room*, as they call it, with a stairway descending from above—he said himself he only did it because it was something idiotic the women had nagged him about. But he couldn't afford to do it, he said. Those were his very words."

Karoline did not know Overhus very well and had never been invited to his home in the more than three years she had been in the town, but she had never heard anything but good about him. Lars had always spoken about the Jew before as a big cheat and a slippery fellow who tried to lure customers away from Overhus. How Lars could now go along with this— that she could not understand. The feeling again came over her that Lars was no longer Lars, but that it was a stranger who walked beside her, and she shivered even though she wore a heavy coat and gloves, and it was not cold either.

When he had walked her home and they were going to say goodnight, he wanted to kiss her as he usually did, but she did not let him do it—he was like a stranger to her. She extended her hand to him—not at all a little hand, but a warm and firm hand it was: "Don't do it, Lars," she said. "At least talk to Overhus first, and hear what he has to say about it—do that now."

Lars gave her a superior smile. It was not the first time she had held him off, but he could get along without her kiss. What did she understand about business? Hadn't Mrs. Overhus always treated him with arrogance? She even thought he was not good enough to be upstairs with them when there was something going on. He could show them that he was not dependent on them.

Great opportunities had opened up for him. Maybe there was much to be learned from the Jew, and he had saved up some money, so the time did not have to be so far off when he didn't have to give a hang about the Jew and could start his own store. And then it might just be that the Jew would have to keep his eyes open if things were not to go the same way for him as they had gone for Overhus.

He straightened himself up and stuck out his chest. Energy went through him like an electric current. It was as though his whole body was full of telephone wires with Lars at every single end and Lars at the switchboard and in communication with himself from all directions. He felt business in his legs, in his feet, in his big toe, in his chest, in his shoulders, in his head, yes, business even tingled in his hair.

. . . Karoline? He had really felt for a long time that he had risen above her or sailed far beyond her. In the position he now held, or, what was more, in the position he was going to have, he could get himself a fine, well-educated girl on whom much had been spent—even one of the *"engelske."* For business' sake it would be even better to have one of the really fine ones who could play the piano and everything, if it wasn't one who demanded too much.

So if Karoline thought it made any difference to him, then she was mistaken. When he had kept things going between them even though she was just a simple maidservant, it was mostly because he felt sorry for her and because she had made the journey over to this country to marry him and he knew that she was terribly fond of him. Now he was sure he could do better if he wanted to—yes, he could have almost anyone he wanted.

As it turned out, nothing came of Lars's plan to move. Something entirely unexpected and unthinkable happened that turned everything upside down and hurled him into new plans for the future.

One thing led to another, but that was undoubtedly how it was supposed to be. When Lars had told Overhus that he intended to accept a position with the Jew and demand the money which he had coming to him besides, Overhus had said, "All right, all right!" as though it did not concern him in the least. Lars could well understand that he did not like it, because he hardly said anything more to him, but had gone into his office to figure and divide, which Lars thought was about time now that he would have to hand out so much money. Then Overhus had put on his coat and gone into town and was away for a long time. He was still upset when he returned, but he asked Lars if he couldn't accept his note for the amount. To this Lars had said—with the pointing finger of the Jew in mind—that he would have to have a guaranteed note that the bank would accept. To this Overhus had again said, "All right, all right!" He would have it tomorrow. Several days had then gone by without Lars receiving either money or note. Overhus went out a great deal, and it really appeared as though he had been drinking—he was bad-tempered too.

He had apparently taken his bad humor home with him as well, because the situation at home became more and more tense. First he was complaining and saying that they would have to put off the rest of the work in the house when the carpenters were finished and get the painting done in the spring because he did not have the money for it. Then both the daughter and the wife wept because the house would stand unfinished at Christmas when the boy came home from the university and Overhus got angry and struck the table and said that all of them were determined to ruin him. He would go out on the back steps and sit there in the cold in only his shirtsleeves; several times his wife thought she would go out and get him if it had not been that she did not want him to think she was sorry or anything like that. Quite the contrary, when she thought about how it was for many other wives who had maidservants and everything, while she had to manage with just one woman who washed and ironed a couple of days a week, then she could not help being furious with her husband. Even so, she was almost on the verge of going out to him. It was her all too kind-heartedness that revealed itself in that respect. When she thought about her kindheartedness, which Mrs. Churchill, Mrs. Donald Lee (sister of the congressman), and Mrs. Dougherty (sister-in-law of Major Green) had spoken about because they were familiar with her difficult situation, then her eyes filled with new tears.

It was possible he was feeling sorry as he sat there.

At other times he could be very affectionate and pat her on the shoulder and put his arms around her and say that she had deserved better and that it was of course his duty to provide what she should have. That was the way he spoke on the Friday afternoon when he returned to his office for the last time. He had even reminded her about the time when they lived down in Chicago and were so poor that they sat and stared at a dime and didn't know if they should buy bread or coal with it—days when she used to meet him out in the dark, narrow hallway when he came home weary from his hard day's work.

It was therefore twice as hard for her when the boy came running up from the store on Saturday morning and said with his breath in his throat that Overhus lay dead on the floor in his office. At first she could not believe it, but it was true.

Lars could not comprehend it. The children could not comprehend it— no one could comprehend anything except the wife, who forgot herself to the extent that she wailed so loudly it could be heard way out on the street, and there was no way to hush her. Nor did she wail the way the mattress-factory owner's wife had done when her Fido died, which up to this time was the only refined wailing she had heard. She wailed without fineness and said, "Oh God,—oh God!" instead of "dear me" and kept up a great noise and commotion.

The newspapers reported that Overhus died from a fit of apoplexy and later revealed that he had no doubt mistaken some bottles when he took medicine, and in the office there were various poisons that now and then were used in the store. It was a grievous affair, for he was still in his prime and was a wealthy, respected, and highly esteemed man of exemplary character and had, in addition, a faithful wife, a gifted son, and a daughter whom he idolized and who had graced his last years. It was something to that effect that appeared in the *Chronicle*, and there was also a picture of him.

The funeral was beautiful and there were a great many flowers and many mourners and among them some of the best people in town. Mabel was striking in her black outfit. She had not known herself, and no one else had known either, how well she looked in black. While the mother fell out of her role and sobbed and wept and blew her nose the way simple women do, Miss Mabel mourned in a more high-class manner, like the mattress-factory owner's wife grieving over her Fido, and pressed a handkerchief toward her eyes with the thumb and index finger of her left hand and made small twitches. The son was there and faithfully attended to his mother. She had collapsed and had lost her fine bearing when, supported by her son's arm, she walked unsteadily down the church aisle following the casket. During the funeral sermon, Mabel found it difficult herself to weep in a refined manner and at the same time prevent any kind of cat cries from her mother, who without considering the many people who were present would start loud wailings, so that Mabel had to nudge her to get her to mourn decently.

Overhus's death occurred on the very morning that was to have been Lars's last day in the store. That is how strange things can happen. Of course, he could not leave the store now. Nor had he received his money. He then had temporarily to take over the operation of the store. Overhus had belonged to several lodges and had insurance, so it was not a little sum which would come the way of his heirs. It also appeared that his indebtedness was not so large as Lars had thought it was. Lars was given the task of operating the store until the estate was settled and now the remarkable thing happened that Mabel offered to take over the office work—which she had definitely refused to do when this had been proposed by her father.

And now a new day was dawning for Lars. What he had heard and seen when he worked in Willum's store would be to his advantage. He began to sell confidentially, and people understood that this was their chance to get goods cheaply now that they could talk to Lars himself when he was alone in the store. He ordered new merchandise but led people to believe he was selling out with big clearance sale advertisements in the windows. Money streamed in. Nothing could advertise such a sale better than the proprietor's suicide.

One day the windows were fixed up and the signs removed. It was the middle of spring and the store glittered with shiny new merchandise and there was a new clerk. Lars Olson was Louis Olson and he was co-owner and manager.

Mabel still wore her black dress, and it suited her well. She was really not needed, since they had another girl who did the work, but in one way it was good to have her there. People knew that she was Overhus's daughter, and when Lars acted as though he didn't know if he could give a discount, then he made it look as if he went and asked her. The discounts he gave were also felt to be more important and precious for the customer when they came through many negotiations and proceedings. The number of grateful customers grew through this little trick which Lars had learned at Willum's.

And the sales grew steadily. Lars was not smart enough to take off on dangerous new roads and not dumb enough to be led astray. He had the healthy average good sense which purchased what could most easily be sold. People as a rule found what they wanted at a reasonable price and often got a little extra reduction.

The Norwegian trade returned again to the old Overhus store. The Norwegians went where they got a little more.

They always do.

It happened, when Lars now and then, with his pencil behind his ear, struck an elegant and pensive pose in the store like that of greater business-men, that he thought of how well he had done for himself in the seven or eight years he had been in America. He remembered well how at one time he had sat on Omley's steps, when they had a baptism, without being able to say a word of English and without owning much more than he stood and walked in. It was different now. He had admired and looked up to people like the Stensons and Nels Hill. What was Stenson? After he lost his place in the courthouse, he had tried to get a job here in the store as a clerk for Overhus. Some big magistrate. And Nels Hill? With a twisted smile he remembered that Nels Hill owed them twenty dollars at the store. And Overhus? Yes—he was now their equal; and—he puffed out his chest—now he was in Overhus's position and did his work. He knew that now a newcomer would regard him with the same respect which he had then had for Overhus, and he wished for a newcomer whom he could impress.

Yes—he could rightly strike an elegant pose and cross his legs, because there were not many who had come from Norway and done so well in such a short time. And—an almost religious feeling came over him out of respect for himself and his own eminence—he had come to the place where he now stood with an unblemished character. That meant a great deal. Many got ahead in this world by dishonest means and all manner of cunning. But he had worked himself ahead by means of honest diligence. What did it profit a man to win the whole world but lose his own soul? It almost amazed Lars that he could have made such progress without doing injury to his soul. There were not many who avoided doing injury to their souls in America.

He would begin to go regularly to church again and—who should go there if not people like himself? Nor would it do business any harm if he went—rather the opposite.

There are so many thoughts which come to a man when he stands in an elegant and pensive pose, with a pencil behind his ear, in a store where he is held to be the most important person.

His glance did not include the netting enclosure which was called *the office*, where Mabel was. But she was there and it was as though she was in a cage. He did not see her with his eyes but as through a hole in the back of his head and he knew that she saw him. The elegant and pensive posture would not have been what it was if he hadn't felt her gaze aimed at him, and it was this which gave him a grand feeling. He had one anxiety, and that was that she would suddenly fly out of her cage. Today he knew that he had her, but tomorrow she could be gone. She was attractive in her black outfit, and when young gentlemen came to the enclosure to pay a bill or ask about something, she tilted her head and smiled and acted pleasant.

He was no longer "Lars," but "Mister Olson." But the day might come when he would just be "Lars" again. The share he owned in the store was, of course, small. Actually, he liked her, too, especially when some young man had stood too long at the window talking to her. Then he would find an excuse to ask about something or say something so that the person would be made to realize that Mabel had other things to do than trifle.

But he did not forget that he was engaged to Karoline and wore an engagement ring. He often forgot her, but not that he was engaged. He therefore kept himself at a respectful distance from Mabel and never let her notice that he was engaged.

The thought of the sacrifice he was making to remain engaged to Karoline could put him in a very melancholy mood. Some instinct told him that if he got married, then it would be goodbye to the store.

When he was with Karoline, there was a heavy atmosphere of manly melancholy about him, and he let himself understand what it would cost him once they got married.

Strangely enough, this melancholy also came over him when Karoline one day sent him the ring and the gifts she had received from him, together with a brief letter in which she said that she wished for nothing more than for his happiness. And when she had realized that she would only make him unhappy, then it was best that she break off their engagement.

There was an element of martyrdom in this for Lars. But he had not broken his word to her. No one could say that he had lured her over to America by a promise of marriage and then forsaken her. She was the one who had broken her word.

So he also sent his ring back and wrote that if he was never again happy here on earth he wished that she must have happiness in full measure and that he would forgive her for making a fool of him for so long.

In the book *Letters for Lovers* he had found these moving expressions of the pain and sorrow which could be considered suitable for such occasions together with a suggestion that there might be a possibility of their being united again—if not here on earth, then in the world to come.

He omitted the part about clearing skies and being joined here on earth without further ado, and after a bit of reflection he also struck the part about being united again in the next world. The most important part was this matter of happiness which was gone forever, together with the forgiveness for the fact that she had made a fool of him.

XXV.

THERE WAS NOT A LITTLE fuss in the Highbee family when Karoline reported that she would be returning to Norway in the spring. They could not comprehend it. To think that a poor girl who had to work so hard for her money should make such a long and expensive journey. They understood very well that she had her loved ones there at home and that it would be a pleasure to visit her home, but the time and all that money! Judge Highbee had himself left his home in New England and headed west. He had not thought of going back until he was along in years, and then it was to his father's funeral. His wife could not comprehend it either, because Karoline lived a comfortable life among them. Both of them dreaded her leaving, because they would never get such a good, attentive girl again.

As the time quickly passed they became even more dispirited. They had cleverly raised her pay and shown her all possible consideration. Karoline went to her work as before—the strange thing was that she did not even seem happy at the thought that she would soon be going home.

No—happy she was not. She had come to establish her own home, she had had her great dreams. They had gradually disappeared. Now it was only the memories that remained.

She still felt as though she and Lars belonged to each other—but that was a different Lars. He was still alive, but at the same time it was also as though he was not alive. It was worse than if she had followed him to the grave. He had changed so much. She loved him—there had not been a day since she was fourteen years old that she had not thought of him—and she thought of him now. But it was not the man who now twisted the ends of his mustache over in the big store. She was through with him. It was Lars, warmhearted and innocent, as she had once known him—he was the one she mourned for.

That he could be so changed! Instead of being innocent he had grown foolish, instead of being understanding and good he had become ruthless and selfish.

But there were so many who became like that in America. That was why so many of these well-to-do Norwegians did not even write to their parents and relatives in Norway, except maybe to let them know what mighty people they had become.

But happy they were not. She had realized that much from the very first. They had money, they ate good food and wore fine clothes, but they were not happy—neither the young nor the old were happy. That could be seen in church and on the streetcar and elsewhere, when they sat by themselves and their faces revealed their natural expression; then it could be seen how grief-worn and how tired and exhausted they were.

It would be embarrassing to come home again—with a long face, her girl friends would undoubtedly say, who knew that she had made the trip for the purpose of getting married. She would just have to go anyway. It had become unbearable here.

Spring came at last and Karoline made ready to leave. Then Judge Highbee played his last card. He presented Karoline with fifty dollars from his wife and himself, and twenty-five from each of the sons—a hundred dollars in brand new bills. Had they been rich, then she would have had more, he said; but it was on the condition that if she came back again, then she should return to them. Karoline burst into tears. They had always been so kind to her, and she would never forget it.

Judge Highbee blew his nose and adjusted his glasses when he came into the living room. Those were gestures which his wife recognized from the time when he had tried cases in court and had won.

"She'll be coming back," he said. "Did she say so?" the wife eagerly inquired. "No, but she will anyway," said the judge.

The same spring when Karoline journeyed back the same way she had come, Lars and Mabel Overhus also got engaged.

It had come about so unexpectedly—on a day when there was no one else in the store except the two of them. The other clerk had gone to dinner and the boy was out on an errand. Then Lars noticed that Mabel was weeping in her handkerchief and that she still used the kind that had a black border in mourning for her father. Lars saw that she wept and after seeing this for a while he asked her what was the matter. It was not easy for Mabel to pronounce the words because the weeping had so possessed her. But Lars understood that someone must have said something mean about her that was so bad that she could not repeat it.

What was it?

Well, it was that someone had said that she was in love with Lars and he did not care the least about her, but she would certainly find out who it was who had started that lie.

Lars also wished to know who it was who had lied about them like that.

They finally agreed it must be Sophy—yes, it certainly had to be her. Mabel was now eager and could produce many bits of evidence that it must have come from her originally.

People were so unreasonable in speaking about others. The "others" were precisely those two who now in a way had to join together against the whole gossiping and malicious world. And then Mabel had a new attack of sobs and leaned against Lars; it is so natural to support oneself against someone else when one cries. But the story of their engagement came from the boy who came in the back way and found Lars sitting in the office with Mabel on his lap with her head resting against his shoulder.

When events determined that they should have been seen in such a position, then it was as though there was a bond that bound them together. Mabel fretted so about the gossip that she was in love with Lars that the only thing that provided any relief for her suffering was to be able to cry on his shoulder between eleven and twelve o'clock in the morning, when the other clerk was out to lunch. When he returned she kept her composure and did not seem affected by the gossip that she was in love with Lars. For Lars, it was as though he had pressed the whole big store close up against his heart.

The wedding was held in the month of June, and among the invited guests were Sophy and her husband. Mabel showed tremendous affection toward Sophy, and Sophy showed tremendous affection toward Mabel.

The bride was radiant in her expensive white bridal gown and everything went according to plan except the moment when, in all her finery, she descended the stairs to the living room. And the error was not hers, but the guests' in that they, as well as the minister and the bridegroom, were busy looking out the windows and doors to see if it was going to rain.

Rain was an omen of good fortune for the bridal couple. The weather looked as if it could do most anything, and that is why everyone got very interested in it and not in Mabel, who proudly descended the stairs that had cost so many tears and dollars.

The *Daily Chronicle* had quite a lengthy description of the wedding. It could have been longer, but Lars was poor at advertising the business he managed. After the wedding, the newlyweds went on their honeymoon and stayed in the nearest big city for a couple of weeks as was the proper custom among better folk.

After their return they made their home in the old house and Mabel took over the management of the household as well as of her mother and a maidservant who was to work for room and board while she studied to become a schoolteacher.

Mrs. Overhus had changed greatly since her husband died. She had become more like she had been earlier, and no longer went to tea parties. On the contrary, she often went out on the back steps, which once had been her husband's place of refuge.

XXVI.

HENRY NELSON AND EDITH PERKINS were married at the same time that Lars and Mabel celebrated their wedding. The wedding was a private affair. All that was known of it was what was revealed on a nice card that was sent in the mail and in an article in the *Daily Chronicle*. It was not a news item but an editorial written by one of Edith's girl friends, who had an aptitude for journalism. It told how one even in our prosaic age could come across really romantic engagements and weddings, which put the most interesting books in the shadow, how these two young people had grown to love each other while they were still in high school and that their love, tested by many trials, had at last won the victory over rank and position and nationality. The poor but industrious young man had worked to obtain the means by which to continue his education at the university, and he now, after the final examinations, had reached his goal and secured the dream of his youth. This piece was so beautifully written that it remained a lively topic of conversation for a long time among the better folk of the town.

Neither Henry nor his bride read the article in the newspaper because they had read it before it went to press, and besides, the two of them were so happy when they left for the coast that they did not need to read about it at all.

Like two carefree songbirds they took their departure into the world—just the two of them and no one else. She attracted attention with her beauty and he with his broad shoulders and his clear eyes. They played poor and they played rich. They bargained and they paid double, they were kind toward their traveling companions and they were disagreeable and had fun with everything. When they didn't have anything else to do they played pranks on each other and bickered and could not let each other be in peace for a moment.

For Henry everything was like a dream. He did not really know how it had all come about—in an unexplainable way he had been plopped down into it—or it had plopped down on him—like a kind of game which he could not understand.

He was not suited to speculation. The only thing he fully grasped was what he could see and touch. And now he had her, and this was the beginning of happiness.

Mrs. Nelson had withdrawn back to her old home. She had not been in the wedding, but she knew that it had been splendid. She would have liked most to begin doing some washing again, but she knew that that just was not fitting when she had such a fine son who had married so well. She was also finished with him now; but she was not quite finished with him, not just yet. When she went to visit the other women, she could tell many things about how splendid he would have it and how fine everything was; and when she was at home alone, which she almost always was, then she thought of him and mumbled to herself.

There came a time—and it came faster than she could comprehend— that her friends grew weary of hearing about him and his remarkable happiness and would rather speak about something else.

Mrs. Dale had even spoken unkindly to her. She had said something on this order:

"But wouldn't it have been nicer for you if your boy, Henry, had married a common working girl and worked with other folk. Then you could have had someone to be with and have a good time with? There won't be any home for you there."

—A common working girl?—When they started to talk like that, then Mrs. Nelson put on her expensive hat and said goodbye and left with such a proud gait that her best friends would not have known her from the back.

A common working girl for her Henry? She would stay away from Mrs. Dale from now on and not go there anymore. But when loneliness pressed upon her, then she went there anyway. It was so awful to be alone and she noticed so many sounds and noises when she sat alone with her memories.

She received many postcards from her son. There were fine hotels, railroad stations, parks, and everything imaginable. And on all of them there were greetings from Edith. She showed them first to Mrs. Dale, because that was just good for her, and then she placed them in her Bible. Often when she picked up the Book to read the divine word, she sat there looking at the pictures instead. Her Henry had been to all of these wonderful places and driven in an automobile and everything, and stayed in fine hotels.

God had been good to her and to her boy and directed everything for the best. It just couldn't be helped that she now sat alone.

She did not much worry about the future now that she did not have her son with her. Life had lost its meaning for her, as it were, from the moment it began to have full meaning for him. What she had striven for was accomplished. Her son no longer needed her—that she had need of him never occurred to her. The obligation lay only on the one side. He owed nothing.

If Mrs. Nelson did not worry much as far as her own future was concerned, this question was like a heavy stone for the Perkinses. The husband and wife were at wits' end as to what sort of arrangements should be made for her. They had thought of getting her into an old people's home—one of the best, for that matter—they had racked their brains wondering if she had relatives in Norway, so they might convince her to make the journey there. But it was probably impossible to get her to give up being close to the boy. They could set up a nice home for her and help support her, but of course the responsibility would always rest on them here where everyone knew who she was and what she had been.

They wanted to do what was right, but when it came right down to it, they dreaded having anything to do with her. She was like a blemish on the family. And the worst of it was that she was healthy and could still live for a good many years and hang over them as a source of discomfort.

The boy was good enough. There was nothing wrong with him. Perkins had work for him when they returned. He was considerate and compliant. Edith could have made a poorer choice, for that matter. But the question of what they ought to do with his mother, that was far more difficult to solve.

But solved it was when the young couple came home.

"Why, of course she is going to live here with us," said the young wife.

It was Edith who spoke, and she spoke like one who was accustomed to having her own way. They offered all kinds of suggestions and plans and raised their objections.

"If you treat her any differently—if she isn't good enough for you, then he isn't either—and if he isn't then I am not. Henry is strong enough to work, if that is necessary, and if I can't cook, his mother can. Don't you think we could manage without you—?"

Their many suggestions fell to the ground. The Perkins couple knew their daughter, they also knew their son-in-law, and there was no doubt that the disagreeable and very controversial woman could wash and sew and cook.

Yes—there would be order.

Would Edith be capable of it?

It was precisely this which was so annoying, that they were so confounded sure that she was capable of it.

Henry was given employment at an iron foundry and machine shop where old Perkins, as in several other industrial enterprises, was director and co-owner. The work was easy. He could not do the more difficult things and the manager was ashamed to have the rich Perkins' son-in-law do the simpler, rougher jobs. Henry's work consisted mainly in wandering around the big establishment and watching others as they worked. The foundry interested him very much. He could defy the tremendous heat and risk his clothes to be in close proximity to the swarthy men who worked half-naked with the liquid, sputtering metal. He could follow the transformation from the big scrap heap on the north side of the foundry to the finished machines in the warehouse on the south side.

It was quite an interesting scrap heap to begin with. Old wheels, the remains of boilers, old rusted pipes, parts of stoves, twisted things, broken things. Things which no longer could be fixed, things which had value only as metal. Objects doomed to rust away if they were not melted down—bits of wreckage from the battlefields of agriculture and industry—a weathered, twisted, and otherwise useless collection scraped together behind outbuildings and along roadsides—most of it given away just to get rid of it and gathered by enterprising Jews in railroad carloads and sold to the foundry.

Henry was no thinker, but he must have thought something because once when he stood with the manager and looked out over the scrap heap he said to him that it appeared as though nothing was too ruined or too bad to be melted down.

The manager had a sense of irony and agreed. He conceded that it was so and added that it was quite odd that only the worthless scrap was melted. He could not recall having seen a single typewriter, an electric motor, a usable sewing machine or piece of farm machinery wander into the melting pot.

The manager was an American and had no great opinion of all the people of foreign nationalities who were hurled ashore on the docks of the big ports back east, but he preferred to hire these people. Those who had Americanized themselves with regard to clothing and language and appearance he looked upon with suspicion—for the more responsible positions he preferred Scandinavians or Germans. A French cook prepared his food, a Belgian kept his garden in order, his clothes were sewn by a Swedish tailor, and a Norwegian girl cared for his children; but at his club he sought to associate with people of his own kind.

The type of machine which he manufactured was his own patent and was, in his opinion, an improved type of that sort of machine. But he did not buy up the machines of others in order to melt them down. He melted only raw iron and scrap. He was not only a clever man, he also had foresight. He knew that one day his machines would also end up on the scrap heap, when the time of their usefulness was past.

He used the melted scrap metal for the coarsest parts of his machines. He did not use it there because he thought this was best, but because it happened to be cheapest. He never melted down the finished products from other factories, but used them to make something out of his own raw material and the scrap which trains and wagons brought in from every direction.

In this place Henry spent his days in boredom. In a way he envied the men who worked half-naked with the glowing metal. It was, however, not fitting that a person like him put his hands to hard labor. He did not think that he had been placed in the wrong niche, and no one said that to him either. He felt out of sorts without consciously knowing why.

But he lived a good life at home. Those two young people followed each other all over the house. A happier wife was not to be found in town than the young Mrs. Nelson and one would have to look for a long time to find a happier man than Henry.

His mother was also to live there and a room was put in order that was her own. It was well located so that she could go in and out by a back stairs without having to go to the main entrance. In their early enthusiasm the young couple had dragged her to the dentist who parted her from her old stubs and filled her mouth, much too full she thought, with big white teeth. Henry laughed out loud the first time she appeared with them, and the others complimented her on her youthful appearance and controlled themselves. Mrs. Nelson was also instructed as to how she should do her hair. When she looked into the mirror she could hardly recognize herself, she was so changed. She also received new dresses and other nice things to wear. She did not like it, and thought maybe it was a sin; but she must not forget that her son was now a fine man. It was for his sake that she had borne those plagues which the dentist had inflicted upon her—she had become so accustomed to offering herself for him. When she was in the house she bore the plague with courage and held herself erect; but as soon as she was out the door or in her own room, her teeth found their way to her dress pocket and she regained her stooped and somewhat waddling posture and was old Mrs. Nelson as she had been before. The worst of it was that she no longer felt like herself. She could not even seriously pray to God or sing a hymn with those teeth and with her hair put up on the top of her head. It occurred to her that God would not acknowledge her like that. Her conscience, or the voice of her conscience as she had called it, had earlier reminded her about this or that and had been her direct connection with God, who so graciously had stood by her. But since she had got those teeth and that hairstyle, the voice had gone away—or it was not the same voice. It said something like this: "Oh, see what a nonsensical woman you have become," or "Now you look like a real sight," or it said,

"Now you are among important people and you must be like them"; but then it could change in an instant and say "Who cares about the important people." It could never be the voice of conscience which spoke like that.

But when she was rid of her teeth and her hair was down and her thin braids were put up for the night, then she could again find consolation in the Bible and sleep—when she could sleep—always certain that she would wake up at the right time. Yet, she was well-off. She unceasingly told others that she was well-off, she had good food and had her own room, could come and go as she pleased and could lie down in peace and get up in peace. She had to repeat this incessantly so she wouldn't forget it. Everything she had came from others, but then these others had got her big, handsome son in return and she knew what he was worth—more than all they possessed. She also saw that he was happy. That she could tell by looking at him. She also saw that his young bride was happy. She could tell that by looking at her. Her only sorrow was that she could no longer do anything for him. There was a stranger who washed his clothing, a fat woman who prepared his food, and a servant who brushed his clothes. She could do nothing more than fix herself up so that he could be proud of her, or at least not be put to shame by his mother.

She heard him arrive, but she was not the one who opened the door for him. She saw him leave, but she was not the one who closed the door behind him. She saw very little of him, because he was always busy and they often went to parties, the theater, and the like. It was not necessary for her to sit up there in her room and wait for them to return, since no one knew that she sat and listened for the carriage, but she did, because that was the only thing she could do for her son.

She had also grown very fond of the young wife who once had kissed her, the first time she entered the house. She had called her Mama and patted her on the cheek and asked if she was angry or anything because she had taken Henry from her. Then Mrs. Nelson could pat her on the back and say, *"He belongs to you now, you keep him all the time."*

Things were more difficult when it came to the older couple. They did nothing to offend her, but they never gave her any joy either. Mrs. Perkins always took hold of her dress so as not to brush against her as she passed by. She looked at her the way a tired woman looks at a big washing she has to tackle. Old Perkins never, or seldom, spoke to her.

At first, she had often gone downstairs when strangers were present. Fine ladies had said many kind words to her and she had wanted to tell them about Henry and how sensible and good he had been when she had taken him along to the places where she worked. She would especially never tire of telling how it was just as though he understood that it was not fitting to cry among strangers and he had waited patiently to suck at her breast until she had the time for it.

But what belonged to Mrs. Nelson's most precious memories did not belong to social gatherings. She did not realize this herself, because she was always very moved when she spoke about these things and did not see how Mrs. Perkins got a headache and used her smelling salts, or how embarrassed and red Edith became, or how embarrassed the others were. It was natural for her to speak about the only thing she had lived for—the only thing that had happened in her life worth thinking about apart from religious matters, but which she did not realize was not fitting to talk about among such fine folk.

Later, it happened they forgot to ask her to come down when there was a party, but then both Henry and Edith came up to her room afterward and brought her something good.

There were times later on when Edith came up alone. Henry had made friends who took up his time. His work required no exertion and his unused energy therefore had to find other outlets. With genuine passion he played billiards and other games with which the town's wealthier men sought amusement at the club. He did not play for money and was very careful about liquor, but he stayed out late.

When he came home he was tired and wanted to go to sleep. It was quite annoying how quickly he could go to sleep and how well he could sleep when he came home from the club. He slept in the chair as he patiently listened to his wife's scoldings.

He never contradicted her—he thought maybe she was right, but with the obstinacy of a spoiled child he went anyway, when the desire came over him to do so.

He did not drink—and that was a good thing; he did not gamble money away, and that was also good. But his young wife felt that she could not be everything to him, and that hurt her, because that was what she wanted. With determination she had acquired for herself an expensive amusement in the shape of a husband—an expensive toy. He was wholly and undividedly hers. She would not give him up to others.

She would not complain to her parents. She had got her way and they might answer her with something like, "We warned you. You've got it the way you wanted it." So she would rather seek refuge with the old woman in the room in the back of the house. She would talk about Henry, and the young wife could not hear enough about him. Edith would have to bear her disappointment by herself.

It was not anger she felt, because he was as faithful as gold. Nor was it anxiety, because she knew he could take care of himself—it was grief that she could not be everything to him, that he lacked something in his new relationship that the club supplied at the card tables and among the rolling billiard balls.

She knew that if she asked him not to go there he would stay home. She knew he had no idea how his preferring an evening at the club to an evening at home hurt her. It was also painful for her to see him unhappy. He did not care anything about books or music. He did not have an ounce of interest in social issues—he was not much concerned about any of this. The fun they had was some playful wrestling or running after each other, the way young animals play. She could bite him on the neck in her frolicsomeness and it was not seldom he took hold of her with such force, if only in fun, that he made bruise marks on her.

But then there were those long days when he would spend his time being bored in the factory and being bored at home.

"He is not much good when it comes to work, but he is a decent, good boy," old Perkins could say to his wife when she would say that Edith had made a rather poor choice after all.

"You should just have seen my Henry work," old Mrs. Nelson would say to Edith when they spoke together about him. "He was the best one to use a shovel—that's what they all said. But what he does now he learned at the university."

"Was he happy then?"

"Was he happy? Surely he was happy because he was earning money and had so much to do."

"Did he used to stay out during the evenings then?"

"No—oh no! He was always at home and sat out on the steps in his shirtsleeves, with his shirt folded down around his neck, and he talked with me and told me about everything he had heard and done during the day and when I didn't have time to talk with him he talked to the cat or with the man who stayed with us."

Edith sat puzzled and fingered her rings. She must have got thinner because her rings slid off and on so easily.

XXVII.

JUDGE HIGHBEE was right after all. Karoline came back, but it took a few years. She was glad to go home to Norway, to her home and her parents. It is true that her first impression was that everything was on a small scale, but this was compensated by the feeling that everything in a way belonged to her. Here she had her rights as nowhere else in the world and the feeling of security and well-being that filled her mind could not be explained with words.

She had often wept during the journey—wept, because there was much that reminded her how happy she had been when she traveled in the other direction—long, long ago. Here at home she could have peace again. Her parents' joy at having her back was also great, and that helped. Mother was really a sensible woman, after all: "Don't you fret, Karoline, that nothing came of it between you and Lars. It is our Lord who is in control of such matters. We never know what we will be spared. We often don't know about things until we stumble into them. But now we are happy that you have come back."

She was not willing to take a maid's position in Norway. The difference both in pay and in treatment from what she had had in America was far too great.

After she had spent the summer at home she went to Kristiania to be trained as a nurse and to learn about massage. This she felt would provide her a means of supporting herself in her hometown, where there was now a public bath and the town was beginning to gain a reputation as a health resort. She was strong, clever, and intelligent, and because of her good knowledge of English she had many patients, since there were not a few sickly persons from England who came to this little town with the ocean and forests to convalesce and regain their strength.

She was as contented as she could be, but there was always something unexplainable gnawing at her from inside. It was the West, the great and mighty West, that pulled at her. She felt a great outburst of joy one day when she saw a steamship sail past bearing the American flag. It waved memories to her from thousands of miles away.

She had no reason to go there. There was only one person she cared about and he now belonged to someone else, who would get to keep him. Just the same, there was something that drew her. She read English newspapers and books so as not to forget the language, and it was not seldom that she dreamed about the big country on the other side of the ocean. She could not say enough about the family in whose service she had been the years she was there. They were the only real Americans she knew, and for her, Americans were the same as the Highbee family. Measured against them, she felt that all the "better" folk whom she had come across here at home fell short. There was an arrogance among some of them that offended her. There was a sort of friendly condescension among others that upset her even more, and not seldom a crossness that she found intolerable. Why couldn't they use the same tone of voice, the same expression, the same bearing toward a person in their service as they used toward those who were not in their service?

Her patients often irritated her. Mrs. Highbee would never have spoken or acted like that, she thought, when she had been reminded of her subordinate position by one or another unpleasant patient.

"Oof! If only I could send all these people to America and teach them some manners," she would say to the doctor at the health resort. The doctor was a jovial and genial bachelor with a bald head and a big stomach. He liked the energetic nurse and would now and then take her hand and feel her pulse to check her "America fever." Some had it once and then became immune, he said; others had recurrences. Other cases, which involved a greed for money, were hopeless. He could in fun prescribe a box of chocolates, and would have it with him the next time she saw him.

If only all the people had been like him, but they were not. He was a fine and educated man. Everyone praised his abilities, but he said himself that he lived off people's gullibility and that he did not have the least bit of confidence in the medicines which he prescribed. The only remedy he considered effective for those apparently sick persons who came to the health resort was one he did not dare to use. Almost every single one of them needed a good thrashing, he said. Sometimes he would say when he handed over a new patient to her: "Pinch her with force, nurse—use your knuckles on her—I'll help you with the court costs if you break one of her arms or legs."

He listened patiently to her when she told about how many poor countrymen had got ahead over there. How big and spacious everything was.

"It is odd," he would say, "they come back to this country, many of them, because they are not happy; but then they can't find happiness here either, and off they go back across the ocean. That is rootlessness. They are ripped up from the one and can't put down roots in the other. I can guess that some of them take hold and shoot up like weeds over there and send up stems and leaves, others are stunted in growth and dry up like so much does when it is transplanted."

Karoline would remind him of the many Norwegian congregations, schools, organizations, newspapers, and the like that they had. Yes—the doctor believed there could be results when they took enough soil with them from home to cover over the most tender roots.

"I don't know much about it," he said once, "but I doubt that you found any Norwegian Americans like the American family you speak so much about. I have heard about a class of Americans from the old New England states, who are described for me as the world's most noble, likeable, and considerate aristocracy. We know something about them here through men like Emerson, Irving, Holmes, and others, but they are a type above the ordinary. Their kind is, for that matter, being swept under by the stream of immigration. It is not robust enough to hold its own. Some traces of it will be maintained through a certain official hypocrisy or the neat, almost religious-toned fleecing which the American trusts understand so well. The fine old New England culture will no doubt disappear just like the strong, religiously inclined Norwegian pioneer."

Karoline had never given such serious thought to any of this. She only understood that the doctor shared all the "better" folk's dislike of America and that it was only her respect for the doctor that made her refrain from giving him a sharp reply.

"But see how slowly people move here," she would answer. "If I don't come today, then I'll come tomorrow. I'll come, but not suddenly."

The doctor laughed. "Well, America puts a little more speed into us," he admitted, but he would really like to know if it was the genuine Americans who were always so busy or if it wasn't the new arrivals who scurried about in order to earn money and get relatives and lovers and such riffraff over to them as quickly as possible.

One thing Karoline had to admit was that people looked better and laughed more in Norway. It was quite incomprehensible how they could laugh and have fun when they lived only from hand to mouth as so many did. Some changes had also taken place while she was away. The youth were active everywhere something was to be done. They built clubhouses, had youth organizations, reading clubs, orchestras, singing societies, everything they needed. She would gladly have taken part in much of this, but the first thing she noticed after her return was precisely the fact that she had grown older. That had happened the day she sent the letter to Lars with the ring and all the rest.

But he was not the one she longed to see again—she was through with him.

Of course she was through with him—but she thought about him every day just the same and sometimes dreamed about him. But if it is true that a person dreams what he thinks about, then she would have dreamed about him every night. And her dreams were nonsensical and silly. She thought he was sick and poorly clothed and she told him that he must not go around like that, or he was sick so she had to carry him as though he was a child and she was his mother. The craziest dreams. But afterward it was as though something was bleeding inside her. She could hardly understand that he now belonged to another, the very one he had always said he couldn't stand.

But it was good to be home anyway. There was mother doing her work around the house—old and bent to be sure, but the same person for whom she had often longed when she was in that foreign country.

As time went on she became more contented with her lot and it was purely accidental that she made a trip back to America. Among her patients there was the wife of a well-to-do Norwegian American. He was a rich businessman, a widower up in years, and he had come to Norway to see again those places where he had played as a child and dreamed the dreams of youth.

It may be that the old man dreamed again, because he found himself a young widow who had little in the way of worldly goods, but was a person of culture. She unfortunately fell ill soon after the wedding and came to the resort to win back her health so that she could accompany her husband on his return to America. She was much improved but there was still a risk involved in her undertaking such a long and strenuous journey, and for that reason it was decided that Karoline should travel with them to watch over her and continue the care which had shown such good results.

The journey, however, ended in disappointment. The rich man was, as it turned out, not rich at all, and upon their arrival in Chicago he let Karoline understand that he no longer had any use for her services nor could he pay her what he owed her. When Karoline pointed out his duty to him and demanded her money, he stood in front of her and threw open his hands and asked her what she was going to do about it.

Karoline did not know at all what she should do or what she could do. The only thing she could think of doing right at that moment was to give him a good talking to, and that is what she did. The man, however, was like steel, because his wife had also scolded him and he had certainly often been scolded earlier as well, since everything she said to him was like water rolling off a duck's back. He did not even show any signs of contrition for his wrongdoing.

Karoline felt bad for the sake of his wife, and the thought of how she had also been deceived contributed much to the fact that she accepted her own loss with greater calm.

But now that she was back in America anyway, she wanted to return to the town that was connected to her brightest and bitterest memories. There she could earn enough money to return to Norway. She knew that Judge Highbee and his family would receive her with open arms, and she looked forward to seeing them again.

It was with sad feelings that Karoline left the train at the station in the town to which she had come years earlier with such happy expectations. No great changes had taken place and it rained now as it had done when she came there the first time, but now there was no one who came to meet her. She had been poor then, but she felt even poorer now. It was difficult for her to hold back the tears. She recognized the houses and the streets and the names on the store signs, but there was certainly no one here who cared anything about her.

After she had found herself a cheap hotel where she could live for the time being, she went off to call on the Highbee family. She knew she would be welcome there. The big, beautiful house stood there as elegant as ever. But a maid she did not know opened the door to her and told her the family had gone to Florida for the winter.

That was the first disappointment. She remembered her old friends Mr. and Mrs. Morstuen and went to find them. Nor were they in town any longer. The wife was in a mental asylum and the husband had been taken by his children to an old people's home after the property had been divided and they had each got their share.

But there were those whom time had not changed. Mrs. Dale was just as talkative as ever. Her family was well off financially. The girls had had a special ability to be led astray by well-to-do men, and a couple of sizeable settlements had put the family on a good financial footing. Mrs. Dale's great sorrow was that she had not got anything for her oldest daughter. But at that time they were newcomers and newcomers had no bargaining power. For the second daughter they had received a thousand dollars, and for the third, two thousand two hundred. There had been more, but the lawyer had also taken a portion of it. But Mrs. Dale struck her clenched right hand in the hollow of her left hand to emphasize that if anything similar should happen to the youngest daughter, then they were not going to get by for less than five thousand; there had to be that much law and order in this country.

Karoline heard a great deal from Mrs. Dale's mouth. The primary thing was how nice Mrs. Nelson had it now. That was how it went when you had boys. Now Henry was a fine man who did not have to do anything but drive around in an automobile. Mrs. Nelson had her own room, her meals served to her, and everything. They were millionaires, though no one knew just how rich they were, but they did have a lot of money and Mrs. Nelson was not even allowed to place her hands on a scrubbing cloth. That was what you call luck.

Lars Olson? Yes—Lars had, of course, married the daughter of Overhus who had done away with himself, and now he owned the whole store himself. Children? No—it had not been God's will that they should have children, but they had both an automobile and a big new house. But he had grown so old in appearance and he worked very hard. He had to, because his wife ran a lavish, elegant house, and there were no doubt a good many who wondered where all the money came from. He almost always sold merchandise for less than what the item had cost him.

Mrs. Dale was sympathetic. She knew very well that Karoline and Lars had been engaged and there had been considerable disagreement about whether it was she or Lars who had ended the relationship. Here, of course, it was right to assume that she had done it, and Mrs. Dale therefore made many sarcastic remarks about Lars. In the beginning he had been so haughty, but now, lately, he had become more meek because he had probably realized that a businessman can't go around with his nose in the air and sell anything at the same time. He had now also begun to attend the old church—at least just before Christmas and again just before the spring season. When he sat in church and tilted his head to one side, people thought things were going badly for him and that he would have to sell at a loss. It was the plumber, if she remembered him, who had said this. When people tilted their heads in church they always had a reason for it and were in difficulties, he had said. Then they always had something to sell at a loss, whether it was one thing or the other. There could be yet another reason and that was a boil on one side of his neck. The plumber and Lars had been good friends earlier, but since this thing happened with Overhus they had not been friends at all. Mrs. Dale thought he was having money problems now because his wife was too extravagant, and he had grown stingy and was not respected more than—so! She made a sweeping gesture with the palm of one hand across the other and it was clear the respect he enjoyed was not worth mentioning.

And the church? Things had gone so badly for the church that it had almost come to a halt. A large number of the older members had gone over to the Norwegian church and there they had built a large new church building to antagonize the old congregation which had completely changed over to English. The finest Norwegians remained anyway where there was English, but it was not so easy to provide the minister's salary. It cost the better folk so much more to live, so they could not give as much as the simpler folk. She had to admit that as for themselves they could not contribute much, the way prices of everything were.

Karoline also inquired about the Omleys. Mrs. Dale glowed with excitement because she could tell the most disparaging things about them. The two oldest boys had gone out west and there was no one who knew anything about them, and Sophy had been divorced from her husband and lived now at home with her mother. But the youngest son was a rare young man because he provided now for both his mother and his sister, and as young as he was, he contracted to do painting jobs and did all kinds of figuring in his head without writing anything down on paper, even though he had gone neither to the university nor even to high school. Yes, it was a shame for the Omleys who had lost so much on speculation—they who had once had so much. Yes, one could say that speculation was a great vice. She would see to it that her husband never did any such thing. If she ever got wind of it, she would put a stop to it. She again banged her clenched fist in the hollow of her other hand. For that matter, she was certain that her husband had no leanings toward speculation, because in that case there would never have been any marriage between the two of them. That she could say with certainty.

Karoline went to see some of the town's doctors to apply for work as a nurse and masseuse. Through one of the doctors she was given employment with the Perkinses. Mrs. Perkins was still poorly and it was both the safest and the most fashionable thing to have one's own nurse. Mrs. Perkins liked her and was not any more unreasonable than Karoline had been accustomed to with other patients. A couple of recommendations from upper-class English ladies had made Mrs. Perkins feel very favorable towards the new nurse.

Here Karoline also met Henry again. He remembered her well and was very friendly toward her. But how changed he was! He was very fat and there was no end to his compliancy, as he kept moving out of everyone's way. If he had any goal in life it must be to take care that his big body did not get in the way of anyone. He ate and slept and sometimes stretched himself when he changed position or got up or sat down.

In a way, Karoline felt sorry for him. She could not help noticing the looks of contempt which old Perkins sent his way. She had never seen so much self-effacement in a person.

She could not understand how a strong, healthy person could live in this manner. His health was excellent. He played golf almost every day to keep from getting too fat and did it because his wife wanted it. He did everything she wanted him to do. In the beginning of his marriage he had worked in a factory as assistant manager, but it ended up with him joining the workers and coming home soiled and dirty, and they did not wish to see him like that. He had been an assistant engineer in construction work, but he had again fallen and revealed his lowly origin by doing rough physical work, and neglected the work he was set to do.

The young Mrs. Nelson had kept her youthful appearance, but had lost her youthful mentality and went about in low spirits. She could not understand her husband, there was something totally incomprehensible about his passivity—this massive indolence. Had he been like others she could have been furious with him, but she knew he was absolutely faithful and his innocent eyes neither pleaded for forbearance nor revealed any feeling of shame. She felt like a mother toward a normal child who for some reason or another cannot learn to walk. In one way she loved him more just for that reason, but what was to blame? Was it her fault? He had not been like that before they were married. Did he have some sort of illness? That she could not believe, because he could run up the stairs carrying her in his arms as though she were a little child. She thought he could shove an automobile as easily as a baby carriage.

Why wasn't he like the other men she knew? They were almost always busy with something and excited about something. Henry could not concentrate on anything. He was kind and considerate, but he could often forget what he had promised her. He could promise everything under the sun and go along with everything possible. She knew that he would stop going to the club if she asked him to. It did not seem to cost him the least bit of exertion to give up anything at all, but when he got involved in a game of any kind it became a matter of life and death for him to win when he had once started. On the other hand, he could very well leave it alone. It was not the game he cared about, but if he once got into it he would go to extremes in order to win. She knew that when it came to his being faithful he was as good as gold, and in that respect she did not want him to be like the "other men," but this gold, as genuine as it was, could neither be struck into usable coins nor made into jewelry. She owned the best husband in the world, she thought, but the world did not seem to have much use for him, nor he for it. There was something unexplainable about it. They could have put their feet under their own table and lived in a house by themselves, but in that case her father would have had to furnish every single cent and that was humiliating. She also thought Henry couldn't care less about where he ate and slept.

In some way or another both she and her parents had put the blame for his lack of ambition on his mother.

Their behavior toward the old woman was influenced by this. Perkins and his wife had never been able to stand her, and Edith put up with her because she was Henry's mother. It happened often, much too often she felt, that he was up there with her and then they conversed together in a lanaguage which she could not understand. It was as though she was being left out, and that she was not accustomed to. She did not want to share him with anyone, and when he visited his mother she would find many excuses for getting him away from there, and the old woman could not help understanding why.

Mrs. Nelson stayed out of the way. She no longer came down to the sitting room. She had nothing to do there. She had gradually come to realize that she did not belong there and kept to her room, where she was often distressed when she heard that there was something going on down below. The fact that she had withdrawn so completely was the only indication that she was in possession of some human intelligence, said old Perkins. People came and went, servants came and went—Mrs. Nelson sat up in her room and had her food brought up to her.

Food—yes! She had a feeling that she had sold her son for a set of teeth and food. In the beginning the food had tasted good, but later it lost its taste for her. The days were long—but later in the afternoon or in the evening she would pass quietly down the stairs and out the back way to go and visit some friends and tell the old, redundant story about how well-off she was and how highly the Perkins folk regarded her Henry.

But there was much fabrication in what she said. She had the whole time regretted the trade, because that is what she thought it was. She had always wanted to have a fine son, and now she had one, and this was the price.

That he did nothing seemed quite natural to her. She had always imagined to herself that fine folk had nothing to do.

She had the feeling that her boy still remained under her protection, that he was among strangers who did not know how to care for him. That was what she wanted to do, but they would never give her any opportunity to do anything for him if they could help it.

She believed the whole while that the two young people were very happy and had no need for her; she felt like a discarded bit of clothing no one had use for any longer.

But Edith was not happy. Her toy had lost much of its lustre. She could envision the day when they would not be able to tolerate the sight of each other.

At least there had once been a time when they were contented. She could not think about it without a feeling of happiness welling up inside her, but at the same time there was something so idiotic about it. It was the summer two years back. The parents had traveled to the coast and their children were to follow. At the time, they were making some changes in the house. The basement under the house was to be dug deeper and was to be extended so as to be under the entire house, which was to be modernized because the interior of the house was no longer in fashion. The stone from the basement was to be used to fill a depression where it was intended there should be a nice tennis court. Everything was off to a start when the old folks left. A hole had been made in the wall, planks were laid down and the laborers had wheeled not a few loads of stone away, when a strike was called and without further ado they came one day and took up their picks and shovels and their wheelbarrows and left things standing just as they were.

Then an untameable work demon had entered into Henry and spread its contagion to Edith's brother, who had just finished the university. They had got overalls and shovels and wheelbarrows and dug and carted as though possessed. The new-fledged university philosophy graduate, or whatever it's called, insisted on clay pipes and Adam's Standard.* They struck matches against their overalls and lit their pipes and worked and

---

*Apparently a brand of tobacco.

sweated in real earnest. But Edith noticed that what was play for the one was dead seriousness for the other. Henry hardly had any time to eat, but when he ate it was almost a disgrace what he could put away. He was completely changed. The other could be tired and name himself "Timekeeper" and chalk off the wheelbarrow loads—just to make a check. But Henry did not tire.

It was fun. Edith made the food for them—the graduate made out his last will and testament just in fun and in it left his real and personal property to the wheelbarrow manufacturer's old-age home, if there was such a thing, as he tasted some of the food which his sister said she had prepared, but Henry thought the food was very good.

It was really an enjoyable week. She had laughed more than was good for her when on the third day her brother showed up for work with an improvised crutch under each arm and Henry had put him on top of the loaded wheelbarrow so he could keep a better check on the work. There was no end to the fun they had had.

But the work was accomplished, and it was done properly.

There were times while this continued that Edith felt some kind of pride rise up in her when she saw Henry work. But there was also an unpleasant reminder of his modest background that was not easy to escape.

But she later remembered more often the peculiar expression in his eyes revealing his eagerness to accept a challenge. It was like a triumphant "Did you see me, what I could do?"

Edith learned something then, and it was that the simple wives who in the workers' section of the town stood by the gate or on the steps and waited for their sweaty and dirty men's homecoming in the evening were maybe not so unhappy as she had thought they must be. There was really something extremely great about a dirty, sweaty man, and especially when he was a big, strong man.

It was not in jest when she had thrown her arms around his strong red neck and said: "Oh, how happy we would have been if we had been poor and you could go to work and I could make all kinds of good food for you."

And the look in his eyes showed that he was made very happy by what she said.

"If it were not for mother, then we could go far away and manage on our own," he often said. And he took his wife and lifted her and swung her in order to reveal his strength. Such outbursts could come when old Perkins had scolded him, which he sometimes did. Perkins was in many respects an upright man, with an aptitude for moralizing and correcting mistakes. He had never found anything to correct in himself, but the need to practice uprightness was so great that it sought an outlet. He did not find much in his own son, wife, or daughter that needed correction either— his daughter had committed an error in marrying a slovenly lout, but other than that there was nothing at which to point a finger. His sense of righteousness then found an outlet in his son-in-law. Perkins had grown old and he had a high regard for his soul and no desire to be lost. He felt no need of conversion, but he needed to demonstrate before both God and the world that he despised idleness, poker, pool, and all ingratitude. When he thus scolded his son-in-law he did it with a loud voice. He had a better appetite and slept better when this had been done. Seldom or never has anyone had a more fitting and hardy subject to moralize over than Perkins had in his large-limbed son-in-law. Henry did not seem to grasp anything other than that his father-in-law was in a bad mood. And that was totally mistaken, because Perkins scolded him when he was in good humor and overwhelmed by his own noble-mindedness, ability, and righteousness. The fact that he was not understood gave him the strength to continue for a long time.

Karoline could not help but make comparisons between him and Judge Highbee. There was no doubt, as the doctor had said, that there was more than one kind of American.

She had her room next to old Mrs. Nelson and often spoke with her. "It is my fault Henry got into this. The boy has not been himself since he came here," Mrs. Nelson complained.

"But he could find some work, couldn't he, if nothing else, in order to get the old man to hold his peace," Karoline once said.

"Work? Of course my Henry will work—why, you should just see him work, but the boy, poor fellow, has got to have something to work for. There isn't anyone here who needs anything. Everything he could earn would probably not even be enough to pay the woman who comes here two and three times a week to manicure the nails of the mother and daughter in this house. What use is it for a man to work when what he makes is just a drop in the bucket anyway?"

Karoline sat puzzled and pondered this. She had not thought of this before.

"It's my fault," the old woman could repeat again and again. "Henry and Edith would like to get away from here and be on their own, but he won't leave me. He thinks I have it good—and I do too—in a way."

"Oh no—you don't need to worry that he would go away as long as you are alive," said Karoline consolingly. But the old woman was obviously not glad to hear it. "Things will never be good for him—either for him or his wife, before they get away and are by themselves. She could be such a good wife because she is a rare person, I can tell you—and she loves him so—she loves him so terribly much," the old woman continued in an almost reverential whisper, "just think, she can't go to sleep when he is out late at night, even though she knows he doesn't drink or ever go on any kind of spree. She comes up here to me and then we sit and listen for him. She knows it is *'foolish,'* she says, but *'I love him so,'* she says, and then she puts her arms around my neck and kisses me here—." The old woman extended her cheek with pride and pointed with her index finger to the spot where Edith had kissed her.

Spring is hard on old people, and it was hard on Mrs. Nelson, who had to take to her bed. But the doctor had good hopes. It was her age, he said. The machinery was wearing out like everything old and Nature ordered itself by something coming to a standstill so the system could rest. He was philosophical and optimistic and was especially contented to have a patient in such a wealthy home. He did not think her life was in any danger at all.

Karoline was given the task of nursing the old woman and sat a great deal with her and read to her. The old woman not only seemed to be resigned to the thought of death, but talked about it with a certain amount of satisfaction: "It will be better for both Henry and Edith when I am gone, because then they can go far away and set up housekeeping for themselves, and then she'll see what a clever boy he is, but of course you can understand he won't leave me."

Karoline could not understand this. Why should they go away and fight for their existence when they had so much and did not have to do it? No, she did not put any stock in that. But the old woman persisted. She knew it was so, because she had heard it, she said. And that would be so much, much better. As things stood now, they could not do anything for each other—not in the least; but then they would be able to do so much for each other and that was what both of them wanted.

She was often occupied with this thought and told about how it had been for her the short time she had been married. She just did not realize how well off she was. She had always believed that people who had lots and lots of money were happy, but it was better to be poor after all, if a person just had the essentials. God had been so good to her, so she had never lacked anything, but she had not understood it at the time. She would not hear that she would be well again and that she would still live for many years.

But this appeared to be the case.

There was a day when the doctor, wearing his triumphantly confident smile, said that when they could just begin giving her something to eat again she would soon be restored to health. He prescribed what she should have. Very little to begin with, but this was to be increased. The medicines had done their work and now they had to build up her strength. The patient was over the worst of it now.

He talked a great deal, because the patient had really been much closer to the brink of death than he had been willing to reveal to them. But now the worst was over because they could begin to get some nourishment into her.

The patient listened to all this with her back turned to them.

Should she really get well again and sit up in her room and listen to Perkins scold her Henry—her boy who endured and took all this because he had an old, helpless mother upstairs? She had never wanted to be a burden to anyone. The food had often tasted bitter to her—and now it was the food which was to save her—food which belonged to old Perkins.

The doctor was perplexed when he returned the next day and read the disheartened expression on their faces, because the patient could not get anything down. The patient just shook her head and made a weak movement with her hand. They had tried everything possible. The only thing she could get down was water.

If she could take water, then she could take milk—a spoonful of port wine. No—she could not swallow anything like that. They would have to start with the medicine again. But she could not take the medicine, either. And the doctor sat for a long time and pondered and stroked his chin the way doctors always do when they are thinking about something. There must be something he had not understood. It was the first time this had happened, and in this case he had been so certain.

The minister came to visit the patient and read for her with a heavy English accent and many incorrect words. He could not, of course, have a dictionary at his side when he knelt down by the sickbed, so he was excused. He was also certain that God excused him. But Karoline did not excuse him, and when he had gone she read to the patient.

The old woman had a striking appearance as she lay there. As emaciated as she was, her face had taken on a look of great dignity. Her nose had become fine and pointed, her forehead and cheekbones protruded outward—she almost resembled a man—a strong and powerful man—a courageous man. It was as though her face had grown larger. It was a face which demanded respect. Edith had to ask herself if this was really the pleasant and continually smiling woman who had stood before them and uncrumpled her hard-earned dollar bills. Mrs. Perkins had been up to see her and had entered quietly but departed even more carefully out of the room. A kind of fear had come over her. There was something overwhelmingly impressive about this dying laundry woman. She felt like a very small Mrs. Perkins when she quietly returned downstairs. She had come up to be kind to the old woman and show in the eleventh hour that she had not disdained her and she had left again with a great deal of disdain for herself.

"It's only a matter of a couple of days now," the doctor had said during a later visit. She will not live through the night, Edith thought to herself. But the old woman lasted out the week and well into the next. Her mind was clear because she stroked Edith's hand when she got hold of it.

She expired while Edith held her one hand and Henry the other. Never had Karoline been witness to such a long struggle. There were two or three times when they thought she was dead, but then she would begin to mumble again and her eyes would grope for her son and daughter-in-law and a triumphant smile would be drawn across her sharp and now so strong face. But her last word, as well as Karoline could grasp it as she wet her lips, was not the name of her son or her daughter-in-law, but the name of Him who had given her strength to live and to fight her heavy battle for her son and who now also gave her the strength to die.

"She smiled," Edith sobbed. "I had to think of her the way she looked that time she stood down in our drawing room and laid out her money— as though she was paying something she thought she owed us."

The sick woman's eyes opened again. "Oh God—she's still alive!— Mother! Mother!"

There was triumph in this look. Now they saw clearly that the old woman thought she had paid for herself and made things right. Karoline carefully closed her eyelids while the young couple looked down at the dead woman.

Mrs. Nelson had never received as much attention in her entire lifetime as she did when she was dead. Old Perkins made glowing remarks about her. "She was blue-blooded," he said. "Just look at that face—I'll be hanged if she doesn't resemble Andrew Jackson. There is blue blood in many of those people from Norway. Some of them would rather go hungry for days than ask anyone for help or go poorly dressed rather than lie and cheat. People whose word is as good as a signed note and who would do anything for you except be a burden. This woman was always so good and gentle and accommodating, but she certainly had an iron rod for a backbone."

Thus spoke old Perkins and meant every word of it. He had never been more satisfied with Mrs. Nelson than now, and nothing was spared for her funeral.

Many beautiful things were said about her by the minister, who spoke to praise both her and those who remained behind. The old woman had had such a good life during her last years. God would richly reward them for all their goodness toward her—tenfold, yes a hundredfold, he would give them recompense.

And the minister was also well paid.

Mr. and Mrs. Perkins soon traveled to the coast, where they were joined by their son. But Henry and Edith headed west instead of east. A letter from them, however, headed eastward. The letter said that they were going to try to get along on their own for a while, and they would be heard from when they had proved they could make it on their own.

Old Perkins wondered where they were going to get any money and was of the opinion that they would soon be back.

But had he seen them as they sat on the train, he would have thought differently. The people who actually saw them believed they were new-lyweds, they were so taken up with each other and so busy making plans for the future.

Karoline did not await the Highbee family's return. She had received a letter from the doctor at the health resort. He wrote that his patients were dying like flies because he could not find a decent nurse. For that matter, he was now in a position to need proper care himself. He could not afford to hire anyone. He would have to obtain a nurse as his wife. That was all he could afford. He had thought to offer her the position.

Between the jocular lines Karoline could read something far more serious. She had come to know him as a conscientious, honorable man—a gentleman in every respect.

Her decision was soon made.

She had seen Lars at the funeral. She had heard much about how far he had come—how rich and respected he was. These rumors had reached all the way to their remote home in Norway.

She ought to have been glad that everything had turned out so well for him, that he had become an esteemed man, but how changed he was! She could hardly recognize him, he was so thin and strained-looking. And in addition he had acquired a cautious and cunning nature. She was seized with the greatest sympathy for him, but she also felt a strong admixture of contempt. It appeared as though someone had struck his head down between his shoulders and it was resting far down and also tilted. He looked as though he was asking God and man for pardon because he had become so successful and rich. But his wife was elegant to behold. There was no one more elegant at the funeral and she held her head with an expression as though she wanted to say: What kind of a funeral is this? Wait till my mother dies, then you'll really see a funeral.

So, was that the way Lars had become?—It was him, and it was not him. Lars, whom Karoline had known and loved, no longer existed. He was gone, had vanished completely, and someone else had come in his place who pretended to be Lars, but was not him.

But what had become of her ideal? Melted down to money and pres-tige, she thought. He had filed himself down, finely planed himself down to be small enough to appear great in his own eyes. It was not a greatness with a dwelling place in his heart, but a greatness which had filled his head to such a degree that it was squeezed down between his shoulders and because of the weight leaned toward the minister in the church and the customers in the store.

How could he have become like this? But this same thing happened to so many. Then they were ready for the great melting pot. First they stripped away their love for their parents, then they sacrificed their love for the one they held most dear, then the language they had learned from mother, then their love for their childhood upbringing, for God and man, then the songs they learned as children, then their memories, then the ideals of their youth—tore their heritage asunder little by little—and when one had hurled from his heart and mind everything which he had been fond of earlier, then there was a great empty void to be filled with love of self, selfishness, greed, and the like. Our Lord had not created men to harbor such things and so they lived with a secret fear of being discovered and tried to hide themselves by changing their names and appearance.

Thus they readied themselves for the melting pot's last great test. There might still be some fine quality about them which could be useful to nature's great household.

Some danced themselves into the great melting cauldron, others went calmly and quietly, because they understood that they no longer had any value as individuals and that they could at least help to fill it up. Others again marched to a full orchestra because they regarded themselves as having so much value that they would create an entirely new metal—they went into the melting pot to become a part of it. Some still went into it thoughtlessly and simply in laziness followed *"the line of least resistance"* and it led them there at last. But Lars was among those who prepared his own unraveling and melted down by ridding himself of his best qualities first. And this was only natural, because the melting pot was precisely for the spiritually stunted, those who no longer had qualities that let people see what they were or what they had been.

Karoline did not have to fortify herself to get rid of these sad thoughts. She had a letter in her handbag written in the genuine and nearly illegible handwriting of a physician. He was going to come and meet her in New York, and then they were going to get married in American style without a period of engagement. They were going to visit the remarkable American family and call it a honeymoon trip.

She had written to Mrs. Highbee and received a letter saying that they would be most welcome and the judge had written in a postscript that he had ordered a Norwegian flag for the occasion.